foreign
parts

'you' 'we' they < or
Bilo on 1st day/2
Cas unsp — tea v tenon

Honors of hamel 8

photos unpushped
& & Cassie an(s)

graves 39
49
113-4

Consid the effects of the
main uncon techs & uses
to render c's "str of cons"

Rhona sleep up 168
171 past. it lesbian
186 year XX c being the male?
(Huff)

by the same author Poss 201

THE TRICK IS TO KEEP BREATHING
BLOOD (short stories)

170 Men

Cassie Burns 107

134 man working woman
185 end of Chris

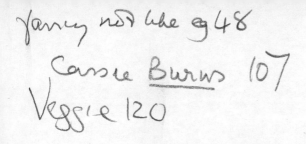

Yancy not like eg 48
Cassie Burns 107
Veggie 120

foreign
parts

mel/yon 36

JANICE GALLOWAY

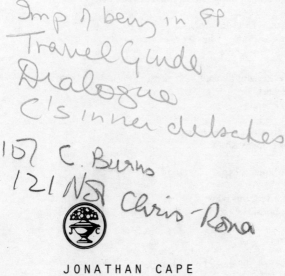

Imp ? being in FP
Travel Guide
Dialogue
C's inner detaches
107 C. Burns
121 NS Chris-Rona

JONATHAN CAPE
LONDON

155 I loved it. You have to care something

Charles

168 mussels with Chris

First published 1994

1 3 5 7 9 10 8 6 4 2

© Janice Galloway 1994

Janice Galloway has asserted her right
under the Copyright, Designs and Patents Act, 1988
to be identified as the author of this work

First published in the United Kingdom in 1994 by
Jonathan Cape
Random House, 20 Vauxhall Bridge Road, London SW1V 2SA

Random House Australia (Pty) Limited
20 Alfred Street, Milsons Point, Sydney,
New South Wales 2061, Australia

Random House New Zealand Limited
18 Poland Road, Glenfield
Auckland 10, New Zealand

Random House South Africa (Pty) Limited
PO Box 337, Bergvlei, South Africa

Random House UK Limited Reg. No. 954009

A CIP catalogue record for this book
is available from the British Library

ISBN 0–224–03980–6

Typeset by Deltatype Ltd, Ellesmere Port, Cheshire
Printed in Great Britain by Mackays of Chatham plc
Chatham, Kent

cockroach drama 73
(Chris) comic/scary

For Alison
all my female friends
and all female friends.

No inverted commas

For hol — detail) irrit smells bad mood
awfulness of sisters Plod prose 184
ines for cems g
female friends
Photographs
Letters 40-1

Death

Death

none

They got off the bus and she was giggling.

She was giggling about something she can't remember what but giggling and running uphill. The main street. She was running on the slope of the main street and the voice behind her shouting her to come back, stop being a bad girl and come back. Her mother's voice getting weeer. Because all the time she was just keeping running, past Mario's lit up on the other side of the road with yellow insides and four big men standing outside, eating. You ran on through the sudden smell of chip vinegar, left it behind, drawing level with the stone soldier, the wee hat and the bayonet edged with streetlight on the corner. The War Memorial. A bayonet and a grey face. The real men outside Mario's not needing to be worried about because you were past. Going home.

She was running because she was going home. The tips of stones in the cemetery became visible. Two streets away. A heart in her ears, drumming. Stop being a bad girl, d'you hear me? Mother with her voice not right making an echo of heels on the road slabs. There was a crack in the slabs they never fixed. You hear her heel sink into the soft moss that grows there, clatter back on the other side. A giggle and the need to run faster but too late. Mother is there with a face like the moon coming down over your shoulder, dustflakes of powder trailing and falling off like stars and her hand pressing you down so the shoulder jars and it is no longer possible to keep going. None the less you are still giggling, an edge of something sore about it but giggling and not knowing what for, starting saying something to fill in the nothing that was coming from mother's mouth. George. The voice of a child breaking the gathering threads of dark. Cousin George got bathed in the kitchen sink with the too wee curtains that wouldn't close right, a big naked boy in the kitchen sink. What had that to do with anything? They must have been there, been to Aunty Mima's, George being washed before bedtime male and separate and vulnerable with a giggling girl in the kitchen. That would be it: the reason for pursuit. For looking. And this was it starting, mother looming out of the blackness with her face crumbling, spitting on a handkerchief. The first thing is gouging. Mother poking the damp hanky at the offending mouth through a haze of sweet spit. Her lips are purple with the time of night, filling up the space between us with a wheeze of asthma breath.

You've to be quiet now, she says. Quiet.

Tail ends of giggles and whines, protests. The exasperation talking to a child who can have no notion of what it is you have to say, trying to pick your words for such a child that only wanted to keep running, to get away. The cold patch on her face where the damp hanky had been almost sore and she looks you right in the eye and says

Your daddy's died.

You see the hanky fold inside bluing fingers, the cold place on your cheek getting so big it feels like your face is tipping over the edge, falling inside it.

Do you hear what I say? Your daddy's died. He's dead.

The man you visit at Aunty Nora's, his sister Nora is your Aunty Nora and he is your daddy that you visit on Sundays. That man. Is it that man she means? The word died rising towards the streetlight like a drawn moth but it won't stop ringing that way, spiralling upwards and further away like wrong snow

You've no daddy any more.

the big scuff on the toes of the red leather sandals moving like worms. The clamp round her wrist is her mother's hand. Crushing hard enough to make marks. And somewhere overhead it starts sounding. Like a shop alarm somewhere over the back of the cafe but not so loud as the sea. You never escape the sound of the sea here. At night with the cars not coming it can fill up the whole world.

There was a bridge out there before you reached the shore. She thought about the chill noise of the waves washing up against the metal girders, how cold they would be. Frozen metal with the water crashing over it again and again. She heard it, repeating and not stopping. Washing solid iron into atoms.

Punctuation: gaps
Cassie in bad temper

one

Driving into the glare of your own headlights on the wall, you
wonder how it would be if she hit the accelerator instead of the brake
how it would be if

ah god

The ferry is cold and the lights too bright for the time of night. You watch the bonnet nose into a space that is too narrow, the window filling up with metal wall. Juggernaut. Rivets on an orange ground, a painted eye that rocks to a standstill when she pulls the brake. Your skin deals with practicalities, contracting as you open the door, helping you fit into the not enough space that is left between the car and this alien brute, this metal enormity muscling up the whole span of available vision. When you stand up, cramming the doormouth, the eye becomes part of something bigger. An orange. An unconvincing cartoon fruit smirking and sooking a straw which is stuck into another cartoon fruit which in turn smirks and sooks a straw which is stuck into another cartoon fruit which in turn decides enough is enough and it kind of gives up. The oranges get even less convincing than they were to start with and aren't oranges at all any more. Just blobs. Pretending. The whole side of the lorry is covered with them. Above, a dancing slogan that might be Spanish: not that you speak any but there's a wavy line over the n. The metal is radiating almost physical lines, palpable as human musk. You find yourself sucking in the diaphragm, your breath shallow: the soft torso folding itself carefully to avoid second degree burns, making room for the door at your back to swing and close. The bloody thing is roasting.

We hear the sound of the other door failing to catch first time, the hiccups and clicks of second tries. Checking locks, our eyes meet through layers of shatterproof glass. OOPS, she mouths. SORRY.

You turn away to not see and a picture appears. On the other side of the car bay, coming and going through the weave of carbon monoxide. A picture of a wee blue man running, representational stairs under his legs. You look at the wee blue man as long as you can bear hesitation then strike out, knowing there is nothing else to trust. You strike out for the promise of stairs, hoping the wee blue man knows where he is going.

2

We/you/they

3rd imp

Cassie and Rona
Rona and Cassie

trip over each other's feet, <u>Rona saying SORRY all the time.</u>
Pelvic bones slither past radiator grilles and rubber bumpers, our
crotches brushing the warm wings of strangers' cars. We move out of
the smell of engine oil, the foot of the stairs rank with urine. Male
urine. Bacteria-infested testosterone.

SORRY.

Cassie clamped her jaw. If Rona said SORRY again, she would
burst. She would just burst.

Cassie wasn't feeling good.

She looked at her watch on the way up the steps and again at the
top, feeling <u>the not good thing</u> getting bigger in her chest and trying
to climb out. It was as far as the throat now, fighting past the vocal
cords. Halfway up the staircase, it won.

I hate these things. These boats, Rona. I don't like them.
I know, said Rona. They're horrible.
They're not horrible, Rona. They're disgusting. All these bloody
fumes and stuff. You can hardly bloody see.
I know.
Ok ok jesus Rona ok ok.

Feet clattering on metal plates.
Cold chips into the silence.

Damn damn damn.

There would be a huff starting in a minute and Cassie knew it would be her own fault. It would be her fault being snappy. On the other hand no it wasn't it was bloody Rona's fault. It was Rona's fault because she kept being such a bloody martyr. That thing she did, making out she knew how you felt and giving nothing away, no clues about what she was thinking. It was always the bloody same. The way she let you just wait, not knowing whether you'd done the wrong thing or what she was thinking because she wouldn't bloody tell you. You were always on your own with Rona, on your own and carrying the weight of too much rope. There was no hope of her saying SHUT UP or encouraging you to behave better in any way at all. She had no sense of social responsibility that way, none. Cassie knew it would happen sooner or later. She would just

SORRY

Rona and Cassie
Cassie and Rona

got to the top of the steps inside the sound of silent bursting and looked up the length of the deck. A pale grey carpet rolled down into unknowable distance, taking a random design with it. Close to, three computer game machines twittered like bottles emptying out at speed: further off, an echo of muzak that could easily have been the Bee Gees. That this was what not paying large sums to Air France meant. It meant this was all you deserved. And it would get worse. It always did. Cassie slipped a sideways glance at Rona. Pink rims round the eyes like a rabbit, broken veins starting on the cheeks and other things better not examined. Cassie moaned, trying not to know she would be looking the same. Rona caught Cassie looking and smiled. Laughter lines ha. Haha. It was too horrible to think about, too horrible by half.

4

A cafe sign, a photo of a cup of steaming tea on the wall.

They hadn't had a drink for hours.

A queue was already in place, a knot of too many people holding out notes which meant the people serving would run out of change. They maybe had already. Maybe that was why the queue was so big. Cassie looked at the queue, the photo, the queue again. And she knew two things. She knew that if she went over, if she stood in line, even if she had the right change, there would be no way of avoiding awfulness. Sugar that would ease under your nails when you tried to pick up the wee plastic spatulas that were not spoons, overfull cups in puddles of their own slops you lifted before you realised you had no hands free for the wee milk tubs, no hands free for the paper bloody napkins while all the time the cups were searing your fingerprints off through the too-thin plastic and the crowd seethed at your back, dunting forwards and not caring, not caring a damn. She also knew she wanted one. Cassie wanted a cup of tea so badly her eyes filled up. She could feel them doing it.

I know, Rona said. I know.

Rona went instead.

Rona went and got the tea.

Cassie watched her go, weaving a route through chaos, finding her way to the counter, ordering. She would be ordering for the two of them, forking out money she wouldn't ask for back. She'd smile when she ordered it as well, smile at somebody who wouldn't even notice, steam blossoming her cheeks with the heat.

Cassie shut her eyes.

Low thunder through the soles of her shoes. They were still in bloody dock.

A finger touched her wrist, handing over a cup. Cassie took it without saying anything. Rona didn't say anything either. Cassie could hear her though. The chink of money being stowed safe in the zip pocket, the sifting noise of sugar being opened and shed into liquid. A sip. Rona said oo and coughed. Gullet opening, closing. Another sip. Godknew how she was doing that. The steam alone was burning the end off Cassie's nose. Rona had her own way with pain, extremes of temperature, altitude and fear. She refused to feel it. It was entirely possible she was searing her taste-buds off and refusing to admit it. A sooking noise. Sook, deep sniff, another sook. She kept it up for five minutes or so then breathed out heavily.

That's better, she said. Tea always makes you feel better.
Cassie said nothing.
We could get the couchette things now if you like.
Cassie sniffed.
Couchettes. I think we should get them, Cassie. They'll be all away. You'll feel better after a lie down.

Cassie thought about leaning towards Rona and didn't.
In a minute eh? I just need a minute, that's all. A minute.

Rona sighed but stayed put. An old man drew level, tinkering with the top of a gold foil box. He pulled out a cigarette without having to look, letting the cellophane fall as he raised it to his mouth. He hadn't even begun to find a match when the coughing started: big deep wheezes like a cat about to bring up a fur-ball. Cassie couldn't look. She heard him though. Hacking. A retching noise. The dull, Chartreuse-coloured splat of mucus on wood. Christ. Cassie straightened her shoulders. Enough was enough. She walked straight to the wire mesh bin, dropped the tea and kept moving before it hit the bottom and poured back out like molten lava. At her back, something that might have been Rona tutted, deep-sighing through the nose. But she was following. Flat, unmistakable foot-falls. She was following all the same.

The only couchettes left were outside the Duty Free. Rona and Cassie sat down on them hard, dropping the bags on to the deck. Rona breathed out heavily, back in. Cassie sniffed.

6

Well, Rona said. The shop can't be open all night. It'll be ok.

Cassie said nothing.

It'll be fine.

She sighed again, then stood up. It took Cassie a moment to realise what the shuffling noise was. It was Rona walking away.

Cassie looked down quickly. The bag was right there, tipping her foot. Wherever Rona was going it wouldn't be far. Cassie nuzzled her foot against the evidence, feeling it push back. Rona's bag. The big brown plastic one that looked like something you fed horses from: flaps all over and a zip compartment, a travel kettle sticking out the top. The travel kettle was red and white with the word *SPORT* in slanty writing between two green lines which throbbed, catching the neon off the Duty Free sign. Cassie knew without looking what would be inside it too. Herb teabags. The travel kettle would be full of herb teabags, plastic spoons and sugar in a ziplock polythene poke. Underneath it, there'd be a box with sticking plasters, Solpadeine, a handful of tampons, insect cream and godknows. In case. And under that, under that and under that, more seams of predictable preparednesses for other in cases. In case. Cassie looked at the bag and its red and white kettle, its multiplicity of flaps. She let a sudden vivid urge to fling the bloody thing over the side flare, create a vision of the bag rising in slow motion, kettle flex flying out behind as it tumbled in mid-air, scattering plastic knives and forks, wee sachets of tomato sauce and crêpe bandage before it hit the sea where it would float upright, bobbing lightly, picnic cups trailing like lobster creels in its wake, then pass. These things happened occasionally. They never lasted. Cassie kept looking at the travel kettle, the brown sides of the bag and didn't move. She just kept sitting beside it. She also knew she would keep sitting there protecting it from interlopers and people who would wish it harm, caring for it because it was Rona's. Just as Rona knew she would. Rona could wander off like that because she knew the bag would be perfectly fine. Because Rona knew who she was dealing with ie an ineffectual big sumph who couldn't do anything as an independent entity to save herself.

Ah god.

Cassie's head hurt. She slid her back down into the cloth of the couchette. The smell of human saturation made her sit back upright again, rubbing the space between her eyebrows with one hand. Ah god ah god. It could be worse, though: things can always get worse. It was something not to forget. THINGS CAN ALWAYS GET WORSE HAHA. She said it out loud to see if it made her feel better. It didn't. It made her feel like a nutcase. It was the boat's fault. You only had to look to see it was not a healthy environment.

FORE: six wee boys battering a Space Invaders machine behind which the DISCO chaser lights periodically illuminated wee formica tables with NO SMOKING signs at one of which a thin woman with a face chiselled out of orange Playdo was lighting up and flinging the spent match into a puddle between two soaking beermats not far from which the BAR seethed already with people crushing each other against the grille while the smaller of their number waved money like marker flags to indicate that though they may not be visible, they are at least here, waiting for breathing space and cheap drink to help blank out the darkness to come while

AFT: a BANK with a queue like a film of DNA cloning itself sat with its shutters battened down against the rival trail of persons with tickets with things wrong with them and miles of salt water beneath their soles waiting blamelessly for the INQUIRIES girl behind reinforced glass to finish picking at one broken nail till it was time to shout at them through protective plastic slats, all the while ignoring the KIOSK where a cluster of magazine breasts made dimpled clouds from which a solitary male torso rose like Venus from the surf, the words BIGGY BIGGY BIGGY a shameless scarlet banner over his crotch and

AHEAD only inexorable lines of rivets, healing the walls into something meant to keep us afloat leading out and away as far as the eye can see. But there is also something familiar, a fine black strand coming through the anonymous rest that is Rona thank christ

Rona,

Rona coming back with blankets in her arms, her eyes too far away for the colour to be clear. But her. You watch her come, stumbling as the floor bumps upwards. It bumps upwards because the sea is under it, the engine boiling up foam. Just within earshot, the sound of casting from the edge of terra firma and, distantly, men cheering. She looks up then and sees you looking, tries to wave. The ship forces her into a railing but she steadies and keeps coming, carrying blankets and a smile. She keeps coming anyway.

And you know you will not sleep.

You know you will blame Rona.

Outside Victoria. Right outside where they've got those two wee Scottish bays at the back. Hicks from the Sticks. You can see he's standing there under duress, me thinking it was ok just to clutter up the pavement with luggage while I got a photo. Rush hour. We had no notion of rush hour at all. It must have taken us fifteen minutes to get across the road, watching to see how other people managed it. Other people spilling off the kerb like treacle over the lip of a tin, melting in through the traffic without even looking first but nobody got knocked down. Every time I stepped on the road I thought something was going to amputate my foot. Chris hauled me across the road by the elbow, made us both run, laughing. He was on holiday. He didn't have to sweat in the glass box for a fortnight.

Jesus this is me making him do it again. Outside the Underground station, guarding the cases. I couldn't believe the Underground: commuters like the kind you saw on sitcoms, rolled umbrellas. We stared a bit I suppose. We were seventeen. He said, Did you see that guy? The guy two seats along from where you were? The right hand side? I kept nodding while he was talking, not all that sure but you want to join in. I thought it had to be one of the pinstripe types. Jesus, he said. Jesus. He wasn't even trying to look like a real woman. He hadn't even shaved his legs.

Flights of escalator I forget how many flights of escalator but I remember somebody had to shove me out the way to get past. The other one like this was just a blur: big grey scribbles. He went to look at one of those maps of YOU ARE HERE to work out what we were supposed to do next and left the Custom Cars magazine on the seat beside me. I turned it over so I didn't have to see the women on the front, legs apart over some car bonnet with flames licking up from painting round the wheels, cradling their own tits and their lips pushed out like piglets with the apples taken out of their mouths. Like sucking pigs. I bought Cosmopolitan. It had the girl with her tits covered up and no car. I thought about the holiday instead. I'd heard of Madame Tussaud's and the National Gallery. Nelson's Column, I suppose. And sex shops. I knew there were a lot of sex shops. Magazines with pictures of men in them as well as women. Chris's was the only erection I'd clapped eyes on. I watched him watching the YOU ARE HERE machine, imagining him beneath the jeans I'd pressed a crease in to show what a good housewife I was and tried to be blasé. All I felt was terrible. Like other people could see what I was thinking and I'd humiliated him in front of a lot of strangers. I couldn't look him in the eye when he came back over. I must have been very preoccupied because when we were walking out, moving off into the night air of the street, I knew I'd left my purse behind. I'd left all the English money I'd been saving up in case they didn't want ours.

10

They used to be really awkward about Scottish notes. I felt it like physical pain: we wouldn't be able to have breakfast or anything till we got to a bank. It was my job to attend to things like that and I knew before we'd even begun I'd have to let him down.

A bus was coming.

No it wasn't.

Boat engine turning over.

Pres

Under the slits of her eyes, Cassie saw only stripes. The couchette. Only a minute ago, Rona's face had been there. Cassie had spent most of the night watching it, staring till her eyes got sore, then shifting the gaze out the window or along the deck before another look at her watch. Sometimes she managed three minutes between looks, sometimes two. Then it was five thirty and the air looked thinner. Like someone had sieved it. There would be changes in the sky out there even if she couldn't see them yet: light coming. She watched the last of Rona's profile in sleep, pointing at itself in the reflected sea. Cassie would be awake first. A position of power. You got to establish your rotten night was the worst if you were awake first: you got to define the priorities. Safe in that knowledge, she must have drifted off for ten minutes and then this happened. The bugger beat you to it. She wasn't there. The bag was away as well. Christ. Cassie turned too fast and something twanged in her neck. The soreness and Rona looking down at her happened at the same time.

Rise and shine, she said. Rise and shine, standing up and shaking crumbs off her front, checking the travel kettle was ok.

Indecipherable tannoy directions burbled up from somewhere too close, cutting off the end of something else Rona was saying. She smiled instead and pointed, risen and shiny as hell. She even knew which way to go.

The cartoon oranges were runny with condensation, cold dripping off and into rainbow puddles underfoot. Cassie touched one of the droplets on the side of the lorry, tracing it down a path it wouldn't have chosen for itself. Freezing. The tip of her finger came away black. She wiped it on the side of her jeans, breathing deep. Icy air filled out her chest. The shapes of her lungs outlined. Cassie coughed, shivering. A cloud of cold came out of Rona's mouth when she laughed. The laughing was good. Took your mind off the creaking in the shoulders from sitting in the same place all night, the pain of collapsed foot arches. Her neck twinged as she ducked for the door but it would pass. Rona was already in, foraging for the clasp, hauling the belt down hard. She clicked it and looked over, checking Cassie was doing the same. Cassie watched Rona checking and didn't care. This morning it wouldn't annoy her. She would fasten the bloody thing anyway. Two men in blue suits walked by the car window, trailing the scent of grease and machines. Moving that lazy way men did between bouts of hard physical work, kicking bits of wood out their road. They walked to join two others, two arrangements of braced muscle under boiler suits, tensing as they worked chains big as carpet rolls to release the door and put the ramp into place. Cassie looked hard at the men, the elongated oblong of another country about to open up under their touch. Something big clattered into place, one of the men shouted. And it was there. Light first. Then almost visible fresh air making green strands through the fug. Cassie was rolling the window down. She noticed she was rolling the window down, nose and lungs sniffing out the newness. She knew fine what she was doing was learned behaviour, more to

12

do with fabric softener commercials than anything else but she let herself do it anyway. They always looked so happy on tv. And so would she. Through the clouds already building up on either side, the choked-up coughs of cold engines forcing a start and weighting the deck with poisoned undergrowth, Cassie smiled. The Spanish juggernaut shuddered, six front tyres shedding water and mud. But the car was rolling. Ahead, someone was giving signals and Rona was following. The light behind fudged out the face and made distance hard to estimate but it was definitely a man, beckoning then on and through, up the ramp to spit into a sudden wash of sun.

BRICOLAGE.

A foreign word on a hoarding. Cassie laughed, growing ecto-plasm on the passenger window, the feeling of doing something dangerous getting thicker.

We're on holiday, Rona said. We're here.

The car wobbled towards the centreline. Two rabbits ran across the road and Cassie squealed involuntarily, sitting up and pointing for christsake. Laughing. Wildlife thrills me to hell.

BRICOLAGE.

The tail end of a drawing of a pile of bricks and a man in the corner waving. Rona hadn't seen, though. She was too busy watching the road, trying to keep it to one side of the tyres, bouncing in the seat.

Cassie looked at her watch.

I don't know what we're in such a good mood about. It's ten past bloody six.

Rona had the dirtiest laugh in the world.

13

Cassie and Rona
Rona and Cassie

wove past hoardings with foreign words on them, not giving a
damn, on the wrong side of the road.

two

Fourteen minutes to and flat as hell.

Je m'appelle Cassie et what was this is this is mon ami was a man mon AMIE Rona un tasse de café UNE tasse de you didn't say tasse you just said un café you just said UNE café and what you got was that coffee with milk in or just black stuff JE DESIRE meant something filthy you didn't say JE DESIRE you said VOULOIR je veux meant I INSIST you didn't say

Cassie looked at Rona and cleared her throat.

It wasn't my idea to come.

Cassie looked at Rona and cleared her throat. She had been hoping something casual and right would come out in French but it didn't. Only the coughing noise.

It wasn't my idea to come.

There was no accounting for it, no excuse. Cassie hadn't been. Not France, not even Spain. Not after those beaches in Greece, after the Cyclades and Antalya and Albania, bored and sweating with the suntan stuff slithering off and leaving raw burnt bits like open wounds, lying next to all those girls in teeny wee plastic bikinis you couldn't believe wouldn't melt, after all that there was no desire to go anywhere hot till Rona came in that day shouting It's only me and making coffee not able to relax starting making coffee saying I'm just round for a minute do you want to go to France?

Rona had eased back against the worktop, pretending to be relaxed while Cassie turned granules in the cup with a spoon. Rona hadn't put in enough. Cassie turned the granules so long Rona had had to repeat the question, rolling a bit of fluff between her fingers, the soft movement puffing the cloth of the pocket outwards. It was like this every time, the holiday thing. No it wasn't it was getting worse. Worrying if you were doing the right thing or if you were just doing things out of habit, if you were being assumptive and lazy. Questions had to be addressed: questions about whether anyone was taking anyone else or themselves for granted and if so whom and why. They always went though. They always came back. Then there would be another question about another holiday and Rona having to roll fluff between her fingers for a slightly longer interval each time.

I maybe said yes but it wasn't my idea.

Six minutes to.

Motorway and place names long gone. It was likely Rona would want to stop soon at some café or other. That meant they would have to go in and order. Cassie had seen Tous les Matins du Monde at the GFT. Hiroshima Mon Amour and Trop Belle pour Toi. She had read The Second Sex and Huis Clos. She could remember

16

Asterix cartoon books, an advert that had started DE QUOI NOURRISIEZ-VOUS VOTRE CHIEN and a sentence she had written about mushrooms glistening in the early-morning sun from a French exam. None of it was any use. Sartre. L'enfer c'est les autres.

They'd manage.
They always managed when they had to.

At least you'd see the place coming, be able to run over the words and phrases necessary for the buying of coffee before the time came. You'd see it coming no problem because the landscape was completely flat. Flatter than anywhere Cassie had ever seen. It was flatter than Holland for godsakes, just nothing for endless miles. Cassie watched five more tick up in tenths. Rona was still driving. Of course she was. Cassie looked into the back of the car. Bags, a box of cleaning materials, a warning triangle and godknows. Nothing interesting.

Glove compartment, Rona said.

Cassie opened it. POTTED FRANCE was edge-on inside the open mouth.

It was a book with a line drawing of the geographical shape of France on a tricolor background, the middle filled in like a delicatessen window. A subtitle, *An alphabetical guide for the traveller who needs to keep tight purse strings,* had a drawing of a purse beside it with wee strings. Cassie raked the page ends with one hand. The line drawings were inside as well. A bicycle leaning against a crumbly wall with ivy on it purported to be PROVENCE. A bunch of grapes and a donkey was ANJOU. NORMANDY turned up without warning.

NORMANDY is an agricultural region, full of farms and meadowland, orchards and rich green pasture

17

> which produces the excellent dairy produce for which
> the region is justly famous. Normandy is a place to
> explore and take time over, full of echoes of the Viking
> past and peasant or fishing present. Merchants,
> pilgrims and sightseers have come in their hundreds
> since the 11th Century.

The rest of the page had historic Rouen, beautiful cathedral, headdresses, the charm of old market places, orchards, pancakes, apple wine. The word CEMETERIES and four lines.

> The north provides many beautiful cemeteries devoted
> to the memory of the Great War dead of several
> countries. Lovingly tended by the French and often full
> of summer blooms, they are well worth a visit.

Underneath the four lines was a small plan raddled with crosses. Cassie had to look twice before she realised the scale. The thing must have covered miles: great blocks of landscape given over to the same pattern. All the way from the coast more or less. It was where they were, now. Cassie looked out the window then back at the page. Farms meadowland pasture Viking peasant fishing pilgrims headdresses charm and pancakes. And these four lines.

Cassie looked back outside. The rolling waves of FLAT kept themselves coming. Cassie put the book down, staring. Letting it click. It was flat because it had been bombed to hell, that's why it was flat. Shelling and reshelling over the same bare yards, earth puréed under countless thousands of army boot soles then flooded with mud that would have dried out like plaster. Sealed and level. Cassie felt the hair at the nape of her neck prickle as though a ghost had planted a kiss there. That's where they were. Now. Driving a trench through all that crucifixion. There had been no sign, nothing to show. Of course not. That was over and done with and this was what you got at the end of it. Yards of bugger all. Oh well. At least it left the locals with beautiful cemeteries and a bit of tourist revenue. That would be a great comfort. Cassie looked at Rona.

I don't believe this thing, Rona. This book.

Rona didn't even look over, just kept driving, flatness stretching out through the glass behind her driving arm.

I'm saying POTTED FRANCE. I hope you didn't pay for it.

What's wrong with it? she said.

It says not to miss the local pancakes or the cemeteries. Egon Ronay recommendation.

Rona changed the position of her hands on the wheel. Her face didn't alter. She was not picking up the irony. Cassie tried again.

Och just these four lines about the war that are worse than nothing. Sort of offhand. When you think what happened out there and this thing sticks in something that misses the point. It doesn't even say why it's so flat.

Rona said nothing.

It's flat because of the war.

Rona said nothing.

The war. They bombed it all to hell. That's why it's like that. And the book hardly mentions it. It doesn't bother.

Cassie waited a minute but Rona still wasn't for biting.

It's just when you're actually looking at it, it makes you think. Those poor buggers coming all this way and realising too late and getting shot to hell and knowing it was pointless. Because they did. They knew only they weren't allowed to say. They shot folk who tried to talk people out of it. Percy Topliss, conscientious objectors. They weren't allowed to object. Jesus. The skin of her back was crushing and uncrushing itself: someone walking over a grave. You think you should be able to feel it, that the place would be charged with some kind of static. Like Culloden. Look at it, Rona. Crawling

19

with folk once who weren't allowed to object to dying. Bombed to hell.

Rona inhaled and rubbed the side of her nose. L̲o̲o̲k̲, she said. Cows.

Cassie held still as long as she could then turned slowly.

Rona didn't often chat when she was driving and it would have been good to encourage her. Cows though. It wasn't anything you could respond to. Cows. Maybe it was just too early in the morning. Cows. Rona's hands were gripping the wheel, knuckles white. It was because she was driving. She would be concentrating on the other side of the road thing, that would be it. It was because Rona was driving she hadn't time to think about all the stuff Cassie's head kept filling up with. Rona was too busy working out things Cassie could not even begin to imagine. Rights and lefts. Rights and lefts were not explicable things: you either knew them or you didn't and Cassie didn't. Cassie looked over at the kind of hands that knew left from right then back at her own. Filleted fish on the jean legs. Unable to drive. Hands fit only to be hurtled over strange terrain down an unknowable side of the road: having to trust someone else to care enough not to plough them into a tree. Rona was a good driver though. She could drive for miles sometimes and not even seem to be awake, the way she drove to the office in the mornings and said O we're here when she was turning into the carpark like it was a surprise. But it couldn't be the case, not really. It was too awful to think about otherwise, the thought that large numbers of people, unbeknown to non-drivers, were careering about on the road, not even conscious maybe, avoiding death by sheer luck. It wasn't possible. Cassie sneaked a look at Rona to check. Unexpectedly, she was looking back.

See? Cows.

Cassie looked out where she had pointed and saw only empty field. Rona snorted, both hands back in place.

Didn't look in time. Too bad. Anyway, she said, I'm needing a coffee. Look for signs.

Cassie snapped the glove compartment open, put the book away. A big wooden crate with petrol pumps came up fast on the nearside. Beyond, a lone woman was trying to thumb a lift. You could watch her approach, come level, retreat. From behind, her whole back and a foot above her head was consumed by backpack. She didn't as much as turn to see if they had slowed. Cassie watched the reflection of the woman in the vanity mirror over the passenger seat eyeshade. Growing smaller for miles

miles

miles.

Photos 2
still London *Pas V*

Pink neon. Ann Summers shop, I think. Leicester Square. Look at him, arms crossed in a desperate bid to look worldly. Seventeen: posing about as a sexual sophisticate and not really knowing why. It was just what you did then. 1971. There was nothing anybody in their right mind would want to pay good money for in there either: eight-inch black vibrators with variable heads, things that rotated and played tunes. I Was Born Under a Wandering Star. Washable condoms with Mickey Mouse on. Anyway we got frozen and sore eyes walking about Leicester Square all the time because we hadn't a clue where else to go at night and that was free. Sex shops and places selling terrible posters, lamps with luminous blobs changing shape inside them, Chinese pincushions and metal puzzles: the kind of tat you think is luxurious when you're a teenager because you don't know any better. Luxurious because useless. Hanging about cinemas looking at what was on and reading the destinations at bus stops. Loving every minute.

Outside the tube. Piccadilly Circus, probably. We got the tube every night, miles out to some motel we were staying at. I loved the tube, thought it was the essence of London life or

21

something but it scared me as well. The first night, running for this tube train we could see from the top of the steps, I got there just in time. I got on with the doors brushing my shoulders then I realised he wasn't there. I hadn't thought that could happen, the doors just keeping closing like that. But they did, with me inside and him out. I'll never forget the look on his face, the train easing away from where he was. Like he'd been hit in the stomach. After he slid out of sight, I was more self-conscious about the other people in the carriage, trying not to let the feeling I was going to be sick show. I got off at the next stop and waited looking what I thought was nonchalant and he rolled up on the next train. I caught the face a second before he saw me, looking terrified. Worse than me. Then he clocked the fact I was there and tried to look annoyed. It passed though. We walked about like Hansel and Gretel after that, making sure. He kept saying he didn't know what I'd do without him. I've never gotten that look out of my head though. Chris watching me slide away on the train leaving him behind.

This was meant to be one of me but I'm not in it. A bit of Nelson's Column and two pigeons. Lots of sky. He used to kid folk on it was an Art shot but it wasn't. He just slipped when he was pressing the shutter release. It would have been a nice thing to have because I looked good then. Fresh as paint. And this. This is in entirely the wrong envelope. More than ten years out, for godsakes. It's a Turkish soldier. Asked us if we wanted to go home and meet his mother and tried to put his tongue in my mouth when he insisted on kissing me goodbye. Western custom.

The window is full of rising dust. Rona clatters her knuckles off the passenger window again, brandishes a packet of Polos. Two petrol pumps and a TABAC sign rise behind her. We are going in.

Dark. Bulbs were on somewhere, not helping much. A dull hissing noise that might have been a radio came and went out of the murk and a dull gleam, like teeth in a halfshut mouth, filtered through from the gantry's upside down bottles and glasses, cellophane wrappers and measure nozzles. All the tables but two had chairs stacked on top, the carpet folded back on itself so only the rubber showed. Behind that, four men hung about in front of the counter, not speaking. They turned and looked at the two women who had just walked in. Cassie tried not to look back and failed. Bellies over the belts of the waistbands, stains on the T-shirts. The stains quivered when they breathed in. The men just kept staring, taking their time. Rona peeled away from Cassie's side, leaving a hole of cold air. In search of a toilet, probably. One of the men watched her walk past then they all turned away, back to their glasses. Cassie scanned the nearest tables, feeling for the novel in her back pocket. It was always good to carry a novel or a notebook in case you needed to look absorbed, a woman not to be trifled with. It was there all right, reassuringly firm and cool under the hand. She walked the two steps to the nearest place, sat then dumped the book on the table. Black cover. White letters. Thérèse Raquin. Zola. Zola in translation but there was no way of telling from the cover. For a horrible split-second, Cassie imagined the thing an attractant: the men strolling over, tossing the Rizla papers and tobacco tins on the table, dumping a full bottle at her elbow in expectation of some kind of literary debate that would involve *crimes passionels*, class war, the misunderstood gulf between realism and naturalism, Camus and football. But she knew they wouldn't. Of course they wouldn't. Even if they could make out the title in this light, if they noticed the thing at all, even if they were desperate for literary conversation, they would not choose her. One look and they'd know her classification. Tourist. Female tourist. And English: they always thought you were English. Anyway, they would leave her alone. It would be ok. It always was ok, just this bit that was always difficult, the initial reminder of the depth to which this was not your place. And it wasn't. Not your language, your currency, your carefully gathered collection of survival techniques or any other bloody thing. Cassie fiddled with the spine of the book, looking stern. Maybe she should write notes: notes about how this always happened and how you came though it, some guidelines for the future. Rona was coming back, though. Cassie heard her bump into a table, the leg of it scraping on tile. No cups.

Did you order?

No. Cassie knew she was trying to look as though the idea was outlandish, something nobody in their right mind would be asking her to do. Rona sighed, walked back to the counter. The man behind it didn't even bother to look up. Cassie watched Rona tap the counter with her nails, the man keeping putting glasses on a low shelf. Out of sight. A blue jaw and hairy hands.

This was short change.
Frenchmen were supposed to be suave.

They were supposed to have close-shaved chins and mesomorphic outlines, suggestion of muscle rippling under the polo shirt material, neat crocodile-effect belts and pleated trousers, side-partings and a flop of dark hair over the one eye. Lopsided grins. Yves St Laurent or Chanel uncurling from manly necks, discreet watches braceleting biteable wrists. But there were only these four men with stains and a rude bugger needing a shave.

National stereotypes

Frenchmen were supposed to be suave.

Turks were sex-crazed. They followed you about, muttering filth.
— Scots were dour but could fuck all night.

Joke.

Rona's voice, half an octave higher than usual, was asking the man's back for café au lait. Cassie turned away. There were cracks on the facing wall and dirt along the picture rail, the cocooned grey corpse of something a spider would come back for later wavering on a thin wire. Cassie thought about stalls. You got them in France: roadside stalls with fruit. They could get apples, a melon. They could buy stuff to eat there and not have to do this again. But they would. Cassie knew fine they would. Rona would come back and they would drink the coffee in silence, warding off the impending tip question and whether they would leave one, how much. Foreign countries jesus. Eight o five. An interminable two weeks of this to come. Rona came back, two wee cups using up a hand apiece. Drinking it took less than a minute. Rona looked over, a foam moustache lining her upper lip. When she started untangling the 500F note from the purse, getting the harmless smile ready, Cassie picked up her Zola and walked.

The sun was getting sore already.

Cassie went to the car, knowing it was shut. It was getting worse, this thing. Only here – what the hell time was it – only here an hour and fifteen minutes and this thing was cranking up already. It was a record. No it wasn't. The time they went to Denmark and Rona phoned up the night before and said You don't need to go with me if you don't want in the premenstrual voice – the time they went to Denmark, THAT was the record. First days were always the same. The windscreen was glued with mashed insects, a light coating of sticky filth. It would need washing every day. Less than one day, less than one morning, and it was a mess already, a mess and locked. Rona had both sets. Rona always did. But soon she would come and open up the doors. They would get into the car and get moving again, thank god for tarmac and the Romans, the road the road. They might even listen to some music. That's what they would do. They would listen to it and feel

Cassie didn't know what they would feel but it might be better.

Through the window, a corner of the personal stereo, under the travel kettle and two polythene bags of polythene bags Rona brought to put dirty washing in. No sign of tapes.

Phôtos 3   2nd hôl— Edin

Ahhh the Alpine.
Sunbeam Alpine. We got the MoT just the day we were due to leave. Edinburgh, I think. Edinburgh. We couldn't really go far with him spending on gasket sets and piston rings and godknows but it was worth it. He loved that car. I was proud of what he could do: out in all weathers, coming back in with the sweatshirt greasy and his hands grey, a big smear on his face and smelling of gunk. I tried going down to learn how it was done but he never liked it. Said I just asked questions all the time. Hanging about watching. I took to watching long-distance, imagining the big square hands on pieces of dirty metal, muscles working against the weight of the machine and nearly burst with love listening to the Top 40 in the kitchen. Me and Ann Nightingale. I hadn't a bloody clue what he did out there. I got to polish the upholstery and chrome. I liked the chrome. Even if I did catch the odd reflection, my own face drawn up like an African tribal mask: I liked to see it shine. I got to fill dents in the bodywork then sand them down. When you felt the sanded places afterwards, stroking to see if the edges were smooth through the chalky powder it was warm: warm, hard smoothness that made your fingers feel like struck matches. It took a whole weekend spraying the thing purple with two guys from work, handkerchiefs over their mouths. All they took for it was two cans of Newcastle Brown. He went out

for a drink with them after and I poured cold tea down the sink before I went to bed. I knew not to wait up. Next day he was late home. He came in pink and sweating, smiling fit to bust. You should have seen her he said, opened her up along the shore road and she goes like a fucking princess. She goes like a wet dream. A bent garage gave us the MoT just in time for his scheduled fortnight. Second holiday. Must have been the Festival I suppose but we wouldn't have known any different.

It was you know. It was definitely Edinburgh. Because here's one of Chris outside the otter house. All lapels. There isn't any otter because it wouldn't come out. I used to have snaps of the whole thing: the zoo, Castle, Arthur's Seat, Holyrood, C&A, Bargain Books. The zoo was the best. He's got one of me throwing sandwiches at penguins. I've always liked animals.

From the side of the petrol pumps, all Cassie could see were more flat fields. Cows and rabbits. Normandy butter brewing inside fourfold bovine guts and apple trees on what had been wasteland, greened over. It was astonishing the way things recovered, things growing out the bombed-to-hellness it had once been. She had read somewhere birds didn't go there for ages after the war. A place with no birds. In the distance, Cassie made out things like huge fingertips poking over the top of a distant wall. A sign. Just legible. Cassie said the words out loud.

Canadian Cemetery.

You never thought of Canadians in the First World War.

All that way.

Cassie looked at stone tips, monuments to bits of strewn Canadian. The flatness on either side, cows and the trees dredging up sap from the ground to make cider and that brandy stuff. Calvados. Australian cemeteries here too. The book said so. Canadians and Australians stuck out here being processed into Calvados by apple trees. The turned earth of the nearside field. Australians to christ. Sucked dry by tree roots.

The TABAC sign, wavering. The door that didn't open.

Heat scouring the back of the neck.

It wouldn't be long now, though.
Not long before there was the thrill of tyre dunting off the gravel, putting the headphones on even with no tape, hearing the hiss of the empty reels turning, staring out at the sky. Everything would be fine when they were moving again.

Keeping going along the road.

three

COCA COLA

KODAK

AKAI   NIKON

SEIMENS   LEVIS

Well?

Beside a line of cars not moving, the ringroad sign. Rona held the wheel, waiting.

Well? D'you want a look at Paris or not?

Cassie had never been to Paris. Rona had: Student Inter-rail from college. Twice. She said Paris was nice but filthy. She had been to the Latin Quarter with the address of somewhere cheap on a bit of paper. It was called the Latin Quarter because that was where students stayed from the year dot when that's what they spoke. She had gone down into the Metro and on to the first train that arrived though it was completely jammed. Rush hour. She said the train smelled funny: at the time she thought it was garlic. Two men had gotten in and started to sing for money, their hands hennaed with holes in the centres for people to fill them with something. Nobody had. Nobody even looked at them. They got off and Rona got a seat. She'd only been in it a minute when a wee boy came and sat on it too. On top of Rona. His father seemed to think this was ok. Two stops up the line, the boy said Madame je vais vomir so Rona gave up. She got off at the next stop not knowing where it was. Lost. Instead of just looking for the first place she buggered about the rest of the day avoiding the Metro and trying to track down the address on the bit of paper. *R's prev hol*

Was it worth it?
Rona looked blank.
When you found it? I assume you did find it in the end.
Silence.
Well? Did you or didn't you?
Eventually, Rona shrugged. Can't remember.

Rona can't do the ends of stories to save her life.

Well, we'll have to decide soon. Is it this place that's twinned with Ayr, the bypass to Versailles or what?

Cassie looked back at the hoardings beyond the traffic line. Preoccupation with electrical goods, jeans and fizzy drinks, fags, cameras, more jeans, more fags, and yoghurt shows all the way over here from the peripherique. The last time I saw Paris.

Rona takes the bypass to Rambouillet, cashes some money and fills the car up. We need to keep driving.

Outside the Wolverine House. Edinburgh Zoo. That's me
rolling on the grass, coke spraying out my mouth like a water
sprinkler because I'm laughing so much but I can't remember
what about. Chris hated that. He used to look sideways to avoid
the horrible truth when I did things he didn't like. Cassie you
laugh like a drain, he said. He ran away from me all the way
down the hill to the Monkey House then ran even faster out the
other side holding his nose. He held me when I laughed that
time, pleased. Further down the hill we found a bear in a
concrete box, pacing along a naked parapet and back again,
hypnotising itself. A man in a deerstalker was there already. He
watched it for a while before he took a paper bag from his pocket
and threw chunks of fruit cake through the bars. Two big
chunks. The bear didn't eat them. The swaying intensified.
There was nothing else it could do. Anyway I knew if I got
depressed I would ruin the day out so I stopped looking and
started walking up the hill to get away. It's only a bear, he said,
it doesn't know any different. It's ok.

Castle. We took the car with its bent MoT first time but I got us
lost. In the end he took the map off me and threw it into the
back and we guessed. Walking. It worked far better. This was
the armoury: guns and halberds, bloody great swords. One of
them was pitted along the edge and taller than me. Serrated
teeth, stained brown. The spikes on the maces blunt as park
railings. I went for a walk and left him in there, rapt in front of a
glass case of rapiers. Nineteen years old, gawping at guns. I
thought it would cheer you up he said. Museum. You like
museums. He meant it as well. That was the first time I asked
him to teach me to drive. I thought if I could drive I could drop
him off somewhere and get out his hair for a while. He said no.
Fair enough. His car. We came back with loads of pictures of
suits of armour. They're his too. Mutual consent.

31

> Following rapid expansion after both world wars,
> ARRAS is today a large modern conurbation giving
> little hint of its medieval weaving past. The fine town
> square is faithfully preserved. ARRAS has a cathedral
> and a fine arts museum. La Grand'Place and Place des
> Heros are among the most perfect extant examples of
> 17th and 18th century architecture in France.

Arras was shut.

Bits of litter in the streets and two dogs sniffing each other,
feathers whirlpooling in the gutter. A man whistling. There was a
Tourist Office in the town square, a Flemish-looking building with
pinnacle efforts on the roof and furled masonry above the oblong
windows. Tourist Office. There was no sign to say when it usually
opened, whether it ever had been. Only a single dirty curtain falling
from halfway up the window and a square of sellotape where
something had been and wasn't any more.

Rona pushed her specs up the bridge of her nose and looked at
the window. She looked at it for about five minutes without saying
anything or moving position. Then she looked at Cassie.

It's shut.

I know it's shut. What do we do though.

Rona looked back at the window. Her specs reflected in the
glass. She hovered on the edge of a word for about a minute before
she made up her mind which one it was.

Right. It'll have to be a Youth Hostel.

Cassie looked at her.

There's nothing else, Cassie. Nothing else cheap anyway.

Cassie managed to keep saying nothing.

Right. That's it then. Youth Hostel. Rona shrugged. Only I
don't know where it is.

She was tired and starving and so was Cassie. Anywhere would be ok so long as it offered a lie down. A lie down flat.

We could just walk about till we find it. Auberge de jeunesse. There's a handbook in the car.

Cassie looked at Rona. Rona must have had an idea they would do this because she knew the phrase. She'd have looked it up. Auberge de jeunesse. The idea of Rona plotting made Cassie's jaw go stiff. Rona knew.

OK you wait here. I'll go.

Dips in Rona's shoulders where her bra straps dug into soft flesh.

She knew fine I would follow.

Cassie and Rona
Rona and Cassie

walked in silence to the car, shaking separate limbs to feel the blood course back. On the other side of the square, a poodle gurried something in the gutter. The poodle was huge. It was brown, tail going like a metronome, muzzle gritted. The poodle's head bobbed up and down with the thing it was tugging getting longer all the time. They crossed the road avoiding the poodle in a big semi-circle. Well past, Cassie heard something snap. Like bone. She didn't turn round.

They took the handbook and both of Rona's shoulderbags and went back. The building was right across from where they'd been standing. A long type of opera glove lay sodden in the gutter outside. Rona found intercom buttons and pressed them all. The third time, the grille crackled like a crisp bag and Rona got in first.

Chambres she said. Chambres pour deux dames.

The brown poodle shot past the end of the road with something in its mouth. Something the shape of a human arm. Light tumbled on to the cobbles in a slim V, fattening to obtuse. The Youth Hostel door was wide open.

The bed looked terrible. Cassie poked it with one finger. Horsehair.

Christ. Feel this.

Rona didn't.

Doesn't matter if it's terrible, it's cheap. Cheap, Cassie, cheap.

Cassie plonked the sportsbag on the hard surface. It didn't even dent.

It's just the one night, Rona said.

She was off already, hunting about. After toilets. Everywhere they went, Rona found the toilets within five minutes of arriving. Cassie always said Rona should write a book on how to do it, a boon for the British Tourist and Rona always ignored her. As she was meant to.

Showers.

Rona shouting. The hollow tile ring behind it said exactly what the showers were like. They were cold showers: cold, white showers with the grout needing redone and halfdoors if any at all and the basins like wash-house sinks. It was that kind of tile-noise behind Rona's voice.

Showers.

This time the rest of Rona came after the voice so the hollow tone was gone. She was smiling: the kind of smile that knew the place was awful but would refuse to admit it. Rona loves showers. She loves games of not admitting hellishness is hellish. It drives me round the bloody twist.

One time

One time we went to Glen Nevis.

Rona and some friends she'd been in the Guides with or
something, went camping and she asked Cassie too. Not long after
Cassie started in the office. Cassie could remember being asked but
not why she said yes. To show willing probably: new girl fitting in.
What you did because you thought everybody did it and you wanted
company. Trying not to look too horrified so they wouldn't laugh, all
those fine healthy women with climbing boots and no make-up,
taking showers every morning and every night even though there
was only cold water, a tiled floor awash with stagnant puddles. Wet
socks all the time. The same knickers for three days. It was terrible,
more terrible than Cassie imagined and she imagined it would be
terrible. The cold water running over your wrists when you ran the
water, trying to magic the warm to start coming through and it
didn't. She didn't take anything off, just went back to the tent with
the one freezing wrist. Rona was there every morning and every
night laughing. Cassie tried like hell twice then didn't care. There
was no point making out it wasn't awful. Cassie stayed warm and
dirty. She stayed away from the shower block.

Now here we are again.

Youth Hostels and hillwalking, going for swims in riverside
streams: discomfort and bluffness, being spartan and British and
making out pain is not a consideration. Horrible beyond belief. I
read a thing about Doris Day. That Doris Day's first man used to
batter the hell out of her and there was Doris making Pillow Talk
and The Pyjama Game with Rock Hudson never asking why they
didn't make reference to wife-beating in the movies. She just
assumed it was one of those things that happened but no-one talked
about. Maintaining a fiction about real life was just what you did.
Doris Day. Doris as Calamity Jane on the Deadwood Stage,
outshooting Wild Bill Hicock in the saloon. Doris covering her
bruises with make-up while Rock exchanged bodily fluids with the
latest boyfriend before his studio call. Poor bloody Rock Hudson.

Poor bloody Doris and poor bloody Rock Hudson. Madeupness. Like camping. A big lie about it being anything other than totally hellish. Things that suggested how many lies nearly everything was based on. It gets me

It gets you

It got Cassie suspicious and angry. And it came out in funny ways like taking the huff about things it had nothing to do with. The way she felt now because Rona was thrilled with the showers. Showers had been ok in Greece. But that was with someone else, someone else entirely.

Cassie thought about Rona through there, testing the water. The water being freezing and Rona deciding to have a shower anyway. Godknew what she tested things for if it wasn't to act on information received. Thinking about Rona not acting on information made Cassie want to punch something. It wouldn't be Rona. After seventeen years it was unlikely she'd start punching Rona now.

Towel. Rona was right there, holding up one wet hand.

Cassie watched Rona rummaging and dripping on the hard bedspread, one hand inside the canvas mouth, zip teeth angled over her wrist ready to bite and she just didn't know.

I think I'll have one before we go, she said, padding off with the towel in hand.

Cassie listened to Rona dumping off, acknowledging nothing, the clank of taps under familiar fingers. One with a bit missing. Poor bloody Rona. Nine and a half fingers owing to being overfriendly with the wrong dog at an incautious age. Cassie rubbed her eyes and lay flat out on the hard boards. It felt ok. Lack of give under the spine made muscles stretch themselves to accommodate the flatness. It was so sore it was soothing. Like deserved punishment. Something to straighten you out. Further off, the sound of water and Rona shouting Shit.

36

Cassie shut her eyes. She wasn't going near the toilets till it was unavoidable. She would last. A sudden gushing noise, Rona shouting Shit. Then something else. A softer noise altogether. Cassie opened her eyes as little as necessary. A girl was moving about on the bunks opposite, covered in yards of orange hair. Undressing. Through the haze of her own lashes, Cassie watched the girl pull off her T-shirt. No bra. The tremor of transparent breasts when she shook the cloth free of her arms, pale blue veins marbling the fullest parts. Where a hand might fit. The girl kept going, slipping white thumbs behind the band of the shorts, stripping them off over her pencil legs. A red ring round her belly where the waistband had been, a shark bite. A flare of pubic hair. She ran a hand down for one sock, then the other, shouting something in an unrecognisable language, Dutch maybe, Danish. But nobody else was there. The girl picked up her fallen clothes, gold hair glittering in the cupped armpit when she stooped and stretched, stooped and stretched. Couldn't have been more than twenty. Cassie felt an internal muscle clutch and relax. The girl didn't even know she was looking. The sound of young feet flat against the cold floor. Cassie lay back on the horsehair and waited, eyes drilling the cracked ceiling. Waiting.

Chris in the shower.
His penis sprays water, drips soap.

HELLO. Rona's voice making conversation. They're COOL. The showers. COOL.

The sound of the shower intensified. The girl did not answer.

Possible trips from ARRAS could include that to the Vimy Ridge and to Notre-Dame-de-Lorette's national cemetery with its 20,000 tombs where eight ossuaries contain the remains of 26,000 unidentified soldiers. There is also a small museum. Not far is a museum-diorama of the battlefields for those who wish to relive the great campaigns.

The café near the train station had a Subbuteo table and a gang of men in their twenties or so. Young things. Rona ordered cheese sandwiches but they didn't have any. Only pizza. They ate pizza with a bottle of wine that was cheaper than two coffees. After the second glass, Rona brought out the blue folder. Cassie poured more into a glass, held the bottle up for Rona. Rona shrugged. A fresh game started up two tables away.

Too noisy?
Too noisy.

Rona put the folder away.

Back along the cobbled bit of the street, none of the shop windows were lit. Cassie said she thought the place was like Kilmarnock on a wet Wednesday half shutting.

Why shouldn't it? Rona was always thought-provoking after a drink. Eh? Why shouldn't it.

Cassie put her arm through Rona's. She was quite right. Arras had as much right to look like Kilmarnock as Kilmarnock had. She was quite bloody right. Rona smiled in a kind of watery-eyed way that made Cassie feel she had given her a present. Going back to the Hostel, she made a mumbling noise and put her arm round Rona's shoulders. Rona tilted her head close and Cassie pulled away. She wanted to confess.

I'm not able to use those showers Rona.
Cassie could hear her sighing into the dark. I know. I know.

38

They walked along the guttering. The opera glove was still there, velvet fingers broken by the running water.

We'll find somewhere else tomorrow, ok?

There was a long enough space of nothing for Cassie to feel too much relief. Manipulative.

Ok. After we look though. After we look for the war graves place.

A crackle and something foreign right in Cassie's ear. Rona must have pressed the intercom button when she hadn't been looking. Rona shouted OK through German catcalls, great hoots of laughter and mock screams. The door creaked open.

No-one else in the dormitory. The noise must have been from the men's bit. The ginger-haired woman wasn't there. Cassie wondered if she should say about her, that she might come back then changed her mind. Maybe she wouldn't. Rona was halfway out of her trousers, sitting and hauling them over her shoeless feet.

Remember that place we stayed in in Amsterdam, Rona? Christ.

It was ok, the place in Amsterdam.

It was ok my arse. That guy that was the dog trainer telling us about the way you get an alsatian to go for the throat and what a mess they made if they were good. That was the word he used, Rona: *good*. Remember his teeth? Funny how you associate Americans with good teeth.

Orthodontist culture, Rona said.

Well he missed out. He must have been skint that guy. White trash. Not a sanctioned part of the American Dream at all. And that other one, the one with the beard from Kent who came and read us his erotic poetry when we were trying to watch the tv. The woman who tormented his mind or something: the way he just assumed it

39

was ok to come and torment our minds with it as well. It was hellish, Rona, class A hellish.

Rona laughed out of a column of cloth. Her shirt was stuck, needing another button loose at the neck.

Admit it. It was the worst place in the world.

The breakfast was good though. It was. All that cheese and different bread. Hot chocolate. You got a good breakfast. The shirt peeled up. Rona's face was lilac.

You always remember things like that. The breakfast for heaven's sake. Cassie tutted. It was a point though. They had been. Rona wasn't finished.

Anyway, it was you they came over to talk to, not me. Things like that never happen when I'm on my own. It's you they like.

That was a point as well.

Cassie undressed thinking about it while Rona turned back her sheets. She always took the bottom bunk. Even drunk, it was what she did. They peed in adjoining cubicles, brushed their teeth side by side, Cassie's skin electrifying with the chill of the tile underfoot. They embraced giggling with cold on the way into bed till Cassie pulled back. Rona's skin was too close.

Are the letters there?

Rona footered with the folder, handed up two bits of paper. Cassie held one up to the light. Opened full it was still tiny, a tiny bit of paper full of tight, right-sloping pencil marks that reminded Cassie of her mother's. Not that her mother had ever written letters but it did anyway. The two postcards, one from Benidorm and one from Tossa. They looked exactly the same. She had to tilt it to read.

Dear Maggie

Just a note to say I arrived safe on the Sunday and may I say I was very lucky to get back as the rest of the chaps that ran away

40

got Royal Warrant and 5 days CB that was only for 1 days absence I was away 2 days I got round the orderly serjeant boy giving him 1/- for a drink so that just shows you how it can be done. Now Maggie we have all been inspected by the General today Tuesday I expect to be on my road to France tomorrow Wednesday so I was very glad I ran away on saturday as I would have had to go away without seeing you I am not downhearted exactly but for the sake of the bairns it is hard times but you will have to try & do the best you can I dont like the Idea if you do start work I hope Maggie you will see the wee chaps all right and you dont mind me saying this if it will help that I will always be thinking of you and the bairns no matter where I go to. Now Maggie I will bid you farewell I hope to be spared to come back & to do more for you than I have in the Past

Yours for ever

I shall write every time I get the Chance   XXXXX Peter

Cassie could hear Rona lying still, breathing. She folded the letter and put it back inside the blue folder, the paper hardly making a noise. It folded on its own, from knowing the lines it belonged in.

That the first one?
Uhu. I only brought the first and the last. That's the first one.

Cassie couldn't think of anything else to say.

Rona lay on for a moment or so longer before she got up and padded over to the light switch. Rona's footfalls hanging in the darkness as she came back, the frame of the beds shaking.
Rona saying goodnight.

Cassie waited a moment or two, listening to lungfuls of dark.

Rona?

The rustle of hard sheeting.

Rona?

The sound of Rona breathing deeper.

I lie wide-eyed wondering why I read the bloody thing out loud, wondering why I think it might be good to cry. I just don't know what for, that's all. I don't know what for.

cotemporaneous —

four

We sleep.
We always sleep.

I can't remember the first time we did that, slept in the same
room and woke together. Rona's place, probably: Chris on one of his
training weekends, away playing football or somesuch bloody thing.
Amateur photography club outing to take photos of gullible lassies
who could be talked into not wearing much. Going round to Rona's
and staying over talking till thon time: it used to happen all the time.
But I can't remember the first; the first time I woke with her
breathing next to me, the other skin generating heat beside mine.
The awkwardness of disengaging, not knowing how to go about the
business of dressing without making assumptions. Some people
don't like their nakedness observed. The first time naked together in
a room, discreetly Turned Away as though by design. The washing
of faces. Cassie hardly lathered the soap at all, worried about the
drying effects and filling her cupped hands only with cold. Rona
scrubbed up like a surgeon then saturated her vest front splashing to

get rid of all the suds, her face prawn pink from being scoured with a towel. Rona watched while Cassie had put moisturiser on, like a wee boy watching a man shave. Cassie had held out the jar and watched Rona dip her finger in, apply it in dabs like Germoline. That must have been early on. That is, if it happened at all. It could just as easy be something I made up to fit what I know now, what I've seen since. A little creative hindsight.

Anyway.

Rona and Cassie
Cassie and Rona

washed up at the sink in a hollow dormitory bathroom in a Youth Hostel in Arras, Rona's enthusiasm for removal of dead skin cells making Cassie feel half-clean and common.

She makes me feel half-clean and common in lots of ways.

Cassie got her own back when it came to brushing teeth though. Cassie brushed her teeth like the enamel needed shifting. Even so they were stuffed with amalgam and six were false. Brushing was no protection from wear and tear. Sometimes she would wonder what the noise was and realise afresh each time. The soft rotary shuffle of molar against molar. She had been known to wake in the morning with her whole face sore from the same thing. Self-control exercised even in sleep. Rona coughed and she realised she was doing it now. Jaw locked. She was grinding her teeth.

Here you go said Rona.
She pushed a card over to Cassie's side of the table.

Things are going fine so far ie Arras. Stayed in a YH last night. This morning they tried to make Cassie wash the steps. She did it when I explained it was the only thing stopping us getting out. Downtown Arras is sunny and we are having breakfast in an unsavoury place that sold us boiled eggs. I have the directions from the War Office and we'll be off as soon as Cassie gets her face out of the coffee. Love, Rona and

Cassie looked up. Rona's hair needed brushing. She looked like a cockatoo, spiky from how she'd been lying all night but Cassie didn't say. Rona had paid at the hostel on the way out and hadn't gloated about the stairs washing business: she was owed something. Cassie took the card and flipped it over. There was a picture of a field on the front and a child looking between big daisies at a tortoise.

I got it for a laugh, Rona said. For mum. She won't know what to make of it. She went back to the other bits of paper, perky.

Rona's cup was still half full. It was also cold but that never worried her. Cassie's had been empty for fifteen minutes. It would probably wait on another fifteen till Rona had checked everything three times. Cassie thought about Rona phoning the War Office. Cassie didn't know how else they were meant to find it but knew there had to have been a way that didn't involve asking anybody for anything. Especially not the bloody War Office. It was what Rona did though: she trusted authority. Like the time she had taken an interest in make-up and bought a book to tell her how. St Michael's. She also bought all the stuff it recommended and used it twice. The book was still there with the old eyeshadow: colours nobody wore any more. Grounds rose to the top of the coffee, sank again. In a minute she would start talking through the route, her voice making maps in the background, describing a series of rights and lefts that meant nothing to Cassie and only made her want to implode. One day she would. Rona would be reeling off directions and Cassie would get dizzy and say Please stop, Rona and Rona wouldn't hear or even notice. And Cassie's limbs would start to loosen on the fourth repetition. Please stop Rona. On the fifth, an arm would drop off. A leg. Then each limb in turn. Please stop Rona. Finally the neck would creak, tilt and split like a tree trunk and Cassie's head would bounce at Rona's feet. And Rona would turn, look at the head, roll her eyes and say YOU HAVEN'T BEEN LISTENING TO A WORD OF THIS HAVE YOU? And start again.

Ah god.

It was the caffeine, likely: hangover of travel or something. The giant poodle came out of a doorway on the other side of the road and checked the gutter. Nonplussed. Cassie kept watching the coffee, waiting to go. She couldn't think why she was in this terrible mood.

Boarding House in Stratford. Chris looking possessive. Territorial. He was in a bad mood with me taking one of him there when he was psyching himself up to be a sophisticate for going back inside. A nice place, found it by accident. They didn't usually do B&B, that's why there's no sign. Anyway he'd had this idea we could swan about English villages savouring Ye Olde Pub Grub, the thwack of leather on willow from the village green etc etc. Draught cider and thatch, driving along country roads to watch the locals scything the hay. I don't know. Anyway it was the height of the season and the place was hoaching with foreign tourists carrying copies of Much Ado about Nothing. We hadn't taken that into account at all. For all we knew, it was always this hard to find somewhere to stay. NO VACANCIES signs everywhere: the four without just hadn't changed them yet. Eventually, a woman cutting a hedge took us in. She had a spare room and sometimes let it out but only to people she liked the look of. She made that very clear. She wanted us to know it was a privilege.

Dining room. Chris taking the top off the butter dish. He'd just told me not to take a picture so he's blocking me out for being common. The house made you aware of things like that:

antiques, flowers in gigantic ugly vases. Twin beds and curtains with rope things to tie them back. Their bedroom was right through the wall and the twin beds squeaked if two people got into one so we fucked on the floor the first night and not at all on the others. He was worried about their carpet. In the morning, we met the husband steering two big labradors through the gates and one of the kids. We got home-made quince jam with breakfast. I think she must have known how young we were. At the end of the three days I was packing up the car. Chris was inside with her writing the cheque. Cheque all right? he was saying. I can get cash if you like. He was laughing this throaty laugh and speaking with a drawl. She said a cheque was fine. I knew he would be hesitating over the pen, picking his moment to start. He wrote his signature fast and had to do it all in one go. If he was forced to lift the pen from the paper he would start all over again, cursing because he'd made a mess. He hated messy writing. Just to me, I heard her say, spelling out her name. I do the B&B side of things so John says it's my earnings.

Haha quite right, he said.

It was definitely Chris. There was nobody else it could have been.

I heard her ask him to say goodbye to Mrs Foster too. Have a pleasant journey. He did the throaty chuckle and said au revoir. Au revoir.

I sneaked a look at the Visitors' Book on the way back in for my handbag. It said Mr and Mrs Foster in his writing. Messy as hell. I looked at him and said au revoir a couple of times on the way home to see if he would react. He pretended he couldn't hear me. I never asked why he'd pretended we were married. I think I knew the answer to that. She must have known though. Twenty-one and doing a been-together-now-for-forty-years routine. She would have known fine.

Little Chef. All these stops on the way back. I told him if I could drive I could take half the burden of that kind of thing but he told me not to be daft. Be realistic Cassie, he said. You've no sense of direction look whose car is it anyway you should never teach somebody you know to drive. Everybody knows that, he said. Everybody. So we're going in for the umpteenth coffee, Chris in a bad mood because he couldn't have beer. That T-shirt though. He always looked good in black.

MU

       MU   F   S

just a smirr at the side of the road.

Rona pulled into the ditch, looked over her shoulder, reversing back. A thing like a viaduct rushed towards the rear windscreen, filled up the side window. MUR DES FUSILIERS, lettering over an arch with columns on either side, a single wall as though the other three had been surgically removed. Rona riffled the paper on her knees, let it drop on to the rubber mat, hauled the camera out from beneath her seat.

Is it the right place then?

She was out the car before Cassie turned for answer, the space where she had been quivering. Cassie watched her friend hare up to the wall, disappear inside and reached for the belt clip, shaking her head. She had had no idea it mattered that much. That it mattered at all, come to that.

The gravel was warm. Cassie followed the echo of Rona's having crunched off into somewhere unseen. Behind the first archway, a platform like a stage led to another arched wall in front. Through a slat in that wall, Cassie saw a flash of green roll out like a ribbon, dotted with white. The dots became crosses: row after row stretching up and out, filling the height and breadth of her vision. White crosses: equidistant, repeatedly the same.

The smudge in the corner of her eye moved. It was Rona, Rona looking up at the wall behind. Cassie turned. On either side of the entrance, the curved wall was lined with black marble. The marble was filled with lateral lines, tiny names carved from top to bottom over the whole surface.

Hello. Rona was looking over, her specs hiding her eyes.
This the place? Cassie took herself by surprise. The voice.
Rona shrugged and looked at the bit of paper again.
It will be. A cool matter-of-factness was coming out her mouth. The kind of voice that paused to draw on an imaginary cigarette, narrowing its eyes in recognition of gritty reality. It wasn't a voice she liked much.
Doesn't look like it could be anywhere else.
Rona said nothing.

A sprinkler whirred in the middle of the panel of the sky and greenery at her back as Rona scanned the first aisles. Cassie looked up then down the carved lists. It could take all day. And if it did, it did: this was what the whole thing was meant to be for after all, it was Rona's thing. Cassie put her hand over her mouth to keep quiet and looked out over the grass. Over the crosses. So many of them. The unnatural brightness of the place, its regularity and precision, the crosses so small. They looked too close together to have people underneath. Then again most of them wouldn't have. How they knew that some of the stuff they must have found on the busted-up fields was even human let alone who it was, which bit of whom. Cassie walked forward a pace or so, keeping her eyes level. Grass and shrubbery poked between the white lines, changing perspective. More crosses emerged from nowhere all the time, sore-thumb headstones popping up now and again between the steady lines. Maybe they were the whole corpses, those identifiable enough to put faces to. One was near enough to make out a little detail: a photograph inside resin or maybe behind glass and sunk into the stone, gold letters making sword cuts against the sun. An Italian, maybe. They did that in Italian cemeteries. Or Greek. The photo was smiling, a boy maybe. Hard to see clearly from here. But she wasn't going any closer. The photo had nothing to do with her. The whole place had nothing to do with her. It was a cemetery, not a fucking amusement arcade. Staring at a photo on a headstone and conjecturing about who he might have been just to pass the time was not in order. The place was full of folk who belonged to somebody but none of them were hers. She had no right play-acting or making up wee sentimental fictions while her pal was busy. Or manufacturing spurious noble sentiments about it either. It was dubious territory indeed, the fantasy you could understand a bloody thing by looking at the likes of this. Rows of dead people. Dead men. Dead boys. There was nothing to understand but sheer, grinding misery: women getting those wee letters Rona's grandmother had got with the rubbish about gallantry. Cassie hovered on the top step of the stairway, further than arm's length from where the crosses began. It felt colder there, better. She was just beginning to enjoy the bleakness of it when

Cassie.

She heard her name.

Cassie.

Rona was waving over, pointing. She had found it. Five minutes here and she'd found the bloody thing. Smiling, standing back and levelling the camera, wanting Cassie to come and see. Cassie started walking over, wondering if she should offer to take a picture of Rona taking a picture of the wall. Rona with her trousers still creased from the suitcase. It could be head and shoulders though. Maybe this was a big enough moment for the trousers to be beside the point. She was on the verge of suggesting it when another noise turned both heads back to the garden.

Between the ranks of crosses, a big man in a flat cap and sleeves rolled up was coming towards them. Hurrying without running. Rona lowered the camera and waited till he arrived. They exchanged a glance while he sat on the low marble wall, panting. He hardly took time to catch his breath before he started waving his hands, miming and making sounds in his throat. Not words. More like gargling with rocks. Maybe he didn't see the point in speaking to foreigners in case they didn't understand. Maybe he didn't have a choice. Rona looked intently at him, shrugging, her hands out-turned. The man shook his head, scattering beads of water. Cassie checked it wasn't the eyes and it wasn't. His eyeballs were yellow but quite dry, cheeks purple with thread veins. Weathered. Fingers like worms round the handle of a trowel. He wheezed again and Rona tried single words to see if she was getting warm. Permit? Appareil? Holding the camera up, looking earnest. He looked through the yellow layer on top of his eyeballs at Rona, shaking his head. It didn't put her off.

Cassie admired the lack of inhibition. Because it was. It was admirable. Rona was admirable. She was disingenuous and open and not afraid of being ridiculous. Cassie knew all these things. She was still as embarrassed as hell and trying not to be was only making it worse. By the time she was able to look back, some progress appeared to have been made. The man was pushing himself upright, waving Rona out the way. He waved an arm at the names on the marble wall, stood for a moment wheezing then flapped one hand as though he was irritated beyond endurance before tanking back down the steps and off. He was away, back through the field of crosses, turning twice to make sure of something but keeping going anyway. They watched till he was out of sight then turned back to each other.

Cassie breathed out. What was that about?
Rona shrugged again.
D'you think he's ok?
Rona looked up at the name on the wall, back again at the camera. Saying nothing.

We'll just wait then.

Rona nodded.

Not as though we're doing anything else.

The cool voice was still there. The silence Rona was making was intensifying it. Cassie also realised she was avoiding looking at Rona's face. At Rona's eyes. That the peering into the place where the old man had disappeared was only to keep avoiding them. Rona was sniffing and Cassie did not want to look round. She did not want to know why. At the third sniff, the man reappeared. Carrying something. A bucket. Cassie snorted as though she knew he'd be back, her eyes trained. He came between the white rows, splashing water. Rona blew her nose as he came back up the steps, the bucket dripping. Suds and a grey cloth floated inside. Rona looked at the man and he looked back, pushing for more space round himself and the bucket. Preparing. When he was ready, he started: lifting the cloth out, wringing it damp. When that was done he put the damp ball down and held out a piece of chalk, waiting. He pointed at the names and kept waiting. Rona started patting her pockets. He shook his head. It wasn't money, then. Nothing to do with money. He held the chalk out and pointed up again. Cassie felt her brow clear. Something clicking.

The name, she said. He wants to know which one.

Rona took the chalk gingerly and turned round. She looked over her shoulder to check and he tutted, shooing her back towards the marble inlay. Rona shooed. She walked close to the marble wall and levered on to her toes.

There. It's there.

Cassie watched Rona push her arm up as far as it would go. It wasn't far enough. The name was too high. He pointed at the wrong one.

No, Cassie said. McSTAY. PETER DOUGLAS McSTAY. There.

She couldn't reach either but it was closer. The old man nodded a lot and took the chalk back. They watched him go over the letters with the chalk, whiting them against the black stone, stopping occasionally to make a clicking noise and flex his thumb.

It's so it shows on the photo. He's saying to take it now.

Rona's nose changed colour.

It's so it shows, Cassie said.

Cassie nodded but couldn't hold his eye for longer than a second or so. This was a bloody endurance test. Rona was moving though, angling with the camera again, hiding behind the viewfinder, her lips frayed beneath the black box. The old man smiled wide enough to split the skin on his mouth. The veins on his arms like garden twine. Rona clicked the camera four times then lowered it again. He checked she was finished by pointing at the bucket, reached up with the wrung cloth to clean off the chalk marks, still wordless. Rona and the man, nodding at each other like Japanese wind-up toys: too unselfconscious by half. Cassie retreated to the open space of the doorway, keeping herself apart. Rona was looking up at the old man working, scouring the corners of the T. Maybe she was even talking to him, signing or something. Rona. There were things you forgot sometimes. How short she was, the way she levered on to the toes to point something out. How slender her wrists were. Occasionally you looked at Rona and you remembered she was another person. Someone else entirely. As Cassie was walking away she heard the man's voice. What passed for one. Je ne parle pas. A dry rasp and vocal rust. Pieces of his throat missing. Je ne parle pas. Rona saying nothing back, nothing at all.

Traffic noise.

The bend of the dual carriageway.

Cassie waited beside the car. The feeling of mild nausea hadn't passed off. Being this close to the main road wasn't helping either. Rona wouldn't be long, though, not now she had her photos. Photographs of her grandfather's name chiselled into a wall. It still wasn't any clearer what that was about. Cassie hadn't understood any of that from the start and it didn't matter. Rona did plenty of inexplicable things. It was just Rona being Rona. The caretaker though. Cassie looked at her feet, the gravel chips pushing up through thin canvas. The caretaker helping, chalking in the letters.

Like he had done it before for plenty of people. Thousands. Which meant they all knew as well. Thousands of people, Rona and the man with no voice all knew what a picture of a dead man's name was for which meant it was only Cassie that didn't. Something must be obvious about it. Maybe you had to be totally stupid not to know: stupid or blind. Or have an important piece missing. A sound of deceleration was getting less possible to ignore. Coming closer. Cassie turned to see a stoury brown car with one green wing drawing up at the edge of the gravel on the nearside, a man rolling down the window. Looking over. Cassie looked back without focusing, not sure how to read the situation. The window was full down now: the man with one arm on the sill, speaking. Definitely saying something. It could only be her he was speaking to. She looked side to side, hoping he'd not push it. When he stayed put, she spoke back.

Sorry? she said. Sorry? working out how to tell him she didn't speak French in French, almost smiling. Then it dawned.

The smugness. The way both hands were perched on the wheel, the mate beside him grinning like a grater. The unsaid, shared thing between them. His voice was a half shout this time, the tone unmistakable. He wasn't asking for directions at all. His tongue wiggled out, licking thin air as the car reversed, pulling back fast with the engine whining. Kerb crawling. Whatever he was saying was deliberately obscene. Outside a cemetery for godsakes. At this time in the fucking morning.

Through the shock, Cassie tried to look world-weary. Her face felt too frozen to be doing it right but she tried anyway. The men weren't looking though: they were too busy crashing gears and revving. She heard giggling as they wheeled from behind her to in front, through more jagged gear-changing as they came forward in a rush, the bonnet pointing straight at her to see if she would run. A joke before they drew away. Cassie shut her eyes and refused to move. Engine stink clogging her nose, tyres revolving with the brakes full on. Then the sound she'd been waiting for. The crouch of the front brake releasing.

54

FUCK OFF.

Her voice cut through the cloud of exhaust fumes and gravel dust as she opened one eye. The other.

A disembodied face still grinning kept moving away behind the rising guillotine of glass. They wouldn't have heard her. Even if they could lip read they wouldn't have been able to see it.

I'M OLD ENOUGH TO BE YOUR FUCKING MOTHER FOR GODSAKES.

The car was already away. Cassie waited a moment to be sure then breathed deep till she was grateful. The smell of fresh leaves and carbon monoxide. Chipped stone.

I'm old enough to be your fucking mother bastards bastards.

Frenchmen were supposed to be suave HA.

FUCK. OFF.

Fuck off was probably the best-known phrase in the English language. The man who had muttered it at her in the covered bazaar when she hadn't wanted to buy his earrings, the soldier who had asked her what fuck meant when it was obvious he knew, the time she stopped to find money for this wee girl with no legs begging on the bridge outside the Galata Tower and this complete arsehole this soldier they were always fucking soldiers licked her neck muttering FUCKYOUBABY they were animals. Complete bloody animals. That shop they found in Germany, full of nipple clamps, leather peaked caps and things for tying up scrotums. You think the war would have made that kind of thing lose its appeal but it hadn't. Holland was mild by comparison: windows full of freesias and kiosks full of oral sex – a nation of flower-arranging pornographers. Danes were depressives and Swedes racked by guilt: earnest souls with birch twigs. Greeks were self-centred, Italians fancied their chances, Turks were sex-crazed and the French were unspeakable bastards.

55

HA. There wasn't a decent national stereotype left in the whole of fucking Europe. HA. Gravel crunched right in her ear. JESUS.

Jesus. Cassie wheeled.

It was only Rona.

Rona coming forward out of the black marble wall, the camera round her neck and her face puffy. Cassie breathed out, trying to look blank.

Why did you just go like that? Rona said, coming closer. Just disappear without even saying where you were going?

Blank wasn't going to be good enough. Matter-of-fact was in order. Cold, even. Cassie found herself shrugging, fighting her face into submission.

Eh? Rona said again. I didn't even know if you were still in there, just came out to see.

Well I'm here. Ok? Just giving you some peace to get what you wanted. I was here all the time.

Rona sniffed and looked at Cassie, her eyes shiny. I thought there was an accident or something. I thought I heard a car noise, a car noise like skidding or something and I didn't know where you were.

Rona and Cassie
Cassie and Rona

looked each other in the eye till Cassie broke away.

After a minute, Rona said, I thought there was an accident or something. You should have said.

Nah, Cassie said. Two guys. Taking the corner too fast. Did you get the photos?

She knew fine Rona had the photos but it filled the space.

Mmhm. The keys in Rona's hand, their click off the ring she wore on her third finger. I got the photos.

Cassie reached for the door handle. Rona opened the door.

Seven. A limp smile inside the voice. Seven.

Something squawked as Cassie levered herself into the passenger side. The old man was standing at the mouth of the wall, pointing at something. Maybe the sky. Rona waved back. She waved all the way across the gravel, twisting in the seat to make sure he could see her. Crazed with friendliness. The old man did not wave back but he stayed put till they were out of sight.

His throat, said Rona. He couldn't –
I know, said Cassie. I know.

A mile or so down the road the car stopped. Rona leaned forward, rummaged under the seat, got out banging the door. Cassie watched her run partway up the road they had come, getting faster. It was the middle of nowhere. The bag was still there, under the driver's seat though. She had to be coming back. Moments later and without warning, the door swung open again and she plumped into the seat smiling.

I bet mum likes it as well hahaha. That hellish thing. I bet she thinks it's nice. Hahahaha.

Cassie looked at Rona.

I stuck on we found the name. Ps.

The infant and the tortoise. Rona had posted it. Cassie breathed out. Rona had been to post the card. She breathed out again. Too much caffeine. The car started, pulling out towards the centre line.

57

A brown car overtook too fast and honked a horn. Rona took her foot off the accelerator, looking round.

What was that about?

Cassie sank back in the vinyl, closing her eyes. Godknows.

Rona checked the rear-view mirror, blinking. I don't know what that was all about though, do you?

Forget it, Cassie said. It won't be anything. Just boys being boys. Being bastards.

Rona held the steering wheel and moved into second.

Waste of time thinking about it.

Rona nodded once and settled back. Bastards eh?

Bastards.

The car was picking up speed. Anyway, Rona said, her whole face changing. Hahaha. I bet mum loves that card.

five

Cassie and Rona
Rona and Cassie

went to AMIENS and didn't stay.

There was a cathedral. That was something nice people did on holiday: they looked at cathedrals. Rona had done all that already: she had dotted about Europe looking at cathedrals while Cassie polished a purple sheen on the Alpine and went to Edinburgh Zoo. Rona said Venice smelt of rotting sprouts. Cassie had to take her word for it. Now they were in Amiens knowing there was a cathedral but not able to find it. Nearly three. They went to a mini supermarket and put four plums, two peaches, two tomatoes and a baguette in a wire basket instead. There were boxes of Camembert not in the fridge. They ate inside the car under a big tree at the side of a public park, sweating behind the windows that kept the outside in its place. Cassie preferred it.

The sun. It gives you wrinkles.

Rona just looked.

I'm very fair. Celtic. I burn.

Rona said oh yes but didn't push it. Cassie told Rona the tree they were under was a sycamore to cheer her up. I won the nature prize in primary four, she said. Noddy and Big Ears book.

Rona knew. Cassie knew she knew: that was the point. Cassie said she won the nature prize and what it was and Rona pretended to be impressed. It was a routine. Not today though. Today, Rona was Not Playing. Cassie watched Rona's teeth bury themselves in a plum. A single bead of juice fattened on the underside of the plum then dropped, melting into the breastbone area of her T-shirt. Rona kept chewing.

Cassie sighed and looked out the window at leaves. Something oozy off one of the trees had landed on the glass and was running, slow as spittle, into the brushy stuff in the recess of the frame. Cassie's nails needed cut, red juice tracing the line of the quick. Neither of them would have remembered to bring scissors. Cassie sighed, pinning her hopes on Rona saying something. Rona didn't. The sick feeling was still there. Maybe it wasn't indigestion at all. Maybe it was redundancy. Rona had phoned the War Office and read the maps. She had bought the warning triangle and painted the headlights yellow before the drive south. Before Rona drove south. Rona = driver, planner and executive agent. Rona = somebody with relatives. Cassie ≠ anything much. Cassie was only there because. Because because. Because Rona asked her. Because that was what she did: she went on holidays with Rona. Rona asked Cassie on holidays because. Because because. Cassie didn't know why Rona went on holidays with her at all. The pretext this time had confused things in some way. It gave the illusion of purpose. Now, they were clueless. No they weren't. Cassie was clueless. Clueless was Rona's normal state and she never minded it. She never even noticed it.

Cassie looked at Rona chewing, a big pink stain on her T-shirt.

That blank look on Rona's face. It wasn't post-climactic confusion. Her head didn't work that way. She was just eating plums: not tussling with feelings of inadequacy, redundancy or anything else. Rona was just eating plums. She was also looking back. Cassie coughed.

Juice on your top.
Rona looked down.
You've spilled juice on your T-shirt. Cassie reached over, poking a paper tissue at the stain, knowing it wouldn't come off but doing it anyway. Bits of tissue made little rolls when she started rubbing, soaked buds flaking off the main part of the tissue.
It's not coming off.
Looking down, Rona patted the paper curds. She turned something over in her mouth, sucking in.
I'm just making it worse.

Cassie felt Rona's hand enclose her own. Her fingers removed what was left of the tissue and crushed it into a ball. They kept tight hold of the ball. Her foot tipped the guidebook on the floor and the plum stone clicked off her top teeth. On you go, she said. Keep you out of bother. Read.

Cassie read.

AMIENS, the capital of the Picardy region, is a textile town, its reputation dating from the Middle Ages. During the Second World War, over half the town was ruined and the traveller will find much evidence of Amiens' architectural restructuring. The beautiful Notre Dame Cathedral with 126 pillars and a spire reaching 112m in height, is the largest in France. The three magnificent doorways, decorated with bas reliefs dating from 1225 and central door showing Christ and the apostles are awesomely large scale. Inside are 13th century bronze figures of the founding bishops and a choir enclosure decorated with effigies depicting the life of St Firmin. The Chapter House holds treasures of 12th and 13th Century gold and silver work christ this is

Christ this is boring.

No it isn't.

It bloody is.

Rona spat the stone out into the paper ball still in her palm. It isn't. It's fine. It gives you an idea of the place anyway. She held the polythene bag up to the light and rooted for another ripe one.

Are you serious?

Rona seemed to be serious.

It gives you an idea about damn all Rona.

It does.

It does does it?

Yes. It does.

No it doesn't. Listen. "During the Second World War, over half the town was ruined and the traveller will find much evidence of Amiens' architectural restructuring." What does that give you an idea of, then? "Half the town was ruined"? It's not exactly perceptive about the nature of human suffering is it? It's a side-issue to this thing there might have been people in the bloody buildings. And who's Saint Firmin when he's at home? Eh? Who's he?

Rona said damn into the bag and chased something deeper inside it. She couldn't care less.

Saint Firmin, Rona. I'm asking if he's a big favourite of yours.

Rona didn't even look at her.

You don't know who Saint Firmin is Rona and you're sitting here listening to me reading out the stuff in this book as though it means something.

The wordless rustle of polythene was making Cassie feel dangerous. She wished Rona would put the bag down. Rona didn't.

Point taken though, Cassie said.

Rona said nothing.

It was good we read it. Saves a lot of time.

Rona sighed. What does?

Reading the book. It saves a lot of time going to see things. We could do it some more. In fact – Rona rolled her eyes and said oh god – In fact we could have stayed at home really. Got some food in and sat in the car, reading bits of this informative book to each other in between spells of map-reading then had our own beds to go to after. In fact, what are we doing here, Rona?

Rona had put the bag down. She was shutting her eyes. Cassie heard her own voice thinning out. What are we doing here?

Rona opened her eyes after a moment and looked out of the windscreen. We're on holiday, she said. That's what. On Holiday. She started gathering up bits of paper and cheese rind.

A dog walked up to the passenger window, sniffing. It held its nose on the glass and went away.

We're On Holiday.

A perfect print of nostrils shimmered for a moment near Cassie's elbow then melted out. Rona sighed.

Come on, let's get this place tidied up.

Outside was getting overcast. They took rubbish to a wire mesh bin. There was a click as Cassie bent over, closing her nose against the whiff of hot trash. When she looked up Rona was a voice behind a lens, pointing. CHEESE she said. WATCH THE BIRDIE.

Coming from a wee country you forget how big other places can be. We cross backroads
   dirt tracks
   farm lanes and
   the same roadsigns twice, pointing back to Amiens.

We take hours to cover inches.

After a half hour search I find the tapes. In the door compartment after all. Rona had put them in a paper bag. Protection from the heat, she said, seeing me looking. She never tells me anything.

63

Be sure it's true when you say I love you
It's a sin to tell a lie

We thought backroads would be prettier.
But coming from a wee country, we forgot.

Be sure it's true when you say I love you
It's a sin to tell a lie

Continuous play.

When it's been through the once, the machine just puts the same bloody thing back on again. You don't even notice if you're not careful. Chris told me goldfish have a retention span of four seconds: that's why they don't notice they're going round and round the same circuit, they keep thinking it's new. I used to believe it. Now I wonder how he knew that, how his source worked it out. Who it was that thought they had a right to say they know what fish think.

I don't want to set the world on fire
I just want to be here in your arms

I take the Inkspots out, put them back in the case, developing a suspicion that goldfish probably know fine. They probably know perfectly well where they are only there's bugger all they can do about it. The Inkspots out of sight. I unearth Callas. She clicks into place as I lie back with Tosca.

Vissi d'arte, vissi d'amore
Non feci mai male ad anima viva!

Backroads
Dirt tracks
Farm lanes

64

The same roadsigns twice.

We thought backroads would be

I lived for art, I lived for love
I never harmed a living being!

And by that time it's dark. I take the headphones off, tuck the machine away. Being careful. I've only brought three tapes.

Rona pulled the brake on full, making the car sound like it was falling apart with rust. Inside a hairpin of engine noise, a luminous triangle from some passing headlamps reared up from the road behind, flaring Rona's hands white against the black wheel. Shadows ticked over the roof upholstery, faded again. Whatever it was had tanked out of sight before Cassie looked in the rear-view mirror. At least the main road was still there if needed. Of course it was. Rona looked ahead, one hand hovering near the ignition key. The track had just stopped. Ahead, inside the twin beams, the two churned runnels of caked mud from some big anonymous farm machine led into scrub then just vanished and with it, the track. No clues. Rona switched off the engine.

That's us then, she said.

The lights cut at the same time. The dark filled up inside Cassie's ears so there was nothing to do but listen. Everything outside was the same thing. Rustling. Fields of it all doing the same thing. She thought about the machinery track and, further back, the road but they were just theory. This rustling stuff could well have been taking over, shuffling forward over the tracks behind like

65

science fiction plants. Maybe it was corn. Cassie didn't know. The nature prize hadn't stretched to cereals. Now and again, metal clanked. The bodywork cooling down.

Do you want to get out first? Rona leaned back, rubbing her eyes.
Cassie looked at her.
To pee. You first or what?
I'll wait, Cassie said. I'm fine.
Cool air came in when Rona opened the door.
God I'm tired. I'm knackered.
The ricochet of slammed door, the car rocking in its echo.

Cassie watched a white cardigan legless in the dark. It shrunk in the rear-view mirror till only a notion of it was left, turning off into what was presumably a field. Cassie watched the bit where cardigan had been. The complacent hum of electricity cables. Another clank. A scraping that might be straw and dried stubble grating on the exhaust. Between times the dry ebbtide of unidentifiable cereal rose and fell. Cassie looked briefly into the mirror again, checking the door locks in passing. The reflection of her own eye catching her out. For christsake. She pulled one of the locks back up. Rona might have to get in in a hurry. She might come running back for a very good reason and Cassie would have locked the door and in the split second of her not being able to get in stop it stop it STOP IT. But it was what you thought. You thought anything to alleviate the bleak monotony of reality, of what was probably more the case. Rona was fine. She was fine and out there scent-marking her patch of this interminable French countryside in the dark. Perfectly content. Probably. Cassie pressed the recliner button and stared up at the roof, knowing it felt the same. It always felt the same. Every time it feels the same and you always forget till it comes again. We have slept in the car in Fife, Leith, bits of Dorset and Somerset, Norfolk, just outside Jedburgh and godknows and it is always like this: just the shrinking car interior, anticipatory stiffening of the joints, not knowing where the hell you are. Wondering if sleep is possible and what the hell you'll do if you can't, how it is to be borne till light comes. What the hell you'll think. Outside the white noise of some foreign field that was forever foreign shifted, a godknowshowbigness of flat blackness at the edge of a road staggered with signs saying there is nowhere to go but where they had just come from. Cassie imagined waking in the car, sun up on a desert landscape. Dry craters and tumbleweed spilling over sand. Your lips cracked, eyes crusted with salt. Outside, a light breeze whips up eddies of dust. You get out, leaving her sleeping, to walk in slow motion towards something undisclosed. Slow pan past sand drifts shoring the sides of the car, its colour obscured by grit and the blinding sunlight, to a huge hoarding. Chipped and weather-eaten, the only sign other human beings had come this way before. Slowly, slowly your eyes lift to read the flaking board. And it would say

AMIENS. That's what it would bloody-well say.

Blackness. Single stalks of cereal wave in the night wind. I listen, staring out at the needles of grass, waiting for Rona.

Hansel and Gretel. Holding hands under a tree. I can't remember who took it, maybe the couple in the next tent. First time in a foreign country: celebration for him finishing the HND. We'd no money but we managed. I remember the heat more than anything: stepping off a plane knowing when you got on it Glasgow was outside and something else when you got back out. Something thick and viscous: the smell of hot fig tree. I hadn't thought another country would smell so different. A blue minibus took us for miles over flat scrub to Tolon and upended us on to this building site full of bits of tent. Unerected. Dawn just breaking. Things with too many legs were making noises even at that time in the morning but we got by. The heat when we went inside. I don't know what I expected but that

67

much sweat wasn't it. Babes in the wood. You sometimes forget you've been that naive.

Ah god first time on the beach. All white self-conscious extremities and the look of bravery under duress. We just didn't know not to go out at mid-day. Clueless. He's looking like that because I've just lathered him with this jungle-strength suncream I found in an army and navy store: like axle grease only paler yellow. Used up nearly the whole tube first day. We thought it was what you did, what you were supposed to do: sitting there frying and uncomfortable for nearly an hour before we staggered in to wash the bloody stuff off and cool down. The shower block reeked of putrefying sanitary towel and male catpee but it didn't matter. Just getting in there, being able to wash all that stuff off my arms was the best bit of the day. It had gotten studded with grit and bits of broken shell and neither of us had brought soap. It never occurred. We didn't even have towels. Same night, Chris discovered he couldn't eat the stuff in the site restaurant place because he reacted badly to olive oil: we didn't even go out of the campsite because he kept being sick till he'd got rid of it all. We got by on a big poke of crisps out the camp shop just before they closed. We held each other a lot that night. Kids. Actually we were twenty-two. Twenty-two. Folk are married with weans and everything by that time, worrying about DSS benefits and where they'll get the money for the eldest's first pair of school shoes. I make these tender allowances for stupidity without thinking these days. Look at his face though: big baby blues over the top of one greasy arm, the chip-white chest. Trying not to give away the fact that he just wasn't coping. He wasn't sure he was going to cope at all.

I hate this one. Chris drinking cocktails made out of luminous liqueurs in the site bar. Happy Hour. Once he found his feet, he took to the bloody thing so fast it was frightening. The thing behind him is a lizard. It's changing colour. I'd just finished taking this when he pointed over my shoulder and there was one right behind me as well. Big green eyes slashed with black the same height as mine. I'd been sitting next to one the whole meal and never knew. My whole skin felt it was peeling off with goosepimples. It's not that I'm scared of them or anything it was just the shock. I fell off the chair and he laughed. Cassie you're an idiot, leaning back being suave with the Chocolate Alexander in one hand, not helping me up. Exchanging glances with the waiter. I didn't know what to make of it. Ended up trying to hold his hand while he threw up into a toilet bowl all night. Served the bugger right, really.

Five men with hats radiated like buttercup petals from a round table, reading form. Just after nine in the morning. There were no other women. Cassie broke the croissant with her fingers, shaking the flakes off before putting it to her mouth. Rona didn't. Pastry tumbled down her front and into a drift on the tabletop. Cassie winced but it was nothing to do with Rona or the croissants. Her breasts hurt. Like they'd been badly stitched on. They'd been hurting since Rona had woken up, wanting to get shifting before somebody found the car on what was probably private land. They'd opened the doors, reflating limbs with their eyes creasing against thin morning colours, hobbled halfway down the dirt track and back. Like Bill and bloody Ben, Cassie said. The laugh sounded fragile. Hung-over.

We're too old for this carry-on, Rona.
Who says?
Me. I said it just then. When are we going to have lots of money so we don't have to do this kind of thing any more? They retire on the bloody stock exchange when they're our age.
They don't have holidays though, Rona said. They're too busy to have friends. Think what they're missing.

Cassie found a peach bruising itself against the rear seatbelts. They had bites each. Before the third bite, a sign appeared, toppled among long grass and yellow flowers at the side of the road. CHANTILLY. Rona couldn't work out how they could have been so close and not seen the lights.

Will we go straight there then? Rona paddled one hand on her top, putting more flakes on than off. The Art Gallery?

Fine.

We can sit here for a while if you like.

Whatever, Cassie said. I don't mind. Whatever.

I thought you said you really wanted to go.

Cassie said nothing.

Rona sighed. I'm not going to say we go there if you don't fancy it. We could go later if you prefer. Or now. What do you think?

Rona now is fine. We'll go now.

Or we could just get on the road.

No I'm fine. Hunky dory. We'll go to the Art Gallery ok?

A long minute of silence.

Ok, Rona said warily. Will I go to the toilet first or you?

One of these days Cassie would, she really would burst.

Past the old eyes and the barman, the chamber waited with an open door. Hole in the ground and soapless. No running water.

CHANTILLY, ancient seat of the Princes de Condé, is famous for its forest and, of course, its horses, 3000 train here for major equestrian events. Visit the Museum of the Horse and the Château, where the chef Vatel committed suicide when his fish course, prepared for Louis XIV, arrived too late to be eaten. Also houses major artworks.

There was no-one else there. No queue, no-one selling guide books. Only a man in a peaked hat glaring. Maybe if nobody came he got to shut up shop and go home. He took the ticket money, not looking up.

Rona and Cassie
Cassie and Rona

walked round the museum looking in cases. Cases of THINGS. Clocks, swords, jewellery. A piano with music that didn't fit the period. Walking sticks and writing desks, quills and carved inkwells.

Pity there's no guidebook, Rona said. A brass clock covered in cherubs reflected in her specs. We could do with one. I mean I don't know what's meant to be interesting about this thing. I don't know what we're meant to be appreciating here at all.

The next room was full of carved chairs and sofas. Rona liked furniture. Alone in the next room, Cassie found paintings. Cassie liked paintings. They're the closest things to photographs, I suppose. I've always liked looking at paintings.

PIERO DI COSIMO: *Simonetta Vespucci*
is a woman with braided hair. Ropes of pearls are woven into the pleating, long yellow coils looping on themselves, her forehead high. Her skin is blue-white, profile pointing left. There is the faint curve at the corner of the closed mouth: there are her blue eyes. They focus on something beyond the edge of the frame. Around her shoulders, a shawl woven in tan stripes covers only one shoulder. Her girl breasts are the colour of milk, the nipples bloodless. Hanging on the luminous breastbone, a snake and a golden chain. Every strand of hair, every bead between the strands is visible, countable. Between the loops and braids, pearls sit like drops of solid water. The tail of the snake fades to a place behind the painting that is not seen. Behind, the trees are leafless.

71

Her hair heavy with ornaments, forehead taking the strain invisibly, she waits. The bare skin, impossibly flawless and too white, does not shiver despite her nakedness: the shawl is not for warmth. She doesn't mind the snake he has painted there, doesn't mind that she can't move her mouth or eyes. She cannot be other than serene. Her feet would be bare if they were visible. Standing on grass, cold blades cutting at her ankles, not complaining. Good girl. For all that, she knows something he doesn't. Her face cuts a white curve against a sky, thickening with cloud. Watching for something to come.

It was Rona.

She said it again. Will we go for some lunch then? Rona standing at the far side of the carpeted room. Are you ok?
Cassie was ok.

They went back to the car. Rona checked the map, making sure Cassie twiddled knobs till the car seethed with hissing. Radio 4. The Archers. Cassie turned up the volume, listened to a weather forecast for the wrong country before the signal died altogether.

Like yesterday. Better in fact. Paros. Same year I started at the office. Two paypackets to play with. This was one of the best times we ever had, me and Chris. Summer 78. I think I felt it was all opening up from there on in. Paros. The harbour. Somebody offered us a room the minute we got off the ferry and we just took it. Que sera.

I know it looks dark but it wasn't. White and plain, just the room and the bed. White makes everything look nice. There was somebody already in the room when we went in: the woman

72

took it for granted we wouldn't mind. Chris said I had too many Presbyterian hangups. He got us another room anyway. The shower was right at the end of the corridor: you had to walk down it every time you wanted to wash. The sign on the door was Greek and could have said anything. It probably did. The first time I went, traipsing down this corridor with no bulb, toilet bag over my arm, I heard scratching the minute I'd shut the door. I didn't think anything about it right away and started the water running, keeping out the way to avoid getting splashed till the cold had run through, but I could still hear this noise ticking away. When I turned round a cockroach the size of a hoover attachment was prickling its way over the white flagstones, taking its time. I think it knew I was scared. I know it sounds daft but I think it did. Because it stopped and waved its legs and started coming straight for me. I turned the water off quick and just got the hell out, left my towel and everything inside. I waited for a minute in that dark corridor between the white rooms catching my breath, then breezed back through. I was too embarrassed to say I'd been chased by a cockroach. Or maybe I thought he'd do something horrible if he knew, persecute me with one of the bloody things or something. Anyway, I didn't want him to know. I just said I'd changed my mind and he could go first. He was away for about five minutes with me listening the whole time: the noise of the water running near and far at the same time. Like Psycho. So I wrapped up in a dressing-gown and went down to make sure he was ok. It wasn't till I was pushing the door open it occurred to me it might not be him at all. It could have been a naked stranger in there as well as the bloody cockroach. But it was Chris: one hand cupped under his scrotum and the other scratching a lather into the pubic hair. Just Chris. A second of confusion and something that might have been anger only then he knew it was me. I said everything ok and he just smiled.

Chris in the shower.
His penis drips soap.

Cassie folded the vanity mirror back behind the eyeshade and saw them across the field. Two towers so big they hazed over in full evening sunlight. Two different towers.

six

.

Jesus Rona we've stayed in some dumps have we not.

A bar with a cowshed on top: crumbling brick and shutters going up the height of three floors. But 50F. Cassie read the black letters sellotaped behind polythene. 50F. It would be a room with deathwatch beetles disappearing under wormy skirting, walls peeling with dark brown flock, mildew marks behind the washbasin and bidet, a mirror bouncing on the wall from the impact of people copulating like bears in the next room and over the bed, a framed oblong of perforated notebook, long since turned yellow and rimmed with brown insulating tape, squint, reading DEFENSE DE CRIER DE JOIE no it wouldn't. It wouldn't be anything of the sort. Cassie looked at the 50F sign and pushed the door.

Three boys with cracked leather elbows and sneakers were playing pinball machines. A skinny man with thick eyebrows and dark hair falling into where his eyes should have been mopped the counter with a cloth. Cassie didn't know she was staring till he smiled: as if his face hurt but a smile all the same. It seemed the first time she had seen that in days, someone who was not Rona smiling. Thin as an anglepoise, two broken teeth showing between bleached out lips. They moved when Rona asked for rooms, again when she repeated herself because she couldn't make him out: the kind of voice that wouldn't be felt through the shirt cloth. Even if you held him tight, hands pressed over his chest, there would only be ribs. Cassie watched Rona peering under the fringe for his eyes, the wounded smile when he offered the keys. Whatever it was like, they'd take the room.

We took the room.

No shower but two washstands and separate beds, a bidet. Cassie took off her jersey and ran the taps hard.

50F, Rona said. It was for the whole room. Not each. They price the room.

Cassie turned. Rona was crouched on top of a chest of drawers, head inches from the cracked ceiling.

He said you could see the cathedral from here.

She looked again to check and shrugged. You must need special equipment. Bargain, though. 50F.

Cassie bounced on the double bed, clanking springs.

> Medieval CHARTRES and the lower town, its hump-back bridges spanning the river Eure has charm and an unselfconscious ease with itself seldom found in the modern world. For above all, CHARTRES is its cathedral: a massive, uncompromising yet serene structure which rises heart-stoppingly out of the surrounding arable plains. Indefinable, indefatigable, CHARTRES cathedral comes close to the impossible ideal of perfection.

Chartres was empty. More or less. The odd soul running with a loaf under an arm, people pulling curtains. Time of night. Rona and Cassie walked along the side of the main road towards more buildings: emaciated houses you couldn't see over the tops of and little shops. All shut. Cassie was going to say it looked like Edinburgh when she saw it. A ring of stretched stone people through an alley width between the teahouses and empty card carousels. A sheer cliff of masonry filling the full height of the close.

Indifferent to being happened upon.

The cathedral.

The end of the close had a forecourt with nuns. The nuns were walking about, mostly backwards, looking up and shielding their eyes though there was no sun. Cassie looked to see what they saw, tilting her neck till it creaked. A crushing height, this close. Dizzying. She took a step back, being careful. Nuns were a hazard in this light, barely visible and milling in an unpredictable kind of way. Rona wasn't among them. She would have gone round the other way, through the bit of garden they had passed on the way through. She would be in there now, smiling at wee growing things, poking bits of shrubbery and trying to remember what they were called in Latin while this thing rose up behind her, monstrous and unnoticed. Cassie looked up again, aiming for where she remembered the top of the wall had been. Too fast. It was still too near. And something was falling towards her. Something big. She jerked her head out of the way, hoping it wouldn't hurt much or at least be clean.

Nothing happened.

She opened one eye.

The other.

It was a gargoyle.
A bloody great lump of masonry jutting out, so huge you

77

wonder how you could have missed it, how anyone in their right mind with their eyesight in working order could possibly not have seen it the minute they turned the corner. She straightened, cast a quick look to see if anyone was watching. The nuns had formed a scrum, all cardigan backs. And Rona was elsewhere. Safe and elsewhere. Slowly, Cassie turned her gaze back up.

The thing was still there.

Fifteen feet or so up the wall, poking from the stone. An animal in the act of springing. The front legs were tensed, suspension forks against the impact of landing, paws tucked in near the joint sockets, back legs lost inside the wall. It looked like a greyhound only fatter, all muscle and lean meat. Only the face didn't fit. A griffin face, a story-book dragon with hollow nostrils, and big eyes, its tongue lolling as though it was dying from some kind of asphyxia. Gas poisoning. The top lip peeled up in two places for the down-curve of what should have been fangs except there was only one. On its back, wings lay like bits of broken umbrella against the back musculature, tips meeting over the ridge of spine. Over the whole body, legs and belly, through the wings too, an illusory network of veins pulsed under non-existent skin. It had no penis. Between the animal's back legs, above beautiful chiselled testicles, just a snapped stump remained.

Cassie stepped back a pace, refocusing. There was another of the things a level higher. Two. Another step let two more appear. Above that and above that again. The cathedral was covered in the bloody things: a whole menagerie poking out of the stone tracery like diseased erections.

BOO!

Cassie wheeled, almost losing her footing.

HAHAHAHA did I give you a fright HAHAHAHAHA behind a black box, then whiteness obliterating everything. In the after-

78

math of spangling dark, Cassie heard the automatic winder and knew what it meant. One day Rona would come round with a photo. Cassie would look and see herself peering, chalked out with too-close flash and scarlet eyes, surrounded by blacked-out cathedral. A mesh of discoloured features was beginning to reassemble, a row of tiny teeth reintegrating in the losing light. Behind that, from the middle of the nun cluster, a single arm rose up, pointing at the sky. A ring of white noses peaked against the dark stone. Rona's melting mouth blew a kiss. She turned, laughing like a sewer and started walking.

We go to a bar full of young things in T-shirts, dayglo designs and contextless words on the front. Rona wears the blue skirt she made from a bit of material out the bargain bin at Remnant King's, the new espadrilles from BhS. I watch her in the new clothes, bringing glasses out to the table, looking fine fine fine. Sometimes Rona does, that burned black hair going grey, the sober eyes. She looks just fine.

Got you a surprise, she said.
Cassie caught a whiff of aniseed. Rona held out a glass cylinder, the liquid inside snot-green with bleeding ice.

I watch Rona watch a tree on the other side of the water for ten minutes without speaking, taking three flash photos of godknows. Leaves maybe. The river in the dark. Insects she doesn't know the names of making dents in the water. On the way back, she walks without looking where she is going, staring at the sky. The clearest night in the history of the universe. No cloud.

Cassie found the way back.

Despite the legend of her rotten sense of direction and how it's better she doesn't know how to drive, it was Cassie that found it. You'd be halfway to Spain this time. Rona, she says: I don't know what you'd do without me.

79

I don't, I say. I just don't know what you'd do.

Naxos. This was the bit off the shore front, if you bothered to look. Hardly anybody did. We were looking for somewhere to eat one night and chanced it. And there it was. Whitewashed houses, purple flowers trailing like ivy, huge wooden doors like coffin lids. Venetians left over from the crusades built them, people stranded on the way home. Coats of arms still chiselled into the walls. We went for walks up there a couple of evenings running it was so beautiful but I didn't like to stay late. Night just comes down in these places, covers everything like soot. He's in that shadow somewhere, hiding and going to pounce and make me scream. I'd have been terrified on my own, high walls and no light, the maze of lanes between the old Venetian houses, not really being sure where you were likely to surface. Who would be there when you did. But I had Chris. He told me not to stare out strange men or drink too much in case I said something inflammatory. It's ok for you, he said: I'm the one that's left with the consequences. I used to worry about that, whether I would start fights without meaning to, what I would do if I did. But it never happened. We never got lost either. He said it was because he had a great sense of direction but it wasn't that. He was too bloody-minded ever to admit he didn't know where we were, just pretended it was a diversion he'd meant to take all along. And I let him. I knew fine but I kidded on I didn't. Just followed at a respectful distance working out lethal things to do with my shoulderbag and the spray mosquito repellant in case. Eventually I made him promise he'd run away if anything happened, look after himself. He took the point. It was easier than worrying all the time. Easier for me.

It was deserted. Shutters up and webby stuff on the hinges of the door.

Is this the right place though?

Yes it's the right place. The car's where we left it for heavensake. Rona looked at the key and tried it again. Like nails down a piece of slate.

Are you sure?

Rona didn't answer. Just kept making noises that scored down the tooth enamel. Again. The kind of noise you imagine rheumatism might make, bone grating against bone with nothing to cushion the AGAIN jesus jesus

Jesus Rona stop that. Stop buggering about with that thing. It's bloody awful.

I can't help it, she said. It won't – Rona's voice muffled with peering into the ancient keyhole – turn. It just won't.

She scraped the key against the door surround, breathed out once. The early stages of huff.

Cassie sucked her lips against her teeth, clamping down to stop the fibres of noise finding the fillings. The noise came again anyway.

It's stuck or something. Rona's voice merged into rust.

Cassie looked into the dark, watched leaves not move on the trees. At least they were back off the road. It would be worse if they had an audience. Cassie looked at Rona's bare legs, the shirt you could see her underwear through. Cardigans. They needed cardigans. Cassie tilted the watch back and forth, settling it like sand to read in the gloom. Nearly one. Nowhere would be open at this time, no public place to get help from.

Shit.

Rona was sifting through the last of a pile of things from her bag. A union membership card and two emery boards sat very close to one foot, as though she'd tried and dropped them. She said shit again and booted the door. Little bits of something scuttled inside the wall, flakes of paint feathering down. Rona shook the hell out of the end of the key with both hands, wrenching the door till it thumped down on the hinges. The door couldn't have cared less. Of course it couldn't. It was an inanimate object. Nevertheless, Cassie was uncomfortable. Somebody might still be in there, another guest. Maybe the patron who had given the key so he wouldn't be disturbed was in there, listening to his door being kicked hell out of at whatever time it was in the morning. Maybe he was in there listening now.

Shit. Another dunt. There's a torch in the other bag as well. The one inside the room. The one you said I should leave behind as a matter of fact. And a pair of pliers. Shit shit shit.

A rustle that sounded like deliberate surreptitiousness, as though someone was watching, came and went.

Shit.
Rona kicking the door again.

Rona's hands streaky with rust and dirt. Cassie looked down at her own. Pale as mushrooms. Bugger it. Bugger being out here in the cold feeling stuck. Cassie had to act. She had to move. It was all kidding on but kidding on was, in itself, something. Cassie stumped round the peeling plaster tower, making a wide arc from the starting point. There was no other door to find or try. Nothing. She moved to the front of the building instead, braving cars that did not appear. The street was deserted, the bar door bolted, laced with thin chains and padlocked. Twice. Cassie leaned against the wall and listened, hugging her shoulders. Rona was behind this barrier of waxy leaves somewhere, on the other side of the hedge. Being silent. The only thing to hear was the rustle and shiver of desiccated things, burned-out grasses and other vegetable matter. No sound at all from where Cassie had left her, on the other side of this clammy earth. Cassie kept listening. Listening harder.

Say shit Rona.

Make the key scream.

There was no sound.

A white hand pushed through the split-end ramble of the bush in front, reaching. It was holding something. Cassie looked down at the hand. It offered a key.

You take this. The key waggled. On you go. I've had enough. Cassie reached. She watched her fingers close round the key. What are you meant to be doing out there?

The hand retracted leaving weight in her palm. A car exhaust coughed through distant catcalls.

Well? A sigh. Then Rona's voice, less certain now. Well? What have you been doing out there? Cassie?
Cassie looked at the key, making her voice flat. I've been round here looking for another door. There isn't one.
Oh. She sighed again. Well, you might have told me you were away.
Yes.

Nobody spoke for a moment.

Cassie said No luck then?
No. No. Just a minute.

The sound of leaves creasing got louder, became dull slaps on paving. Rope soles. Rona came round the hedge, her face grey under the streetlight, talking. See? Over there. Where it says restaurant? There's a light. I'm going over. You see if you can make any difference with that thing. She nodded at the key.

There were pink curtains where Rona had pointed. Rona stumped over the road towards them, the black scuff along the side of the white canvas feet glowing in the dark. Cassie looked down at the key, then up at the lit window, back at the key. She retraced her steps back to the door. The key filled most of the inside of her hand, three prongs like fingerends. It went into the lock badly. Cassie shoogled it self- consciously, tried a turn. It squealed and fought back so she stopped. Rona might be a while. She tried again, more forcefully. The key hurt her finger. There was a mark when she pulled it away. Cassie stood in the moonlight under nearly silent trees and waited for Rona.

Me posing in one of the Venetian doorways, cat looking over a veranda. He put the flower in my hair. He was in the middle of taking that actually when the guy shouted over. Thing like a trap door swung up right behind Chris's back and this man of about fifty poked out. White hair and a good tan. I pretended I hadn't seen him but he shouted over again, hailing us like we were a taxi. In German. I think it was German. He must have thought that's what we were, Chris being so blond. And Chris turned round. I thought it was going to be the fight I'd thought about so long, my head racing through ways to escape. But Chris turned round. There was nothing I could do to stop him. Two minutes later they were knee-deep in the same language, talking shutter speeds and variable filters, chummy as hell. He said he was Danish. Rowed himself over in a kayak all the way from Scandinavia to study something or other and now he was here living back to back with a closed sect of orthodox nuns. People weren't allowed to look at them, he said. He and Chris exchanged amused glances. But he could. He could see over their wall from his bedroom. I think you'll find it of interest he was saying, can I offer you a drink? Chris was down the trap door like that. Before I opened my mouth. The Dane slid past me to pull the trap over. I remember looking up, noticing it was already dark up there. Bits of purple flowers and whitewashed gables before the lid came down.

It was down two flights of steps, a circular white room with books all over the floor, a mattress and the biggest camera I ever saw. Leica. Chris was thrilled to hell about it, nodding as if him and the guy were related long-lost brothers or something. Your wife he said, gesturing over with one hand, a full glass for Chris in the other. I didn't want anything. I just wanted to stay near the wall. It was flaky and damp, chalky stuff came off on my blouse. But I stayed put. When he and Chris went round the corner to spy on the nuns I took a good look at the mattress, the stairs and the trapdoor. The monstrous camera. Getting the lie of the land in case. I think I had an idea the drink was drugged, that me and Chris were meant to have sex and let the guy take pictures or the guy was going to set the self-timer and join in. The nuns might even join in. Whatever, I couldn't wait to get out. When they came back I smiled bright as Doris Day and said we had to be on our way. I was ashamed when he helped me up the stairs, knowing he knew I was terrified of him but it didn't change anything. I just couldn't wait. Outside, Chris was furious. What the hell was the matter with you? He was just lonely for heaven's sake. Shaking his head because he didn't know what else to do with me. I locked the door on our room myself that night. Maybe I thought they'd made a deal when they were round the corner pretending to look for nuns. I don't know what was wrong with me. But I wasn't right for days. So that's the last in Naxos. Me in the doorway of someone else's house, on the verge of losing trust in everything. Went back and got all my hair cut off before me and Rona went to Glen Nevis. A stab at looking streetwise or some such shite. Pathetic really. No trust at all.

Rona was coming back. Two men following behind her in rolled sleeves, one with a cough. All smiling. Nous ne pouvons pas rentrer, she said. La porte ne marche pas. It sounded wrong but fathomable. It was fine. Rona held out her hand for the key. Voilà. Cassie tried to smile an aware-of-the-absurdity-of-the-situation smile, hoping it looked ok. Nobody was bothered. Rona was pointing at the lock, the men peering at it hard. The one in the checked shirt knelt, looking closer. His arm rippled when he moved the key, a muscle flexing. Black hair covered the whole limb from where the sleeve ended to the wrist, curled partway up the back of his hand. He looked up. shrugging at the friend. Rona moved out of his light. The friend took the key, looked at it, flipped it over, leaned to put it in the lock for himself. Hair coiled over the back of his shirt collar. The key screeched twice. The hair retracted, the friend tilting upright. The kneeling man stood up, knelt back down on the opposite knee, took the key back and started again. Intent. The friend looked across to Rona and smiled, gesturing like the assistant in a magic act. Rona wasn't even looking. She was creeping up on the key-holder, making cooing noises. Fascinated. The friend stopped and coughed, hooked his hands at his sides. Finer down along the inside of the arm where the hair thinned out. A shirt button missing at solar plexus level. He turns to look at me.

I know from the look on his face. He is standing there feeling as daft as I do. Coughing now and again. A gust of fading aftershave coils towards me when he shifts on the spot, changing weight to the other foot. I smile, trying to think of something in French, something reassuring. Licking my top lip to start. And Rona says

OOOOOHH.

OOOOOHH.

The door was open, Rona shaking the checked-shirt wearer's hand, saying My Goodness at the door handle as if she couldn't work out how he'd managed. Cassie offered her hand to the friend.

He coughed but took it anyway. He took it and the thing was a joke after all. Men and women who did not know each other or speak the same language shook hands outside a broken-down hotel after one in the morning. Roles were reliably in place. They had finished a night's work. The door was open.

The door-opener dusted his hands on the sides of his trousers, started moving away. Au revoir. He waved and nodded his head as though he'd taken off a hat. Au revoir. The voice fading already. Cassie watched them hack their way into the hedge, getting ready to step through. Leaving. And without thinking, Cassie spoke. Loud. Je voudrais vous baiser, monsieur, je voudrais vous baiser. It meant a kiss, I could kiss you, or something like that. She hoped it meant that, laughing in case it was full of mistakes. There was a silence then one of them shouted back.

YOU SHOULD BE. CARE FUL WHAT. YOU SAY.

Guffawing and the odd escaped snort. Laughing getting fainter.

You should be. Care ful what. You say. English. The bastards had been able to speak English all the time.

What did you say there? Rona touched her elbow. What was it?
Nothing.
No, I didn't catch. The French thing. What was it you said?
Just I was glad we'd got in. Cassie's face was fixed in a smile that wouldn't go away. I told them I was glad it worked out. That's all.

Rona looked sceptical but didn't ask any more. They went inside.

Undressing in the dark, casting clothes in undisclosed places, Cassie muttered bastards to herself twice, smiling wider each time.

87

Je voudrais vous donner un baiser. It would be obscene all right. Filthy. Somewhere, behind that pink curtain, the two of them would be sitting finishing a bottle of something, doing impressions of her accent and snorting like gnus, the way men did at women drivers and heels caught down drainholes. Whatever she and the other man had traded eye-to-eye forgotten, insignificant. He was where he belonged now. Knowing things she didn't. What in christsname was it she had said she wanted to give them?

Sorry? Rona dunted into her, not able to see. Come again?

YOU SHOULD BE. CARE FUL WHAT. YOU SAY. Able to speak English all the time. Cassie tilted her head up to the invisible ceiling and laughed out loud, feeling terrible. Bastards.

I just wish I knew what it was I said.

seven

Chris in his knickers. Some awful hour of the morning. There weren't any curtains so we woke early. Everything was white outside. Except the sand. Volcanic ash. Santorini? Anyway, 1982. I remember because he bought this Greek paper with something about that sickening wedding a year after the event. Charles and Di. For some reason I thought we'd be far enough away from that, that it wouldn't count there. The downside of the Global Village. Anyway, '82. Every morning, that's where he was. Looking out over the tiny market out there, a rickle of crates and boxes with peaches on thin wood scaffolding, holding itself together to hold the fruit. You'd go past it and the fruit would be warm to the touch: not even nine in the morning. Baking. I bought a kilo first day: I didn't know how many it was. Dripping out this bag as big as a bin liner. Pages of my novel got stuck together and put me in a bad mood for days. But I liked the early morning, lying on in bed, steeling myself for another day on the beach. Except magazines, Chris didn't read. Not anything. Well, except for that Greek newspaper. I needed the novel to give me something to do while he was turning his face to old boot leather, sticking to page rations to make sure I didn't run out. I don't know what I thought would happen if I did: I just knew it was very important not to let it. The novel was company. He didn't talk when he was sunbathing. He didn't do anything at all. Then we'd go out for the evening, sitting in bars avoiding the disco. I remember wondering what would happen when we ran out of islands, whether he'd agree to somewhere with ruins or museums: things to look at. Cassie I get two weeks to relax, two weeks: I can do without museums. It seemed reasonable at the time. I didn't say two weeks was all I got too.

Church. One of those wee white boxes with blue domes they have everywhere over there. Greek Orthodox. That's me outside wearing a towel over my shoulders and a straw hat. A towel. I knew they wouldn't let me in without the hat but my shoulders were uncovered as well. Chris whipped the towel out of his beach bag and attended to the drapery. Making sure I was decent before we got inside. Taken such a lot of care over the outfit then had to wear his beach towel he'd been lying on all morning, smeary with oil and stuccoed with broken shell. Fetching shade of shit-brown: he said it went with my eyes.

The cathedral, with its distinctive asymmetrical spires, towers over the wheatfields of Ile de France like a stegosaurus. Built over a period of only 30 years (between 1194 and 1225) its architecture manages an integration of styles and a palpable aura of unity, grace and calm. The towers and stained glass, the choir screen and side porches exhibit work from other centuries.

Three coaches were emptying out, another reversing up on to the gravel beside the postcard-stand. Germans maybe. The name on the coach was not certain. From the other side of the road, Rona angled a shot of the group from behind a rubbish bin. Another busload clustered at the notice board with times of service, making Japanese noises. Rona took a photo of that too. On the way back, she skirted a man lying out flat on a bench in the narrow bit of park. She didn't take one of him.

Rona and Cassie

sat side by side in the park outside Chartres Cathedral, letting the busloads go first. Cassie peered at the spires but couldn't see much. Sun was making her eyes water already, gritting salt in the corners. It was sorer with them shut. The only option was to look down. Rona had kicked off her sandals and dug her feet into the dust under the bench. Her toes resurfaced slowly, testing the air. She had beautiful feet, Rona. Downy hairs on her legs and smooth skin over the anklebones, prehensile toes and neat wee nails. Beautiful. Cassie looked at Rona's feet till Rona's hand ferreted into the picture and picked at the skin of her big toe. She tore off a strip of nail leaving a ragged white line and an ooze of blood in the nearside corner. Rona just didn't care. She didn't even know she had beautiful feet.

I got us this. Rona held something out, newly plucked from the horsebag. CATHEDRAL GUIDE: ENGLISH.

Oh yes. The pamphlet was in Cassie's hands. Rona had put it there.

The kiosk over there. She pointed. Cassie couldn't see for sun. There's more as well. That one looked good though. I got us that one.

Are you wanting to read it first? Before we go in? Is that the idea?

Rona shrugged. Whatever.

D'you want a look at it then?

Doesn't matter. Later maybe.

Cassie breathed in. You bought it Rona. What did you have in mind?

Och anything. Doesn't matter. Rona wiggled her toes in the silence. Just I thought it would be a nice thing for when we got home. If we don't look at it now. Souvenir. But you might want to look at it just now. Do some finding out. You usually like to. If you want to look at it just now on you go.

Cassie looked at the pamphlet, Rona's feet, back at the pamphlet.

I'll have a look then, will I?
Ok whatever you like.

Cassie couldn't work out how she'd done it. How she did it every time: worked things so they looked like Cassie's idea all along. Anyway, the book might be interesting. It might be full of fascinating things worth knowing. Possibility.

Possibility.
It gets me every time.

A note by the Author:

Notre Dame de Chartres is one of the most magnificent churches ever built to the Glory of God and Our Lady. Grand but without pomp, precise in all its proportions, the two magnificent steeples soaring in an invitation to prayer, the cathedral uplifts the soul and shows, in its severe beauty, a proper scorn of meritricious vanity.

How can we ignore strong emotions! From the moment we arrive in the nave, it is impossible! Yet there is no impression of being crushed by the stone blocks hanging 115 feet overhead, for robust piers lend their support and give the whole building its solidity and feeling of equilibrium.

Down the aisles one walks on as if garbed in bejewelled raiment from our unparalleled stained glass till evening, when the last beams of daylight filter through from the darkening skies and powder the stern walls with golden dust. Is some medieval sorcery trying to bewitch us out of our senses? Is it so? No! For

Cassie didn't want to know this. She didn't want to know about the insides. She wanted to know about the outsides, the thing directly in front. There was a picture two pages on. Cassie looked at the picture, back at the cathedral. The queue off the buses straggling round, obscuring the steps but it was definitely the same thing. THE WEST OR ROYAL PORTAL.

The three doors which open into the nave are decorated with a telling range of sculpture. On the right, the descent of Christ into our world; on the left, His ascension. The central tympanum shows His second coming while His life (as relates to His birth and death, the incarnation and the Passion and Resurrection) is rendered on a frieze of over 200 figurines.

1. Joachim and Anne rejected because they are childless.
2. They leave in grief.
3. Joachim tending sheep and visited by an angel.
4. He and his wife at the Golden Gate.
5. Mary washed in a tub by two women.
6. Joachim and Anne bring her to the temple.
7. The three journeying together.
8. Mary climbs the steps.
9. The parents return home.
10. Mary taken to the altar by a high priest and St Joseph who holds a flowering stem.
11.

Two young things from the Chartres parks department started hauling out dead plants from the verge opposite. A man in a straw hat stood watching them, wavering like a sheet caught in a light breeze. Cassie flicked over a page.

The archivolts show the seven liberal arts, depicted twofold: allegorically by women and historically by the men considered to be the outstanding exponents of each art.

1. Aristotle and Dialectic.
2. Cicero and Rhetoric.

3. Euclid and Geometry.
4. Arithmetic and Boethius.
5. Astronomy and Ptolemy.
6. Grammar and Priscian or Donatus.
7. Music and Pythagoras.

The archivolts of the Left Door house the labours of the months alternating with the signs of the zodiac.

A shower of somethings shot past Cassie's ankle, scattering on the path. The boys from the parks department wielding trowels in an incautious manner. Flicking earth from her skirt, Cassie looked up. The man in the hat was looking back, spitting into his Volvic bottle.

Enough.

THREE   arches and big wooden doors so plain they looked like night shutters;

TWO   steeples on either side, one plain and the other tortured, teeming with irregular lumps;

ONE   bloody great targe of glass between the towers, shattering outwards.

The gargoyle was still there.

Of course it was.

And other things. Maybe they hadn't been visible because of the light last night but they were visible now. Thousands of them. Beasts and birds all over the walls and steeple, the arches round the doors crushing with different sizes of people. The main pillars were made of tall, skinny sorts with soft faces, four of them women. A high average. Maybe they were queens, saints or somesuch. On the other hand, maybe not. There were no crowns or haloes, nothing set apart about the faces, the dour serenity about the eyes. They looked like women waiting in a bus queue in the rain, women in rainmates who had trained themselves not to notice the water falling on them, minds elsewhere. The one with her breasts ground away and hair in braids, the low sash over her hips. If Cassie stood up on her pedestal they'd be the same height. Nose to nose.

Cassie shifted focus to the stone above the door, the smaller figures on the lintel. A shepherd with his friend and four sheep, talking to someone headless. Their clothes gathered at the waist in full, deep folds, the way thick fabric folded. More figures round the door arch: someone reading, ropes of beard falling into an open book, somebody ringing bells with a hammer, holding an instrument with countable strings, a woman with two children hiding in the drapery of her skirt. Some kind of nativity scene was taking place in the middle of it all, the baby Jesus sturdy as a two-year-old on mother's knee. She held out both his arms. Her face was missing but the child's wasn't: a wee face radiating the kind of stoic preoccupation you saw only on the faces of real weans, the faces of real two-year-olds in fact. Three figures or so along, a woman in a scarf looked over, shawl up to her mouth to hide the smile. Chipped noses, smashed shoulderblades, missing hands and hipbones. From the faces though none of them knew.

Cassie looked hard at the smiling woman. The way the shepherd touched his friend, the bend in the arm of the mother of God. There was something shocking about it. Something that rankled. They were all too at peace with themselves, too untroubled for comfort. The Dark Ages. They were called that for a reason.

Black Death and fear of damnation, hellfire, the wrath of God. Fear of superstition and torture, fear of every bloody thing really. People dug their own graves at the sides of roads and lacerated their own skins for public display, scourged, whipped and purged themselves, watched for blood dripping from the eyes of plaster statues, gouged stigmata in their own flesh. They wasted the limbs of their own children to make them better beggars and burned animals alive in metal ovens too emulate the screams of the damned for purposes of social control. They drowned witches and burned people alive, starved others in wicker cages and let them wither, die, rot and slither through the slats in public view. Magic, persecution of disfigurement and difference, dancing bears and leprosy, leeches and wasps in glass bottles over open wounds. Unmarriageable rich women locked away for a lifetime, married women locked up in chastity belts that dug raw weals into the skin every time they stooped, sat or lay down to sleep. Scolds' Bridles and stocks. Starvation and terrible tax burdens. Quiet book-learning in monasteries and ethereal music, sonnets and courtly love – that stuff was all fantasy and veneer. Buildings like this even. You couldn't afford to let the beauty of the thing seduce you too far or you forgot the truth and the truth was always hard as iron bloody bars. Because to produce something like this people had been broken into bits, toppled off its towers and scaffolding, crushed to mush under fallen masonry, lost limbs or eyesight chiselling and drawing plans by inadequate light, embroidering cloths they would never see complete. But Cassie's eye kept being drawn. The fingers of the musician in mid-stroke. His assumption of ease. The shepherd just looking you right back in the eye and at his feet, sheep who safely grazed. You looked and you saw this. Not knowing whether to laugh. Or.

A step nearer.

There were more of the bloody things.

Over the heads of the columns, figures so tiny you hadn't seen them at all till now. Hundreds upon hundreds in groups of two and three, cutting cloth, sleeping, dancing, playing music. A stone-mason, carving more of his own. The cathedral crawled with tiny people not knowing how hellish their lives were, how little they knew or understood. It drew the breath out of you, even thinking about it: the hopeful journeys over the yellow fields taking days it must have taken days to get here, weeks and months. For some, even years. The hazards of travel and how long it took, the anticipation of getting nearer. Then reaching a clearing and this thing appearing on the horizon, rising up out of the flat earth like judgement. And closer to, covered in themselves.

Big, isn't it?
Rona's head was tilted back, peering up at the steeples.
Why d'you think they're like that? Not symmetrical? Is it symbolic?

Behind Rona's back, a dog patrolling a parapet over a shop. A window display of children's clothes behind the glass, empty limbs dangling on threads. Road accidents hung out to dry.

The door at the front is massive.
Vast.
We push it open and go inside.

We couldn't see a bloody thing.

Just night
twilight
and the nails of something huge forcing into the sky.

Rimmed by tunnels of arches, the shape of empty space pushed itself, fingers first, out of the stone floor. On either side, people milled and mumbled like the sea, drawn like flotsam towards the aweful vortex of

glass glass glass glass glass glass

glass glass glass glass glass glass

glass glass glass glass glass glass

glass glass glass glass glass glass

glass glass glass glass glass glass

glass glass glass glass glass glass

glass glass glass glass glass glass

glass glass glass glass glass glass

glass glass glass glass glass glass

glass glass glass glass glass glass

glass glass glass glass glass glass

glass glass glass glass glass glass

glass glass glass glass glass glass

glass glass glass glass glass glass

glass glass glass glass glass glass

glass glass glass glass glass glass

A hand.

Rona's hand.

Waving.

It was fine once you got used to the level of light. Of dark. Cassie nodded at Rona, then walked off in a different direction. Down a side aisle towards what was now a row of cane chairs, a table with a cross on a scarlet cloth, three candles guttering black smoke. Round the corner, a shock of yellow light. A whole battery of candles burned in solid rows, flicking occasional dots of soot as they melted down, the dark metal spikes and bars of the frame they were impaled on hellish with flame. No wonder it was hard to see, candles licking and guttering like industrial chimneys all those years. Centuries of charcoal that had furred the arteries of the distant ceiling, adding its extra weight to the support beams that were the only thing keeping tons of rubble and sky from crashing onto the people beneath, pulping our heads like ripe melons. People didn't look at the ceiling though, they looked at the candles. All the candles did was melt. Pour, drip, crust, melt. Faces slithering and folding on the other side of a cloud of visible heat, waves of warm air rolling like tumbleweed and twisting features out of shape. The watchers persisted only so long then drifted off into the cool cave of the interior, or bunched near a hatchery of boxes lining the facing wall, choosing fresh candles to replace those steadily wasting away. 5F and 10F: the prices in black lettering on white card, a childlike hand some 6 inches high. The sound of money falling into a dry box said there was still more wood than metal inside it. The cast of flashbulbs and someone singing under their breath. The people at the boxes were in no rush. Choosing the right candle was a serious business. Cassie had a notion candles were prayers. Maybe you were supposed to buy the dear one if you had a lot to be taken into consideration.

100

Maybe on the other hand prayer had nothing to do with it. Maybe they just looked better. Maybe tourists bought them so their pals could take pictures: This is me lighting a candle for the cat in Chartres, drunk on atmosphere and shameless. It seemed entirely likely.

The frame glowered steadily in the foreground, plenty of spikes still free. Not all the candles were burning though. Cassie could see a few that had snuffed out prematurely, still whole. Others had burned down only partway then stopped. Awkward wind currents. Nobody relit them. Maybe you weren't supposed to. Maybe that was cheating. Maybe the prayer only got one go and relighting it was not permissible. Perfectly useful candles. It would have been good to think the people who cleaned up this thing after the place was shut used them through the back for something, but it didn't seem likely. People bought these things for reasons, invested the candle with some sort of power. The people who worked here were supposed to understand that which probably meant the candles would not be reused. Throwing them away didn't seem right either. The whole thing was unfair, somehow. The idea of coming and choosing the candle, taking your time to get the right one, saying the right magic words over it and waiting long enough to think it was ok, walking back up the aisle and behind your back the thing dimmed, darkened, snuffed out. Only a coil of black smoke by the time you'd got to the end of the street and you oblivious, whistling tunes as you walked home thinking things were fine fine fine while behind your back, God had stopped listening. Without you knowing. Without your ever knowing. Cassie looked at the nearest stalk. Still more or less intact. The tapered part at the top was hardly dented. Cassie looked. Nobody would notice if she did it. If she went forward, lifted it, relit it from the next in line and put it back in place. Nobody would care tuppence. Cassie watched the cold candle, imagining beginning. No-one was looking. A child's head poked into the space she was focusing on; a child going up on his toes to reach, the length of wax longer than his arm. He lit it carefully from the others, then took his time, jamming the thing hard on an empty spike before he

101

stood back, crossed himself, looked behind. His mother nodded at him from further away, a smaller child keeking out from behind her knees. Then he turned back, watching the flame. Quite still, just watching.

That was where Cassie wanted to be. She looked at the candle he had lit, the place behind it waiting. She could still do it though, just go over and reach in. You didn't say excusez-moi you said pardon. Pardon. And the boy would move aside, let her through. Any minute now she would go over. Any minute.

The wee boy, his eyes burning.

A pair of specs appeared over his head.

Rona's specs.

Rona was there behind him, flames clustering on her lenses like yellow lashes. Rona smiled at the burning frame, her earrings frazzling like sparklers. She was holding a candle. A fresh one, the wick still white. Rona and child coloured in the same soft light, the same mouths, lips partly opened as they watched. Rona had a very small mouth. She lit her candle from his, put it among the others. Cassie watched the two of them, not bothering with each other much and clutched the camera tighter, looking at the tips of her shoes. It was a near thing. The relighting idea. It would probably have been awful, broken all sorts of taboos: stealing somebody else's paid-for blessing or something. Folk thinking you were doing it to avoid paying. Doing it to try and join in somehow, trying to join in with something you didn't even understand. That was probably how religion worked. The triumph of loneliness over intelligence. And why not? Why shouldn't religion be exactly the same as everything else? Faith, hope and charity: as relevant as serving suggestions. A trio of dubious constructs that only somebody daft, soft or desperate could think had any bearing on reality past adolescence. Fairytales for the hard of thinking. Bloody lies. Cassie held on hard to the dead metal shape in her hand, waiting for her breath to slow down, the tight feeling in her head to pass. A watch beeped. Then a chorus of electronic signalling echoed round the cathedral and beyond, striking hours. A fragment of *In the Mood* was in there somewhere. The heat from the frame got hotter. Cassie turned away, her jaw hard as hell. A near thing.

Across the paving, straight ahead, a Madonna and Child appeared. Perched on top of a dark column, surrounded by a bower of Hollywood starlet bulbs. At its base, a man in a denim jacket, prone. The studs on his jacket glittering, clear words emerging through the spangling mesh in dot-to-dot pinpoints of light. GRIM REAPER.

Rona was there round the curve of the next bend, pointing.
Look.
Colours reflected from the rose window, glued to the floor in blobs the length of the aisle. Look, she said, Mysterons.

Cassie and Rona walked silently round the back of a curved frieze, statues of the circumcision and stabbings and godknows, to emerge unscathed. The wee boy was there at the other end, gazing up at the Virgin on a stick. His mother stood behind him, her sari glinting with leftover radiance from the electric bulbs, the child of indeterminate sex howling with grief, unheeded in her arms.

Photo

Rocky's Taverna. Chris eating. They only had one dish every night and it was always good. Empty bottle of raki on the table. Probably why he's smiling like that. Seriously well on. You have to look hard, though. Probably ordered another bottle after I took this. Can't remember but it's likely. There was a garden; big pink things like bells pushing out over the tablecover, like garden cloches with frills round the bottom. Every night after we'd eaten you could sit and watch bees on last-ditch pollen raids inside them. The frills on the ends of the flowers were getting tighter and tighter, drawing in like shirring elastic. You could see it doing it but the bees couldn't. They just kept coming. After a while they'd need to shoulder in and back out, leg sacs so full they couldn't fly straight. Like drunks. The minute one was out, another was wrestling with the bloody thing to get in. Eventually one of them got stuck. It got in ok then couldn't open the thing again. I remember watching the shadow inside, cramming against the pink closed mouth that just wouldn't let him go. It tried backing against the thing, then poking its legs at the seam from the inside. Nothing. Then the strange thing happened. Another bee that had been hanging about outside the flower started fiddling with the thing. Like it was trying to help. Little black legs pulling at the petals trying to prise them apart but it was hopeless. The thing was just clammed for the night. I told Chris about it but he said I was nuts. He'd been watching a scorpion and wasn't really involved. He said more likely the other one was just annoyed it couldn't get in itself. They were programmed that way he said. Cassie, you're nuts. In retrospect he's probably right but it depressed me anyway. He seemed too pleased about it for me to be comfortable. In the end I suppose the bee stayed there all night. We left but I kept wondering if it would drown. I wondered off and on all night. Hanging back, watching the shadow inside the bell while Chris was settling up bills. He had to shout for me to come. The shadow not able to give in.

When the prints came there were six of the scorpion. All his.

> Once a sophisticated Neo-Classical city, TOURS,
> today, is a place of light industry, research and data
> processing as well as being a tourist mecca for the
> thousands who visit the Loire Valley chateaux every

I vote we give Tours a miss, Cassie.

Rona took the last mouthful out of the bottom of the cup and
turned back to the map, exhaling.

There's this though.

> DON'T MISS AZAY-LE-RIDEAU, one of the most
> elegant and inspiring châteaux in France, reflecting
> itself in its own lake amid the shade of beautiful trees.
> The corner turrets and machicolations are not func-
> tional. The interior makes this wonderful building a
> Renaissance museum.

And it isn't as far. Will we go there then? Azay-le-Rideau. We
could go there. If you think.

Rona and Cassie

sat outside the Café de la Cathedral listening to old Beach Boys
hits among the remains of cheese sandwiches and an empty wine
bottle. Well after five the sky still that high blue colour. The dog on
the parapet wasn't there. The sun over the North Door throwing
cool shapes over the park. Cassie lifted her sunglasses and looked at
Rona. The ice-lollies advert behind her was less livid now, KIM
FUZZ and RADIATOR rocket-shaped next to DINOSAUR, a lime
green monster with two sticks. A yellow and pink knobbly lump with
nuts was called NELLY. NELLY had a star with NOUVEAU over
the bit where the stick went into the lump but it didn't add to the
appeal. Rona saw none of these things. After a moment, neither did
Cassie. The waiter came out and eased the board free from behind

Rona's chair and took it inside. Cassie lowered the glasses again and followed the sheen on the arse of his black trousers with her eyes. Safe. A brass plaque behind the counter shone from inside: Servis compris 12% la maison ne fait pas de credit. The waiter turned and polished it anyway. Killing time.

This is interesting, Rona said.
An open page of the pamphlet reflected in one of her lenses, map of the cathedral interior in the other.
This thing. Did you read it? This thing about the zodiac?

Cassie shook her head. The route map was on Rona's left, highlighter pen on the right. She hadn't touched her second coffee yet.

The zodiac signs are carved with the labours of the month. We could go and pick out our signs. Gemini and Sagittarius. They're opposite on this thing. Know what your labour of the month is?

Cassie put one elbow up on the table and watched three figures on the North Door she knew nothing about, late heat on the back of her neck. A clatter from the restaurant next door suggested laying of tables.

It's sitting at the fire. Look. It's a wee man doing it. Sitting at the fire. Mine is mowing the hay. Inner archivolt, bottom left.
Sliced in two by shadow, their profiles extreme. Extremely something. Cassie looked at the faces and tried to think what it was. Three men almost smiling.

The church received from King Charles the Bald the tunic of the Virgin it says. That black thing with the fairy lights round it. It's called the pearwood virgin or Our Lady of the Pillar. She replaced Notre-Dame-la-Blanche, a seated virgin of gold and silver that was in the main chancel. 16th Century.

Benign. That was the word. Benign. One of the faces almost wasn't. Corroded by the wind and the rain, eyeless and nose-free, most of the hair chipped off, yet the tracery of a half-smile was still there, radiating nine-hundred years across the road to Cassie Burns, spinster of some other parish entirely, hemmed in at this table with the plastic cover held on with clothes pegs, surrounded by second coffee cups and flakes of bread, a bottle of cheap plonk entirely finished and a bit of cheese Rona had left on her plate. The same smile given to the empty air every day, a tireless, dependable and beautiful thing which was to the absent black dog merely a commonplace if the dog had any inkling it was there at all. Which it didn't. Of course it didn't. But Cassie did. She was here watching it in the here and now, this moment of knowing the present, being smiled at by a lump of stone made seductive by a long-dead sculptor who knew somehow she would be here – at least that someone would be here – to see. It was astonishing. It was –

You're not listening are you? Rona put down her specs and looked over, rubbing her eyes.

Eh?

Not listening. I'm saying will we go to Azay then? What do you think?

Cassie turned from years and miles away and saw Rona. Rona on the other side of the table, surrounded by the cosmos. At her back, a waiter making bigger clattering noises, bringing out shutters; overhead, the veranda over her head where the dog had been and would be again; at her feet, dust full of gravel chips and chunks of unidentifiable masonry, the perforated edging from a strip of stamps, plastic circles that might have been the tops of bottles rolled flat, gold foil, ring pulls, straws, cigarette filter tips and a baby's teething ring. Pleasing evidence of Reality. The gutter led off into places unseen, the sky likewise. Now she had purged herself of daft romantic ideas, Cassie felt clean. Bruised but pure. Cassie could see into the middle of next week from here if she had been in the mind for it: a timeless vantage point with herself at the heart of the whole. She also knew she had thought that before. Glimpses into the Meaning of Life, Truth, Beauty Ha!

The light was shifting fast. No twilight. You got less warning here, less notice it was about to turn pitch black. A hiccup and a click. *Help me Rhonda* switched off in mid-phrase.

Cassie looked up.

Rona had asked a question. Azay. Cassie couldn't remember what she had said about it now but it would be fine. It would be more than fine, it would be elegant and inspiring reflecting itself in its own lake amid the shade of beautiful trees, waiting for them. Like the time they went to Cerne Abbas and the Giant's monstrous erection had appeared shamelessly over the brow of hill, carved into the chalk. Cassie's French would be fluent and the food affordable. Azay would be just fine.

Across the road, the three men were already changing, expressions melting out into flatness. The pansies in the park borders were wilting and the man with the Volvic bottle had come back. Cassie took the sunspecs off and looked across at Rona, bridging time, distance, light and space.

Rona. I have seen infinity and it says DON'T BE GREEDY. I think we cut and run, go while the going is good and don't chance our luck. Rona, we go to Azay. We drive.

eight

DON'T MISS AZAY-LE-RIDEAU, one of the most elegant and inspiring châteaux in France, reflecting itself in its own lake amid the shade of beautiful trees. The corner turrets and machicolations are not functional. The interior makes this wonderful building a Renaissance museum.

That must be it in the picture. The same advert in window after window, one travel agency after another. The picture looked like Ambleside, the place they couldn't get into the pub for Swedes in hillwalking boots singing nautical-sounding songs but it wouldn't be. It would be here. Ahead, the row of cars stayed tight and unchanging, bumper to bumper like a string of beads, quivering lightly with engine vibration, ticking over. Every so often, a cough. Choking up. Occasionally, arms uncurled from windows to flop beside shut doors, trailing through the low cloud of exhaust fumes as it wove through the dull glitter of chrome. Nothing else moved. Rona worked it out. Friday. The French holiday had started and was inching en masse up this particular road. Only one turnoff ahead, unmarked. Nobody was taking it. Cassie took the map from Rona and looked at where they were supposed to be. She couldn't work out where the turnoff was or where it was going. But it didn't matter. Anything was better than keeping in line with this, people trapped inside their cars because this was just where they said they would go, sticking with this even though they knew it was hellish rather than take a risk. They didn't have to. We didn't have to. We don't.

It's fine, Cassie said. Take the turn.

Rona turned and looked Cassie in the eye. She knew. She knew fine Cassie didn't have a clue. She looked long enough to let Cassie know she knew and sighed. Cassie sighed back.

Christ Rona. Does it matter?

Cassie watches the gap stay the same, the bonnet of the car shivering. Ten cars or so up the line, another car opens up like a moth, doors flapping while someone inside holds their hand down hard on the horn. The doors shut again before the car body jumps off the leash, reverses far enough to bump the car behind, makes enough space to turn, roars over the verge and on to the sideroad. Keeping going. Applause. People applauding as the car tanks out of sight.

Cassie looks at Rona looking at her.

I don't know, Rona sighs, flicking on the indicator. I don't know.

But we turn. We turn unobtrusively, Rona's way, as though we meant to do it all along. Behind, growing smaller in the rear window, the abattoir queue of cars looks almost benign. It can go where the fuck it likes. We are not tied to the same fate any more.

Choosing not to chase a promise any longer than is good for our health, taking a risk we cut loose,

light

free.

Me washing shirts. Last day in Greece. Last time, come to think
of it. The last day of the last time. Me washing shirts anyway.
That was all my thing: my job to make the packing lists, get the
wee sachets of shampoo and the suntan stuff. His as well. I liked
bits of it: the feel of his jeans folded for the case, those thin
cotton shirts for the heat. Travel wash. That was the thing
about the thin shirts. Short shelf-life. When his things got dirty
he'd stand there looking down at them regretfully and I was
meant to come to the rescue. I didn't mind, I suppose. I mean I
did like something about it, the washing and the open air. It
made me feel part of a tradition of women doing the same thing:
stoic and purposeful or some such rubbish. Scarf tying my hair
back. Probably to hide the fact it needed a wash. He said it
made me look Greek. Ancient Greek. Jesus though look at me.
I'm only twenty-nine and look at me. Bashing shirts off the
roadside with that grim determination on my face. I look so
bloody old in it.

Modern CHINON has more than a reminder of its
Medieval past in the ancient streets, the most notable
of which is named after Joan of Arc in memory of her
momentous journey this way to meet the Dauphin and
alter the course of history. The ruined fortresses and
many fine old buildings rimming the banks of the
Vienne make CHINON well worth the time to explore.

I told you. Rona stretched and retracted. It's lovely.

She finished what looked like nothing left and put the glass back near the empty chip plates, scattering spilt salt off the edge of the tablecover.

Cassie had finished ages ago. Cassie drank drinks. Rona could sit all night with one, sipping. There was a sort of biscuit barrel in her flat always half-full. She ate single chocolates if you offered her the box. Peanuts and whole baby beetroot the same. It was beyond Cassie's ken. Rona leaned back, sighing out.

Want another one? We can have another drink or go back if you like. I don't mind.

Lights along the water, done up to look like Chinese lanterns. Flying things were battering into them if you looked close, but far enough away not to be a threat. Couples along the waterside. Cassie looked in the waiter's direction but he didn't see. Rona waved and called HELLO. He turned and nodded. They were staying then. Rona settled back into the chair, letting a man surface into view behind her shoulder. A man in a checked shirt sitting on a bar stool, squashed against a skinny girl in shorts. Now Cassie saw him, the voice started connecting. The bits of words and American twang hadn't been certain before but now they were unavoidable. Almost too loud. *Don't get me wrong, I like Europe. For one thing the women have a little more mystique. French women know how to do that stuff.* Pale purple ears, all lobe. The waistband of his trousers too tight. The back of the girl's head gave nothing away. *They're not aggressive about their sexuality. They know the meaning of the word feminine.*

Cassie looked to see if the waiter was coming. He nodded, gathering money up off a newly-cleared table. Cassie picked up the empty glass and put it back down again. Knotless. Rona had put the horsebag up on the table and was rooting around as well, not really

112

settled. Crushed paper hankies fell out with the purse, and something heavy. It landed at the waiter's feet. The blue folder. The waiter stooped at the same time but Rona won. She picked it up herself, ordering brandy to give the guy something else to do. Rona didn't often order brandy. She put the folder on the table and said nothing by way of explanation. Cassie ordered brandy too. The waiter moved away.

You can take a French girl anywhere because she's got respect. She's not looking to put you down all the time because she respects a man for being a man. Respect. That's a rare commodity.

Maps and stuff, Cassie said.
Rona sat straighter in her chair, one ear cocked.
Arras. You got all those maps and things. We were hardly there any time.
No. Rona looked down. Och well.

The check shirt was leaning nearer to the girl, fanning its face with one limp hand. Cassie wished she could stop catching him in the corner of her eye but she couldn't. *You must have plenty of boyfriends, beautiful little thing like you. Sure you have. I have a daughter must be about your age but she wears a brace.* The voice seemed to be getting louder.

I don't think I'd have liked to stay longer though, Rona said. Arras. Finding the place was plenty.
The waiter arrived with the drinks.

I mean that was the only reason to go there. I'm glad we left when we did.

Cassie waited till he had finished serving.
When he walked away she said. Was it like you thought? The cemetery?
Och I don't think I thought it would be like anything. It wasn't for me really. I said to my gran ages ago I'd go. It was for her, I

113

suppose. Guilt. Rona picked up her glass, looked down. She had loads of them, though. Rocking the brown fluid back and forth. He wrote all the time. I only brought the first and last though. They're my favourites: the bit about bribing the sergeant or whoever it was. He must have bunked off to see her before they got posted. A shilling to get off light.

Rona made a kind of smile, picked the folder up and skimmed through. Here it's:

and may I say I was very lucky to get back as the rest of the chaps that ran away got Royal Warrant and 5 days CB that was only for 1 days absence I was away 2 days I got round the orderly serjeant boy giving him 1/- for a drink so that just shows you how it can be done. Now Maggie we have all been inspected by the General today Tuesday I expect to be on my road to France tomorrow Wednesday so I was very glad I ran away

That bit.

Rona folded the letter again, started rolling fluff between her fingers. They're nice letters.

Nice breasts too. You don't mind men admiring nice breasts and saying so. Not afraid of a little honest appreciation. I couldn't say that to a woman at home. I couldn't say that to my wife.

I'm not sentimental about them or anything. They're just nice. It was the photos for my gran I really wanted. She's not great just now but she'll know what they are. Well, I think she'll know what they are. I'll take them anyway. There wasn't any need to spend more time in Arras though. No need. It was fine.

Rona takes a sip of brandy and coughs. She coughs again.
Christ, her eyes roll, watering at the corners. I don't know what I ordered this for. I don't even like the stuff. Christ.

Maggie just a note to let you know I am still in the land of the living I have been back in the trenches for days and am at present in the line to be relieved tonight we have been lucky this time we did not get much shelling but digging from 6pm to 4am Ill be glad of a sleep The weather is not very good some parts of the trenches we are up to the knees in it We do not get to take off the boots since our feet would swell up and not be able to get them on again so we just got to wait to get out to get our feet dried you might send a good simmet as I find it very cold I dont suppose you will have any at Killie but maybe you could buy something at Agnes and maybe a parcel We are always glad of the food Now I expect Maggie dear you will be finding it hard if you are getting the same weather as us but maybe the boys are able to give you a telling off for coming home wet I wish I could see them There is talk of us going down the line but I do not see it until we are full strength Anyway I will close now and hope you and the wee chaps are well Your very loving husband xxxxxxPeter

I lift my eyes from the letter I took without asking, guilty. Rona has stopped coughing, started sipping. If she minds, it doesn't show. She maybe didn't even notice. What age was he Rona I say and she says twenty-nine. He was twenty-nine. Behind her back, the man insinuates an arm around the skinny piece. *I always think you can find out a lot about yourself away from home. You miss them to begin with but they get along fine without you. You go back and they don't know who the hell you are. I've been everywhere so I know a little about the subject. I say when in Rome. Can I buy you another drink? Believe me, sweetie, you're something else.*

The Bosphorus. Asia on one side, Europe on the other. They call it the Golden Horn because in the evening, the sun sets on the far edge and the whole river turns yellow, like melted butter. I saw a postcard of it in Athens airport and wondered why the hell we kept going to Greece all the time. Well, I knew and I didn't, the way you do. You just don't push enough for change. This reminded me there were other places. Ok he said ok. Humouring me. I had to threaten to explode if we did another Greek beach, but he did consent. Istanbul then further down the coast: place called Antalya that was just a resort. Compromise. I was so excited I bought a Turkish phrase book the day after we got home from Santorini, started learning up. By the time we got there I'd forgotten the whole lot. Anyway. This is it: postcard of the Golden Horn, Istanbul. A river washing two continents. I got shots of the real thing once I was there but not as good as this. I must always have been looking the wrong way at the critical minute or something. I could only ever get it to look like water. So I kept this. Postcard from Athens airport. It gives you a better idea of what it was like. What it was supposed to be like.

Rona in the rain. The blob perched on the kerb. Like she's falling through bloody Niagara.

Rona.

You are putting the camera in your pocket to save it from the wet when she steps off the pavement, looking the opposite way. Rona's profile pokes beyond the rim of scarf covering the sides of her head, too much noise from the junction with men drilling under a tarpaulin on the further side of the roundabout and you know she can't hear a bloody word. The white lorry takes the corner too fast as you knew it would. It won't see: she won't hear. You leave her for five minutes and this is what happens. But Rona is in no danger. She is in no danger because you are there. You watch your arm extend,

116

your hand claim her shoulder and haul her back. Rona's face furious
inside the goldfish bowl of the scarf then her eyes changing, whole
body juddering beneath your fingers as water shears up from the
road and the crush of the front four tyres, catching her full on the
crotch before she comes backwards to you again. Safe.

Bastard. Did you see that? Bastard.

Rona's face was running with water, eyebrows touching.
Muffled and raging inside a sodden scarf, the black fringe making
sharks' teeth into her eyes.

Complete bastard. The eyes creasing up when she laughs. The
dirtiest laugh in the world. She starts to run.

Cassie and Rona
Rona and Cassie

ran with the pavement pockmarking endlessly under their four
feet. Haring out of the rain.

Rona came back with coffees and two paper plates. Pizza.

Today's Special, she said. Not indigenous but cheap. Here.

It looked fine. Rona was fed-up with the rain. She hadn't
brought knives.

They ran out. I couldn't remember the word but they're out of
them anyway.

Couteau. Cassie knew the word but it was too late now. She held
the cup hard inside one hand and tore off bits of pizza with the other.
Every so often the rain battered worse on the roof, the noise of the
people coming out the supermarket tuning in and out like rotten
radio reception. Muzak from the speakers over the servery hatch
filled up any leftover space. Daydream Believer. In French. Rona
took off her scarf and sprawled it over the back of the plastic chair.
Her hair looked painted on. Cassie took a picture.

117

Smile. You're on your holidays.

Christ. Rona took too big a mouthful of tea, coughed and took another one, her cheeks going pinker in the heat.

We got the stuff anyway. The money. And directions for that place.

Good. Water was running down the back of Cassie's neck. Getting slowly warmer. We can get the messages then.

I need to phone. I think I need to phone the woman and check it's ok to come out.

I thought the place phoned. When we said we wanted it in the Tourist Office place, they phoned her.

We should let her know, though. Ourselves.

Ok. Then we can get the messages.

A sigh. Ok. Then we get the messages.

It was Saturday. Cassie needed a supermarket. She needed to squeeze tomatoes and check apples for age spots, fondle cabbage leaves, flex plastic packages of carrots, scan bean tins and thrill to money-off labels. Every Saturday Cassie got the housewife out her system. Every Saturday, saying she didn't want to, Rona came. They took the car to the hypermarket at Darnley then wandered off on independent forays. Rona's always included butter, a single bulb of garlic, dried peas, two lemons, toilet rolls and herb tea. Rona didn't eat enough. But Cassie liked Rona to be there. Even bored and checking her watch, Cassie liked Rona to be there. Trying to get her to pick up bars of chocolate at the checkout, the odd malt loaf. Rona liked malt loaf but needed Cassie to talk her into it. For that reason alone, Cassie knew she did Rona good. They stood in the checkout queue, grateful together: Rona because she was getting out and Cassie because. Because because. She didn't know what it was but something about it felt good. The shopping and the company, the sense of purpose. All the way to Saumur, with the single sighting of what might have been the Loire as they drove over a bridge, swollen with floating junk, through the noise of the wipers on full stress, Cassie had been looking forward to the supermarket. They had gone to the Tourist Office together and found a place no bother.

118

Farmhouse to rent. Self-catering. Shopping. Cassie had known all the words in French. Amazing what came out of the back of the memory when it had to. When you were on home ground.

Rona put the cup down. It wasn't warm any more.

Ok. We can do it here. Might even get the phone bit here as well if we look. Damn.

She was reaching into her pocket and bringing something out. A piece of lined paper with wet seams.

It's ok. Just I can't read this writing. He wrote it down for me in the TO place himself. Wouldn't spell it.

Cassie looked at the bit of paper. The kind of writing someone writing in their own language and not bothered whether anybody else could read it looked back. Cassie traced the letters with one finger and one eye shut, trying to imagine the act of penning them, what, if her own hand had made them, the marks were meant to read. She did it twice.

Bugger it, Rona. The number's clear enough. Just do the phoning bit.

I could go back and ask him to write it again. We should know the name of the place for goodnessake.

Applause and bullets on the roof. Rona looked up. She sighed again. On the other hand. Ok. I'll phone.

Cassie pushed back a strand of drowned hair and smiled.

We are going shopping.

We stack

                              eggs
               mushrooms   cherries   coffee
          bread   garlic   tomatoes   onions
          cucumber   radishes   carrots   brie   yoghurt
          putty-coloured cheese wrapped in leaves   parsley
     peaches   plums   oil   mustard   vinegar   butter
       milk   orange juice   two chocolate bars   biscuits
   three bottles of wine   a bottle of cheap brandy   Grand Marnier

                          in a trolley

                and carry, like a babe in arms,

                    the biggest lettuce in the world.

        It takes up a whole carrier-bag on its own. Leaves like seaweed.

         I don't care what it tastes like, Rona, it's a work of art.
         Rona just looks.
         And when we come outside, the rain is battering more

and more
and more   and more

and more   and more
and more   and more   and
and more   and more   more
and more   and more   more
and   and more   more
               and   more

                                        more
                                        and

Halfmoons fill up on the windscreen, reappear,
         fill up on the windscreen, reappear.

                              120

Watch out for signs to the TUFA CAVES and semi-subterranean troglodyte dwellings dug out of soft lime-stone along the borders of the Loire, the Loire, the Indre and the Cher. The village of TRÔO is partly carved from Tufa which, in this wine-growing region, makes superb wine-cellars. It also provides ideal conditions for mushroom growing: *see also* MUSH-ROOM MUSEUM.

Breath mists up the windscreen from inside when I laugh. Rona frowning, not able to see. Keeping driving.

Past the end of the same road for the fourth time, she was still there. A Bosch figurine with a coat where its head should be, stick legs poking out the bottom. Rain skited off the top of the coat, hard as hail. One arm came out every so often to point at something. Cassie tried but couldn't see what. Rona slowed this time, strain-ing forward to see when the arc were clear on the next sweep of the wipers. There it was in a gap off the main road. Cassie saw it too. It came, blotted out, came back, blotted out. A dust-track off going down behind the main farmhouse. The woman ran to the side window, arm stabbing towards the gap. Cassie tapped on the window without rolling it down, letting her know they'd seen. Taking it on trust, aiming for the opening that showed for less of a second each time, Rona tilted the car. It seemed to climb, find a lip, drop sharply. There was no telling what into. All Cassie could see was the blunt shape of the woman under the waterfall, her specs covered with prisms, making something like a smile under a sag of sodden canvas, leading them in out of the rain.

Not Chris — Rona !

Big room full of knackered old sideboards and things, two bedrooms off to either side, dresser with a soup tureen the size

121

of a wardrobe. Toilet with a window and a tap. I was soaking but I took this before I did anything else. I just knew right away I was going to love it.

Kitchen. It never takes me long to find a kitchen. That thing on the floor is a box with washing-up liquid and dishtowels and stuff: Rona unpacking it. First thing I found was a drawer full of medieval implements to crush garlic, zest lemons and godknows. Look at me. Happy as a sandperson/ housewife/ pig in shit. On my holidays.

I prepare
       mushroom soup
       bread and cheese
       cherries and peaches on a plate, alternate colours,
and take this photo of the table.
Elsewhere, banging doors, Rona shouts We could live in this at home. You should come and see. It's a find. Her voice cracks on the crescendo. We could live in it no bother.

View from the top of the lift at Heathrow, some hellish time of the morning after seven hours on the train. Teetering on the brink. Like the first time we flew anywhere only it wasn't. He's not smiling because we'd just had a row about something, godknows. We'd just eaten too much because of flight delays, pigged out on crisps and cheap drink till we both felt iffy but weren't saying. He hated saying anything that made me ask if we weren't too old for that kind of carry-on yet. He liked to think he was just a boy. It's not a holiday without a tan and a good drink, Cassie, carrying this bloody windsurfing board through customs. <u>Thirty-one</u> going on fifteen. Godknows what he saw when he looked at me. Godknows.

R initiates sR

What about a walk then?

In an unfamiliar room surrounded by ancient dark furniture under the sixty-watt bulb, dried flowers inside an unused fire, Rona turned and spoke. Her feet were up on the edge of the table, toes waving about near the fruit bowl. One elbow nearly inside an ashtray full of cherry stones. She spat them out still fleshy. Like pulled teeth.

We don't need to go far or anything, just get our bearings.

The mirror over the mantelpiece showed the back of Rona's dried head, hair sticking up in sixteen directions, the table covered in demolished bits. Half past seven. Unbelievable. The same level of light all day. At least it had stopped raining, the background wash of cold noise was gone. Cassie could see her own face in the mirror, looking at itself. Saying nothing.
Cmon. We'll get the coats on and just have a look round. See what's what.

Rona picked at her teeth with a splinter of wood, her feet up on the table. Winning.

Up the side of the farmhouse and along the side of the river, the road went naturally downhill into a sort of village square with three houses and some shut shops. Something that might have been a pub was shut as well. A hairy dog with an undertaker's face looked out of a barn and went back inside again. Nobody else, no cars. Back at road level, a bridge became visible: asphalt and metal railings. Rona and Cassie walked the hundred yards or so to where it started. Underneath, the river was engorged, brown with boiled up silt. Cassie saw something move in the gutter. The size of a beetle only not. The way it moved made it not an insect. A frog. It avoided the open palm of her hand and tried to walk round. Rona came over and looked down. She had forgotten the camera.

We could take it back, said Cassie.
What for?
Train it up till it's big then eat it.
Rona rolled her eyes and sighed. Cassie kept looking at the frog.
Well? Rona sighed again. Will we get to the other side of this bridge then? Something might come. It's not all that clever standing on the road in this kind of visibility, Cassie. Cmon.

Cassie watched the frog make slow small movements along the gutter in the opposite direction. It would probably still be there when they came back, slogging away at crossing the bridge without knowing where it was going. Cassie put another hand down to help and the thing just stopped. All she was doing was confusing it.
Are you coming or not?
In a minute. I'm for shifting this thing.

Cassie reached forward and picked the frog up by the sides. The tiny fluttering under the skin. It was so bloody fragile. A verge ran down steep on either side. Maybe that's what it was looking for. Water. Frogs lived near water. But you could never be sure. Maybe it knew fine where it was headed and all she had done was make its life more complicated. Cassie plopped it down in the longer grass anyway and watched. Rona came up and watched as well. It didn't move.

Shoo. Cassie put her hands in her pockets and pretended to glare at the frog. I'm putting myself out for you here. Making difficult moral decisions. On you go. Jump.

The frog sat still. Its sides beating in and out. It was probably terrified. Rona put her arm through Cassie's and started to walk. Cassie looked back only once.

The rest of the road was just road: no turnoffs and nothing on either side except wet green stuff. Getting chillier. They turned and walked back. There was wine at home. They would heat it up with sugar and go to bed with their teeth pink. On the way back over the bridge, Cassie saw the asphalt bubble, a tiny piece of it shifting sideways. The frog. Ploughing back the way it had been going in the first place. Cassie stopped and stared down. Thin yellow stripes pulsing over the fingernail-size ribcage.

Look at it. Look. Clueless.

Rona shook her head. Leave it alone for godsake Cassie. It's fine. It's probably more fine than you are. Leave the bloody thing alone.

There was no-one else on the road at all.

We're the only folk left on the planet, Rona.

Rona snorted and kept walking.

My room is on the right of the door: the room with floral wallpaper. Rona's has stripes. There is a damp feel to the sheet, more cloying as my feet go down. Maybe just cold. A bunch of dried flowers hangs on a hook next to the wardrobe, thick with dust.

Cassie lay back on the pillowslip, hearing the ends of her hair crunch, her own pulse thumping about inside the flattened ear. The wine. You heated it and put sugar in and drank it like lemonade, not even noticing. Heartbeat filling up the fingerends as well now. If she concentrated hard, she could feel the jugular: she could count the strokes. Elsewhere, Rona opened and closed something, creaking a floorboard as she moved. It could be ages before Rona went to bed.

125

Sometimes, the time we went to Devon she had buggered about till after three in the morning, checking her packing again and again. Maybe it wasn't Devon. Maybe it was Copenhagen. Hamburg. Anyway Rona had buggered about till thon time for no explicable reason then snorted in her sleep like a camel till they had had to get up, the noise carrying through two walls. Rona. She drove you gaga if you were sleeping in the same room and gaga if you weren't. She did it all the time.

The moon would be up just outside those curtains. Cassie wouldn't get up to look. Better just leave it there than have Rona hear her moving around too. Blond hair falling over the pillow. Every time I admired the length of his hair he cut it. It's ok for some Cassie but I need to be practical. A sudden clunk, bedsprings. I picture Rona through there in the green floral nightie, sitting up with her specs on, looking at maps. Christ Rona. Rona.

Cassie listened for the crease of paper but couldn't hear anything but the over-loud crackle of her own hair on the pillowslip. The perm: they made your hair brittle. Especially when you got older. The sheets still cold. Maybe that chill in the sheet was damp right enough. Her hand shook when she reached to feel. Pumping with something. Too much adrenalin. Cassie, he used to say, Your chemicals aren't right. You should drink more. HA. Too much these days. That was the problem: Cassie knew she had drunk more than felt good. Rona padding through the kitchen again, running a tap. Feet shuffling back, switching the light off and on a couple of times. Cassie closed her eyes.

Opened them again.

Total darkness.

The occasional drip from the guttering on to the sill.

126

Cassie listened till she was sure then swung one foot out of bed. Both feet on the rush matting, the hem of her nightie tugging away from the topsheet. Nighties. When had that become usual, to wear a nightie? Cassie walked toward the window in the nightie, pushed the blind to one side. The dim chunk edge of the farmhouse where the woman stayed. Possibly a husband. They would be asleep: farmers were like that. They went to bed early because they had routines that weren't optional. Their room would have a crucifix and probably a sacred heart over the bed, white sheets, shutters on the outside windows. They might even say prayers. They wouldn't read in bed or talk much, just put out the light. He would snore on his back and she would sleep with her hands holding a sheet close to her chest, long grey hair loose over her shoulders. They no longer made love in the morning with the picture of the Virgin watching from the facing wall, only very occasionally, in the dark and in silence, so not even the bed creaked. Cassie thought about the farmer's wife, her face lying silent on the pillow. Whether it would be a calm face, serene after a lifetime together with the man or whether

Something rang out.

A metallic thump from what would most likely be the back of the cottage. Hard to say. Unlit by streetlamps or headlights from the road, there was no way of telling what shape anything was in such blackness, where anything was in relation to anything else. What there might be in the utter dark outside this wall she sheltered behind, listening.

Without thinking, Cassie looked up.

Above her head, the black burst into clear stars that shed no light. Rising for unimaginable miles.

nine

A red yard
green wire fencing
a brown dog

and no rain.

Cassie looked out past the curtain and thought about Rona in the other room. Unconscious, her hair an inkblot on the white bolster. Being up first and Rona not knowing what was out here and waiting for her made Cassie feel so good she wanted to wake her up and tell her only that would have missed the point. Cassie looked out at the dog and the sun. A boxer. Gravel drying out making a fine mist over the ground. Cassie wanted to do something nice. She wanted to do something nice for Rona.

Slate. The kitchenette floor was freezing. The taps turned umpteen times before a limp stream of water peed forth. A rising scale as the pot filled. Cassie put the pot on the back ring, trying to work out which dial was which. Electric cooker. She wasn't keen on electric cookers but this was holiday. You made do. Vacuum pack of coffee on top of the pyre of shopping. No filters. Cassie looked round, shivering. There were no jugs. Under the sink, she found only a grater, a thing like a trumpet with a ratchet handle, a pair of small metal folding legs with a scoop, a tea-strainer, a flan ring and a jelly bag. Other things were impossible even to guess at. At the back of the living-room dresser, a thing that might have been a cafetière came to light only Cassie didn't know how a cafetière worked. Bits fell out the middle when she picked it up: a spring and a metal rod with a collander on the end. She put them back inside it and the lot back where it belonged. The bread knife by the side of the sink, rusting along the cutting edge; bread going solid in its polythene poke, butter with a skin and no jam. Still no jugs. Cassie looked round, shrugged. What the hell. She'd manage. She usually managed when she had to. That was when she saw the vase. A vase on the sill, empty. The pot on the electric ring squealed, getting hot. As Cassie moved towards the vase she saw something behind it, something yellow on the other side of the glass. Cassie walked to the door hatch, slipped the bolt and levered on to her toes to see.

Sunflowers.

Field after field, turning open faces towards where she stood in the doorframe, looking back. The odd smear of poppies through the hail of stems. The slink of chain. Bleating and the click of hoof on gravel.

RONA.

There is coffee in a vase. Milk, butter, two cups, one saucer, a plate of bread, odd bits of cutlery with every handle different. A blue bowl filled with peaches and two poppies pulled from the field. Ready.

Cassie shouts RONA again, RONA

129

and waits

radiant behind a hairtrigger shutter, till Rona staggers into
view, her hair a shocked sea anemone, into the daze of late morning
and Cassie, roaring

RONA THERE'S A GOAT OUT THE BACK DOOR

crazed with possibility

taking pictures.

Nervous I don't know why I was so nervous about that holiday
maybe because it was somewhere different, maybe because I
knew. I spent a lot of time telling myself not to be silly. I told
myself it was going to be fine. Istanbul would be laid out like in
Kismet: Topkapi with golden domes and flags waving from the
top, muscled guards with oiled pectorals. At night we would
look out over the Bosphorus, the river joining one continent to
another and clink glasses, watching the crescent moon and the
stars reflected in the Golden Horn while dubious sorts with
two-day growths and shifty eyes slid past in the background, on
their way to somewhere else. There would be no hamstrung
animals and no mutilated children with open palms at the side
of the road; no people offering to be kinder than I could bear it,
being patient in my language when I knew nothing of theirs.
Nothing would be complicated or sordid, too beautiful or too
real: it would be a big Hannah Barbera puppet show and
Disneyland and fine fine fine. I didn't have to face a thing if I
didn't want to. Everything would be

Cassie put the top back on the suncream, watching Rona search out the key. Rona wore shorts: Cassie, an ankle-length cheesecloth thing with sleeves. Long sleeves. And a cardigan. In case.

Mild outside. A light breeze and the red gravel almost dry. Cassie and Rona opened the big wire door of the big wire fence round the farmhouse and walked to the shut village of the night before. Still shut. Shut boulangerie, shut bar, houses with shutters down. Nothing else.

Sunday, Rona said.
Sunday.

They walked back to the cottage. On the other side of the mesh, the boxer dog was sniffing the tyres of the car.

Look at it, Rona said. Filthy. I'm washing that thing before we go anywhere. It's completely filthy. She meant the car. Then we can go for a Sunday drive. It'll be relaxing.

The boxer dog had come to the mesh, looking through. Quivering. Rona said Hello Boy in a squeaky voice and turned the key. She had time to say Hello Boy one more time before the boxer dog lunged at the foot she had put across the threshold, eyes rolling. Rona pulled her foot back and giggled in an unconvincing way. She looked at Cassie.
Oops, she said. Oops.
Cassie moved in front, angling herself to slide through first.
Ok, I'll distract it and you get the front door open. Just slip by when I open the door and take your time.

Rona stared at the dog. It had leaped back a pace or two, put its head down and was waving its arse in the air, drooling. Cassie slid past the doorframe in one movement, trying to look calm.

131

Ok Rona. Shift.

Rona looped behind Cassie, clutching her bag. The dog brought its head up and watched her, on point.

On you go.

The dog turned and looked at Cassie. Cassie looked back, holding her hand out in what was meant to be a soothing way, smiling. The dog couldn't have cared less. It ran at her ankles, stopped short, galloped round to her other side. It made two semi-circles doing the same then hared off round the farm building. Rona was still standing on the step, ferreting in the bag. Woofing sounds crescendoed, the dog on the home straight. It was back before Rona had the key in the lock, heading straight for Cassie. Cassie looked round fast. There were no sticks, only gravel chips. There was no point throwing a gravel chip: the dog wouldn't even notice the bloody thing let alone chase it. She was bracing herself for impact when the goat appeared, stumbling round the side of the cottage. The dog heard the chain and turned, saw the goat, reared like a rabbit and buggered off back round the farm building in the opposite direction. Cassie and Rona got in in time to hear the thud of boxer carcass hitting ancient wood.

Christ. Rona looked at Cassie. Christ.

The sound of breathing.

It's only a pup, Cassie said. Listen. Behind the shut door, a thin whining had started. Listen.

Pup. Rona looked at Cassie. She shook her head and took off her sunglasses and shut her eyes, massaging the red score over the bridge of her nose. Pup. Christ I could do with a cup of tea.

Cassie ran water hard into the kettle, smiling.

You put your feet up. Nice rest, that's what you need. All that driving.

The sound of Rona snorting in the living room.

132

Cassie and Rona
Rona and Cassie

playing house.

Getting his shoes polished outside the hotel, just as we were arriving. Doorman, the works. I'd never been in a hotel before: tavernas and pension kind of things but not a hotel. When I think back they must have fleeced him for that shoe-shine but he was happy enough. The boy called him sahib. He told me I was paranoid to think it might be a joke. Then when we went up there were flowers in the room. Plastic ones but still. Even with the air conditioning on it was warm in there so I sat by the plastic flowers, pretending hard. The colours were a help. He went for a shower: shouted through for me to put something nice on and I knew from the shout what kind of nice he meant. The plastic lid of the case hot enough to blister from the window heat.

THE END.

The next page was an advert for other books, then two blanks. The blanks flapped on her knee, refusing to let the back cover fall shut.

You couldn't work out whether he thought she deserved it: whether Zola wanted you to think badly of her. There was something in the writing, an implied unpleasantness about the physical you weren't sure was meant to attach to her too. And if that was his game he could forget it. Cassie's sympathies were definitely with Thérèse. Camille and his hellish mother, useless Laurent and that shower of hangers on: she was surrounded by complete bastards.

133

Smug buggers, complacent swines and bastards. A passionate woman a passionless universe: a soul as big as. As big as. A soul as big as something very big indeed stuck in a shoe box, a coffin. And it was Zola that did it. He put her there to prove something but there was no being sure what. Cassie flicked to the front of the book. 1867. "I simply applied to two living bodies the analytical methods that surgeons apply to corpses." What he thought that meant. What it meant to a twenty-seven-year-old man with regard to female reality. It felt safer being suspicious: a man writing a woman was always suspicious. And he was all she'd got. Poor bloody Thérèse. Without a soul to trust in the world. Not even her creator. Especially not him.

Cassie looked over at Rona. Rona was staring into the middle distance, the butt-end of a smile left on her face. A book flopped open on her skirt, pages riffling. Cassie shifted from one buttock to the other, full of redundant energy. It was no good. Cranking up a conversation about the book was a non-starter. Rona hadn't read the bloody thing, and anyway, ordinary conversation wouldn't do. Cassie didn't feel ordinary. She felt fired up, needing to know what was true. Own fault, though. You made the choice to read, you lived with the consequences. Alone. You were on your own with whatever happened to you as a result and it was your own fault. Cassie looked at Rona knowing it was her own fault and resented it anyway. Her eyes closed that peaceful way, as if she had flicked a switch and her head had just stopped. As if nothing was tormenting her at all. What's more, she knew. Rona knew fine what Cassie needed at these times. When good films came on the telly, her job was to come round and watch it as well, be dunted on the elbow and reacted at. At the very least to be on the end of the phone, listening. Watching a movie alone was pointless. Books were worse. Rona read for pleasure: Cassie for some other reason entirely. And whatever the reason was it needed participation. Rona already had a list umpteen books long marked THINGS YOU HAVE TO READ. Every so often Rona pulled it out of a filing cabinet and shouted over LOOK WHAT I'VE FOUND, laughed and put it back. Rona was too lackadaisical. Too bloody easy-going.

The book flapped again, two pages turning over completely. That look on Rona's face as though she was thinking something she wasn't for telling anybody. The silence, waiting to think of something to say that wasn't querulous. Own fault. Own fault on several counts. Cassie had asked umpteen times to go somewhere and not have to run about like hell SEEING things and Rona had said Ok then the next holiday they ran about like hell seeing things only this time holding books. Not this time though. This time Cassie made herself a force to be reckoned with.

I mean it Rona, nothing as a real possibility.
Ok, Rona said. Ok.

Agreeing gave Rona all the aces. Now here they were sitting with books in the sun, a sunflower field stretching into infinity, a kitchen two steps away, a goat even nearer and it still wasn't right. Something just under the skin kept wrestling its blankets off, refusing to sit at peace. Worry about the sun, about the dog, about Rona interrupting just when she had settled down. Now the book was finished. It was finished and there was no way of starting another one, not this soon. The other two were inside and would stay there. At least for a while. Rona's were all under her seat. Be Your Own Houseplant Expert, Promotion Strategy for Women, Bleak House, Healthy Living 40+, two maps and a free leaflet about exotic fruit she had picked up in the supermarket the day before. The trapped bird on her lap was a car specifications manual. And she was looking at none of them. Just staring into space. Creasing her eyes against the sun while single pages fluttered on her knees, unnoticed.

Your eyes will get wrinkled, staring like that.

Rona just kept staring up at nothing to see.

Don't come running to me when you've got sunburn, chum. I won't be there. You'll get spots before the eyes Rona.

Rona laughs, staring up, elsewhere. Too bloody self-contained by half.

Room interior. I took it to see if the camera was loaded. He shouted through from the shower: no maps. We were going out and taking a risk, seeing where our noses led. Safari shirt on top of the case there. On top of the shirt, three postcards of belly dancers, paste jewels in their navels and eyes caked with black stuff. One of them had blonde hair. Like Dusty Springfield on an old album cover. He must have bought them in reception on the way up. Cheating. I was looking at these postcards, dizzy from the scent of molten plastic and the air- conditioning not working when he shouted again. Put on something nice. When he came out, I was posing in hoop earrings, pouting like Carmen, the kind of thing you wear on holiday. The kind of thing I'd learned to wear on holiday. I watched him drop the towel, lever his shoulders into a new shirt without taking his eyes off me. Rolling back his cuffs from still-pale wrists. Wonderful, he said. Wonderful. I lathered both my arms in tinted suncream, put on perfume. We were going out.

SAUMUR, the "pearl of Anjou", the grey pencil tips of the château's turrets visible for miles on the beautiful liquid tresses of the Loire, is justly famous for fine wines, mushrooms and its celebrated Cadre Noir riding academy which has schooled generations of equestrian militia and their mounts. DON'T MISS the Decorative Arts Museum, the Cavalry Museum and, of course, the Museum of the Horse.

How come we missed all that, Rona? How come we didn't see the pencil tips of the turrets or the beautiful liquid tresses of the Loire?

Rona's mouth puckered with concentrating, not saying shut up.

Rona how come we missed it though? the pencil tips and beautiful liquid tresses? Eh? How come?

The windscreen wipers came on suddenly, went back off. Rona turned, glared at Cassie and sighed.

Rain. That's how.

Outside the passenger window, the river came into view. Peat-brown and fat as fudge. Cassie checked. No frog.

You think so? I don't see how the rain could have obscured pencil turrets visible for miles. Or indeed the beautiful liquid hairiness. I'm not convinced by that argument at all Rona, not one bit.

Maybe you had to come out the supermarket to see them. Does it not say?

Cassie looked at Rona.

A touch snappy there, Rona. Veering horribly close to sarcasm.

Rona said nothing. Not Playing. Driving got her crabbit sometimes. Crabbit and fussy. The car had slowed down so much it was finally not moving. The end of the bridge was outside, the mouth of the T junction.

Which way then?

Cassie looked. One side had a milestone with S on it, the other nothing at all.

Not up there anyway. Cassie nodded at the milestone.

Rona looked at her.

Well the S will be Saumur. It's just Saumur that way so there's no point. A, we've been and B, we know what's there: we just read it. Besides. C. It's Sunday. It'll be shut. So we go the other way.

Rona was still looking. Cassie sounded the horn.

Cmon. Voyage of discovery. You're only young once.

Rona shook her head pretending to be longsuffering, her face relaxing out. Any minute now she'd choose. She'd choose whether to pull in and start rooting in the back for the map, look it up and take ages and all the spontaneity out of the bloody thing or she wouldn't.

I assume responsibility, Rona. Cmon cmon. How lost can we get?

The car eased off the brake, almost imperceptibly, the wheel slipping inside Rona's hands.

Right, she said, choosing. Foot on the accelerator. You said it. Just remember it was you that said it.

Rona and Cassie
Cassie and Rona

turned off into an unmarked sideroad, living dangerously. Another Sunday evening drive.

We drive for miles.

The road gets narrower and banked with trees whose branches meet and make a canopy. One is set apart from the others, a tree in the shape of a torso: thick trunk and the roots like arms levering upwards, a man struggling to pull himself out of the earth. Rona drives with both hands on the wheel, checking the fuel gauge. The sunflower fields are full of closed green fists, dark heads sleeping like children; tufa cliffs carved with holes like a row of Mexican skulls. The road goes on past the line of the water which is not the Loire, fraught with sudden loops and turns. There is a feeling of having been here before, maybe of having turned full circle without knowing how. The sky gets darker.

We walked without knowing where. That was the fun of the thing: choosing not to be sure of our territory. The threat of the new place was less because I was with him: I thought it would be ok. It always had been. The hem of the new skirt brushed his hand as we walked. Short, he said, it's very short, keeping going. We couldn't have been out five minutes before it started. Just an uneasy feeling in the back of my neck, then footsteps. I could hear footsteps too like our own, an exact rhythm. Then when we were standing at the kerb to get over the street, a huge street wide a shipping lane full of the downrush of traffic.

SHIT.

Shearing the edge off the pavement and turning the wheel like hell Rona shouted it again. SHIT. It wasn't just annoyance. Not the usual readiness to be furious with other drivers for not taking into account the fact that she didn't trust them. It was something else. Rona was scared. Something dunted the back of the car hard. Rona hiccupped forward then snapped round, glaring at the back window.

Did you feel that?
It wasn't a question. People started cheering again outside, arms waving the length of the road.
Bastards. Bastards.

Rona jammed her hand on the middle of the steering wheel. The horn. Hellish and loud. Rona hated people sounding horns. She had probably thought of getting out and shouting but there were too many folk: dripping off the kerb and jumping around in the bit that was meant to be for cars, waving scarves, tooting unplaceable wind-instruments and shouting at no-one in particular. Cassie could feel her guts washing, adrenalin panicking in the veins. Jesus. A judder through the whole car frame as something hit the bumper again. Two men hurled themselves off the kerb and dived at another who was hanging onto the tail end of the float in front, pulling him off. The three of them rolled on the road for a moment or so, almost into the bonnet. Cassie thought she could feel something thud against a tyre. Rona looked able for biting somebody.

Bastards. Stupid idiot bastards. Serve them right if they get hurt. Serve them right if I bloody accelerate.

Rona wouldn't accelerate. She was just scared. Her eyes wide, scared and surrounded by people who weren't. The float in front was awash with firemen, singing and holding up sparklers, the things children had at Guy Fawkes. Cassie would have found it touching if she hadn't been this close. Sweat visible on foreheads, risen veins when they yelled like that. A hand flattened itself suddenly against the windshield and Rona jumped. The hand flattened out some more, levering a man into view. He smiled in at them through the glass, rolling his eyes. Rona looked slapped.

Right.
She clamped her hands on the steering wheel, mouth tight.
I'm stopping for nothing. Bugger All.

Another face appeared, this time at Cassie's side; luminous, waving a match. Hopeless. It just didn't give a damn out there. Surrounded by chaos, people behaving in a way that did not make itself amenable to reason or explanation, Rona reduced to idle threats that couldn't even be heard by the people they were supposed to impress. Two men in the crowd looked like police but

140

were likely just part of the carry-on. Dressed up. Even if they weren't, even if they were real police, this kind of thing probably came under the heading HARMLESS FUN in the Gendarmerie handbook. And so it should. If the definition of harmless was agreed by democratic means, that's what it was. But from in here, from inside the car, wordless, directionless, ignorant, it didn't feel harmless. It felt terrifying. Terrifying and fathomless. Maybe they were all drunk. Maybe something wonderful had happened and Cassie and Rona were the only people on the planet who didn't know what it was. Maybe it was football. Godknew. Whatever, it was alien. Outside Cassie's ken. She tried to think of something that might lead her to behave the way they were and came up with nothing. Not a thing. Meantime, the car had moved forward about a yard or so. A junction beginning to come into view. All they had to do was wait. After one in the morning. It couldn't be long. Something banged somewhere too close. A firework maybe. Under the car. Whatever happened, the important thing was not to let the fear show: no matter how close the whites of their fucking eyes got, they would manage. They always did.

It's ok Rona. It's ok.

BASTARDS, Rona shrieked. IF THAT GUY JUMPS ON TOP OF THIS CAR

The sound of breaking glass.

Two soldiers looking over. They were still with us when we stepped on to the huge street, running to stay with us. By that time I knew it was deliberate. By the end of the road I knew there were more than two. The short skirt bouncing when I walked fast, catching at the skin of my arm. Chris was walking faster. I had to skip every so often to keep up. I knew he wasn't meaning to leave me behind but he was faster none the less. I

141

thought about making a joke but couldn't think of one so we just kept quiet, crossing another road not knowing where we were, hearing more feet speeding behind us, keeping close. Chris turned into a lane, a kind of mesh of backstreets, keeping changing direction. When we got back out on to where the road was wider again, he looked back and they were still there. He didn't say I should have known better than to go out in this skirt in the first place but I knew. At least a dozen men were filtering through the crowd, coming towards us, some running. We were going as fast as we could without looking and it wasn't making much difference. So we stopped. They were getting closer. None of them smiled. I remember thinking I'd have to keep walking with my head up, Chris spitting into the gutter. He spat and said YOU'RE ON YOUR OWN.

It didn't occur to get a taxi. I didn't know how much it would have cost and anyway, I didn't want to get in a car with anyone. They don't have female taxi drivers in Istanbul. So I kept walking, with all this catcalling behind me, keeping going forwards till I saw a place with long dresses in the window. I didn't care what colour it was. I just got the first kaftan I could afford and put it on over the top of what I was wearing. Chris hadn't left me. He was outside the shop, waiting. We walked back to the hotel and nobody as much as looked twice. Back in the room, the map we hadn't taken, like a sectioned wireless on the bed. Blameless.

Cassie closed her eyes. It would be all one in a hundred years. Eventually the noise of fireworks would become fainter, the car pick up speed. And they would get back to the farmhouse, to things where they had been left and the kitchenette. Hot chocolate and brandy. They would last. Grinding their teeth and getting by, the way they always did. Cassie closed her eyes imagining the present moment as something long gone. It always came true eventually.

ten

Chris in a towel. A very wee towel. Most of Chris. Not dried. I
was waiting, angling the camera at him from bed when he
came out but he just smiled. Chris always took a shower first.
That was my reward for all the bloody sunbathing: the
showers, the need to put on lots of body lotion. If he was in the
right mood, he would take the bottle and look at me. Once.
And that look would make my stomach do a butterfly dip
because I knew what it meant, this willingness to get his hands
sticky. Drips of water tracing down my spine off the ends of my
hair. If I was sore from the sun and he hurt me, if I was too
sore to touch I could push him onto his back and take over, get
my hands slippy working over his hips and belly, inching
towards his penis. Absolutely smooth, that first touch of skin
and lotion and skin, peeling the foreskin down over the warm
shaft inside. One hand after the other after the other, slowing
down just enough to keep the tension right. I got enough out of
that. Making the glans appear and reappear, generating heat.
A touch of oil if the bottle was near enough to reach without

having to change the rhythm. Then that added resistance under the fingers, a warning to change gear before he shifted his hips up to meet me, his breathing catching the back of his throat. Letting the ejaculate burst and slither between the fingers of one hand, the other still working near the tip. I took a pride in that, the fact I'd thought it through. I liked to do it well. Even after all those years though, I was never convinced the next stroke would not be the one that hurt him or when he'd push me away. It never was. Not in that context anyway. When it got to the part where he tilted his head to one side, opened his mouth that way he did I knew we were ok. Second day of holiday. We hadn't been sunbathing at all but we did just the same things. He never mentioned what had happened the day before, not then, the next day. That was a routine too. I got comfort from knowing I could do something he really liked. He seemed to really like. I still tried to get enough out of that.

Jesus Rona this animal.
It's ok. The voice came back thin, through a layer of car door. Boxers get like that. Excitable.

Rona wound the window down, inching the handbrake off, pulling up the catch on the passenger door. Cassie made soothing noises, watching the car crouch and start rolling closer. The dog kept its eyes level. Cassie put a hand out, waited still enough for it to come forward and lick. Licking calmed the beast down. It was ok really. Just unpredictable. The car was level now, door nudging her back. Clicking as Rona opened it from the inside. Cassie chose her moment, turned and coiled inside. Closing the door, she felt deceitful. She felt distinctly underhand.

It's going to be hot, Rona said.
The dog looked in the side-window, forehead in velvet furrows.

144

Roasting.

In the rear-view mirror, through terracotta clouds, the farmhouse started rolling away. Receding white walls and green mesh fencing, a dog growing smaller.

Cassie reached for the seatbelt.

Jesus. Look, Rona. Look at its face.

I know, said Rona. I know.

It is easy to love ANGERS. All it takes is the time to know the city and soon its melange of characters, from the Tapestry of the Apocalypse and the Chant du Monde to the giants from the Toussaint Church, live in the mind. Take a leisurely visit and do not let Angers' natural modesty lead you to miss the hidden architectural jewels: the Angel indicating the Great Whore with whom kings have fornicated and who has intoxicated the inhabitants of the earth with her wine of lasciviousness (Tapestry of the Apocalypse, scene 64, text from St John) forgets to indicate that masterpiece of soft porn which is "woman caressing a chimera" beneath a tree in the garden.

Christ's teeth Rona.

Cassie put the book back into the brown bag and looked over the parapet. Sheer. A green swallow dive from the top of the ramparts on to the spotty backs of deer. Babies. Only the babies had spots. Cassie knew that from Bambi. The moat was full of baby deer and rabbits, waterless. The drawbridge was no longer functional. Goodknew how old the chain was, links the size of dinosaur kidneys oozing black bitumen but completely bloody solid, not even tepid in the sun. And it was bleaching here. Ferocious. Threatening to burst through the top layer of skin.

Cassie looked at her shoulder, its similarity to uncooked dough.

The dress was a mistake: not only sleeveless but floral. The material had looked ok in the shop: the kind of thing it might be nice to swan about poppy fields in, chewing the end of a piece of straw. This morning in the mirror over the fireplace it looked more like a paint rag. A long paint rag. The hat with the same material round the brim had been left behind. It should have been the other way round. She should have brought the hat and left the bloody dress, that's what she should have done.

Rona, in khaki shorts and green T-shirt with RIVER RAPIDS written on it, was looking down the green hole on the other side of the turret, angling the zoom. She was probably still in a huff about the parking. Umpteen times round the same bit of town centre looking for vacated places which never appeared getting honked at by Angevins who weren't keen on trailing about their own city at 5mph. Kph. It was the honking started it anyway. Rona hated being honked at. It made her face change colour and her whole body rigid. That on top of the carry-on from last night. There was another honk, Rona shouting BASTARDS and stopping the car. The honking had got worse. Rona restarted the car, stalled it twice, started it again. All the time Cassie had just sat there. Not able to drive: having to watch Rona apoplectic in charge of the vehicle you both shared, unable to act to save either skin. Eventually, a square of dereliction behind some warehouses down some unrecallable backstreets made an appearance and they had stuck the car there. Cassie carried the picnic stuff and one of Rona's bags, keeping her distance. A long walk. Directions were not a problem: the sore thumb of the castle always straight in front. All they had to do was keep pointing towards it, walking past three carparks. Full.

Cassie peered out from behind her shades, one hand flat against the grainy stone. The carparks were out there somewhere, in the dots and dashes of buildings and streets, hemmed in by the magnesium flare of river, avoiding being looked at by Rona. Sun searing a tonsure on top of Cassie's head. They'd move sooner or later, buy drinks with ice frosting ferns on the glass and sit

146

somewhere shady. Maybe with music and a cool white tablecover, a waiter with drown-in eyes. There would be telling of jokes, the return of lightness and possibility. Soon. Rona opened the camera, put in another roll. A fresh 36 to go.

Solid enough to resist the wear and tear of time, the Castle is built on solid quartz slate, its steep face reflected in the Maine. The Chapel was transformed into a military and civil prison which once housed 200 English sailors. In 1815 it was occupied by Prussians then used as a munitions store in WW2, evacuated by the Germans just before the first Allied bombardment. Even so, the roofs and a vault in the chapel were subject to direct hits and destroyed; the restoration work you see today was carried out after the liberation. The unobtrusive modern Gallery housing the remarkable Tapestry of the Apocalypse was opened in July 1954: the garden in the French style in 1948.

The garden was too hot as well. Of course it was. Rona had chosen a specially hot bit. Even the bench: slats cooking the arse as you sat. Cassie rummaged in her bag. The suncream tube was flaccid, unhealthily warm. Even through the layers of canvas bag. Cassie placed the nozzle on her upper arm, squeezing. A fat white worm oozed out, viscous solids separating from a surround of clear stuff. Like creamed suet. Cassie didn't care. She rubbed it over the too-warm skin surface, trying not to hear it crackle.

Phlox. Phlox paniculata.
Cassie turned round and back again not looking. Her fingers were sticky.
You didn't see it, Rona said. Look. The stuff I've got out the back door near the whirly. The pink flowers.
I can't look. I need a tissue Rona. Tissues.
Rona patted one shorts' pocket then the other. A flattened scroll emerged from the second. Here, she said. Here.

147

Three rolled together. Cassie used them one at a time, rubbing between her fingers. Rona sighed and looked back at the plants.

There. They've got it three colours. I could get some for that window-box you've got. Put something in it that isn't dead. What do you think?

I'm starving. Can we eat yet?

Cassie crushed the tissues into a ball inside one palm, holding it there. No pockets. Rona sighed, took the tissue debris and put it back into the shorts' pocket.

Like talking to a filing cabinet. You couldn't care less, could you?

She hauled two bags out from under the seat. Rona handed over the brown one.

Here. Make yourself useful.

Half a white cob loaf, a brown poke mushy in one corner, two separate bits of cheese wrapped in paper, two tubs of mango yogurt and an empty tube of paper off an absent bar of chocolate. Cassie put them in a neat line. Rona hauled a flask out and set it upright near the bread. The hellish blue flask with the spare cup. Rona anchored a polythene poke under one of the bits of cheese and said For rubbish, darkly. Cassie said nothing. A cherry fell out of the mush-cornered poke, bleeding. One of the cheese wrappings had uncurled, showing a pale yellow wedge weeping under a greyish crust. Rona looked as well. She looked for a full minute, raking for something then emptied out the rest of the bag. A rainmate, three prunes, four pens with THIS BELONGS TO RONA stickers, specs, stamps, travellers' cheques, nail clippers, indigestion tablets, receipts, used paper hankies and a saved-up Dutch biscuit she'd been given free with a cup of coffee in Byres Road. The other bag offered three sets of keys, a penknife, two passports, empty film drums, another pair of specs, the Chartres guidebook, two plastic knives, postcards, map, saved-up sugar sachets, Oxfam recycling labels, a rubber shaped like a rabbit, more receipts, an address book, a wool band and lots of blue fluff. She looked and sighed.

Never mind. We can drink it.

She meant the yoghurt.

Cassie made token gestures though she knew she didn't have a spoon either. Novel. Lip salve and the suncream, two pens and spare film. A comb and a tin of sweeties they'd bought by accident on the ferry. The tin had pine trees on the lid. Cassie had seen them and thought they meant pine as in fresh as in mint. They didn't. They meant pine as in toilet cleaner. Dettol-flavoured, shaped like Yeti's feet. Rona had said not to throw them away in case. Cassie put the tin back into the bag with the rest of her things. The novel was no temptation in this heat. Rona repacked her stuff except for the guide. She pulled a piece of brie off the end of the wedge and sucked it, angling for the light on her face.

Might as well work on a tan.

The guide to the wrong place lay at her elbow, CHARTRES glaring up in white.

Cassie tore a piece off the loaf. People went past the end of the garden pointing at grass and birds. Cassie watched, chewing. No-one else was eating bread. No-one else had carrier-bags or rows of food melting in the sun. A hot rubber smell suddenly filled out under Cassie's nose. Rona holding up the flask. Cassie could see an old couple advancing behind Rona's back, a child between, holding their hands. Rona held up the thermos. Chipped Tippex that had once read RONA'S still clung grimy white on the neck. Rona raised the thing like a wine bottle, looked quizzical. A stain on her T-shirt. Again.

Cassie and Rona
Rona and Cassie

have eaten sandwiches in Amsterdam and Gouda, Copenhagen, York, Warsaw, Munich and Lerwick, under trees, in fields, off the side of main roads on steps to bowling alleys and cinemas and in the shadow of the great organ of Haarlem. It's what we always do. We get no richer, no more sophisticated, no more included. We know our place: that proper holidays are for proper people with proper money and that real travellers, in denim bermudas of uneven leg length, travel to real faraway places in search of real poor people enduring real life in the raw. We are neither real nor proper: just fraudulent moochers in other people's territory, getting by on the cheap.

Cassie watched a small pebble, rubbed smooth like beach glass, near her foot on the path. Individual strands of grass rimming the path border. The shadows of the old couple's shoes drew level, walked past. A moment later, the child's, little bites of breath on each downtread, running. Out of eyeshot, someone laughed. Trying to stifle the sound but laughing anyway. It was quite clear. Cassie tilted her head sideways. Rona was pouring another half cup from the flask, sipped, sniffed, wiped her nose with the back of her hand then turned to look out, her forehead smooth, into a place higher than Cassie allowed herself to see.

That's nice as well. That buddleia. I'm definitely getting a buddleia when we get back.

She waved one sandle-free foot in the air, smiling at nothing at all. Rona, inside the jewel case of roughly beautiful walls and towers with an unobtrusive modern gallery housing the remarkable Tapestry of the Apocalypse. The Imperturbable, Queen of All She Surveyed.

Woven by master craftsman Nicolas Bataille between 1373 and 1380, the ornate TAPESTRY OF THE APOCALYPSE was reconstructed after being torn into pieces during a period of disfavour. Almost two thirds of the original masterpiece can be seen in the castle chapel.

You feel you should go and see the major attractions. There must be a reason why they're major, after all. Whether they're authentic or not, cobbled back together to maintain an illusion of the wholeness of an original still intact, you feel you should go. It seems churlish not to.

Two seven-headed animals on sea and land.

A devil spewing up frogs.

Fire pouring into water.

A bowl of blood on a background of flowers.

A palace floating in the sky.

St John and the Son of Man. All those candles. No, I don't know why St John has a sword through his face. It doesn't say.

The one I remember best: woman combing out her hair and looking in a mirror. She looks like a shampoo commercial. The detail on the oak tree. The Great Whore it says. Vision der großen Prostituiren. You're supposed to know from her looking in the mirror I suppose. Vanity.

A bunch of complaisant angels hanging out of the sky to stab a dragon and a baby dragon. Smug buggers. They only had the German version of the guidebook so I had to guess what things were about. I bought these postcards because they didn't allow you to take photos. I thought it was a great idea: not being able to distance through a lens, you'd really need to take the thing for what it was, its existence in the moment etc. And it *was* beautiful. I remember telling myself it was beautiful, awesome, strange. But all the time I knew it wouldn't be as beautiful as it would be when I was somewhere else, remembering. And that it was equally possible I wouldn't be able to remember a single stitch of the bloody thing unless I bought these. You don't remember just by telling yourself you should, by sheer act of will. You don't get to pick and choose. The same way you don't get to forget. Memory. A bastard really. A complete bastard.

What's next then? You've got the book. What's next?

We can visit the Chant du Monde
               Chapel of Yolande of Aragon
               Church of the Saint Serge
               Place de la Laiterie
               Church of Saint Martin
or the
               Tower of Saint Aubin

but we go to the

               Museum of David of Angers
                             instead.

Just picked a card.
Any card.

The place was full of naked men.

Cassie and Rona
Rona and Cassie

did the rounds of male thighs keeping close together, not meeting each others' gaze.

It's all men. Rona said.

There's a woman at the entrance, said Cassie. Woman with a hat on and her breasts out.

Rona's feet clattered off distantly then came back.

You're right, she said. Being cuddled by a big man who's caught her just as she's about to faint. He's somebody noble and she's symbolic.

Ah, said Cassie. That explains it.

Rona had found a sheet of paper. They were free in a perspex box at the door. Cassie took the sheet.

> This sculptor whose name is often confused with that of his native town was an admirer of male virtues. Inspired by the spirit of the Revolution, he wanted to bring life to the idea of the Grands Hommes, the poets, painters, writers and philosophers who would be the new heroes of France.
>
> *"The shape of the foot of a distinguished person has nothing in common with that of a vulgarian."*

I can't make head nor tail of this, Rona. You read it. Look.

Rona looked. She read the sentence Cassie's finger was attached to and laughed.

What kind of feet d'you think we've got haha?

Two perfect toes wiggling out of the tip of her sandal, nails filthy right down to the quick.

Women's feet, Rona. Not in the running at all.

Cassie watched Rona move on, saying nothing. Maybe making fun of it was unfair. Maybe the quotation was out of context, a bad translation. Maybe she was misunderstanding terribly and Rona knew and that's why she wasn't joining in. That possibility should always be borne in mind: the danger of misunderstanding terribly. Cassie heard a story about translators at the UN. Every so often they did exercises to find out what happened to meaning through umpteen languages and back, what happened to the untranslatable. After all, the importance of nuance in those circumstances: wars could start if they weren't careful. So they got an American, a German, a Russian and an Egyptian lined up and told them to get on with it. The American told the German the first thing that came into his head. I like travelling, he said. That way my wife is out of sight, out of mind. The German told the Russian and the Russian told the Egyptian. The Egyptian put it through the final filter and reported back, smiling. The American liked travelling, he said. And women are invisible idiots. Ok, maybe it wasn't true. But then again, it probably was. That kind of thing went on all the time. Even when you thought you were being at your most lucid, making yourself heard. Especially then. Between foreign languages was the least of it. Cassie walked along the row of statues again, filled with fresh awareness and cautious tolerance, knowing how easy it was to misunderstand.

Noble profiles striking grittily determined poses, sinewy limbs etched with striving, turtle plates of muscle on the belly and visible hip bones sloping down to the crotch, chiselled curls circling soft, sleeping penises. It was right enough. We weren't in the running at all.

All men are homosexuals, Rona.

Rona flexed one leg at the knee, angling her sandal up for inspection. She had chewing gum on the sole. Sorry, she said, digging with a fingertip. Sorry?

All men are homosexuals. It's a contentious statement meant to engender discussion. What do you think?

Rona put her foot down, levering it back and forth. The sound of stickiness smacking on tile.

All men are homosexuals. It doesn't mean anything. Does it?

Cassie said nothing.

Beards and jutting jawlines. Blank eyes.

Brass. Brass and gold and godknows: the Old Bazaar. The place was full of big plates, plaques with sailing ships hammered into them. My mother had lots of that kind of thing. Horse-brasses etc. I got to Brasso them when I was wee. Anyway looking at them made me ask Chris if we could get a couple for the flat: masochistic nostalgia, I suppose. I could just see myself buffing them up, squirting polish on like rogue semen, smearing it in with the cloth. Those soft yellow cloths, the kind that were only ever meant to be dusters and not the kind made out of cut-up clothes. I was going to buy real yellow cloths for them, catch the polish dribbles in the egg yolk weave and rub it into surfaces till they shone your eye out. I was fixated about cleaning then. I loved it. You have to love something. Glass and mirror. Tile. Ceramic surround on the cooker. And chrome. The way it came up glittering. You can see your own effort with chrome: it shows. Anyway, I was thinking all this rubbish and had the two picked out and he said Cassie you're joking, they remind me of your mother's. Anyway it's my flat. He bought a leather cushion after a long debate with the guy about the cost of shipping a hubble-bubble pipe, a tin of dubbin. You can polish this instead, he said. Housewife manqué. I didn't know whether it was a joke or not.

And this is

   this

    I don't know what this is. Skyscape. Probably a plane in it somewhere. That blob in the corner there is probably a Mig Fighter or something. How should I know. Fucking wee boy manqué. His photo, not mine.

The whole of Dido and Aeneas, another spin through Dido's Lament. Change cassette. I Don't Want to set the World On Fire finishes just before the turnoff for the cottage. Two bits of paper posted on the milestone. One for the tank museum and notice of a firework display. It's Bastille Day. The 14th.

Turkish cat. There were hundreds of them but this one came and sat at the empty chair when Chris went off for a pee and stared at his dinner. Red snapper. I took the photo instead of giving it some. He came back and chased it away so I got the photo and the cat got damn all. Terrible priorities. I always know after the event.

Chris chatting with a waiter. That's me in the corner, being terrified. Man at the next table took it to distract my attention I think. Chris was trying to hire the guy's moped. Drunk. I had visions of him haring round on the bloody thing with no helmet and the bare arms, being thrown on to boiling tarmac. Pictures of him minus his whole skin surface and calling out my name. He didn't get to hire it in the end but that's me while negotiations are proceeding. I look demented. I look

round the side of the door.

No dog.

Rona and Cassie left the dishes behind on the table and sneaked round the door to the car. Cassie heard herself giggle for no apparent reason. It was possible she was mildly drunk. Sunstruck. It was possible she was that as well.

Bastille Day, though, Rona. It just isn't possible to frame the meaning of such a thing: what it must have been like in there.

The click of metal in the belt lock, Rona getting in and sighing.

Rona think though. Under the level of the ground. Not able to see or hear anything that reminded you of anything, not even knowing what day it was. Even if it was. It could have been any bloody time. How would you know? You wouldn't. You just wouldn't. Not even knowing why you were there, why they'd done this to you. What it was for. But they had. Without it having to be justified to a soul, that was the thing. Any recourse to logic: ethical rules of crime and punishment, justice and everything out the window. They just *had*.

Cassie's mouth was moving the way it did when it could go on for a long time. She wasn't even sure if people had been underground at all in the Bastille or if that was the Count of Monte Cristo. Or something else. Her mouth couldn't have cared less. Just kept going.

Terminal confusion. Angst. Terrible guilt where you wondered if you deserved it, if God singled you out to serve you right. Christ christ. There being nothing you could do to make the thing any better or any different. It doesn't bear thinking about. Hell on earth. Indefinitely.

Rona was looking at the steering wheel, preoccupied.

Imagine though. You can't. They must have spent ages praying: running over the concept of divine love. Praying then praying harder thinking you still weren't doing it right because every time you woke up you were still there, chained to the wall or some other rotting carcass and up to your neck in your own excrement. Filth and despair. Wondering what you had done wrong and not knowing. Being punished and caged up with the only stab at life you'd got running out, not knowing. Knowing you might never know.

Rona still keeping her eyes on the road. Maybe she couldn't concentrate because Cassie was talking so much. At least she wasn't doing Rona any damage.

Simple folk. That's the ones you think about, the ones that wouldn't say boo. What the hell did they think was going on jesus. Then the door getting battered down and it's by. Over. The noise though. After you'd been in there quiet for ever then all these doors battering down and people coming in *not to kill you*. That's the most amazing thing. Not to kill you after all. Half the poor buggers probably died of shock.

D'you think we go straight on here or what?
There were other cars on the road ahead now, not many but more than before. Cassie looked down at the map. It wasn't even the right page.
Rona trust me. It'll be fine. In fact, it is. Look.

SAUMUR.

White on green. The word hovered over the top of a bush, caught in the headlight. Rona accelerated towards it and stopped for another look. She looked back at Cassie, smiled. The indicator ticking. Cassie looked back and couldn't see the sign any more. The light was too low. Her night vision wasn't good.

Imagine being colour-blind though. Jesus.

Mouth keeping going, refusing to slow down for anything at all at all at all.

People sit along the bridge. We sit there too, sleep on and off on each other's shoulders, getting colder. At midnight, torches start moving around behind trees and bushes, held up by invisible people

158

on the other side. I dunt Rona and she looks up. Feux d'artifice I say.
Voilà!

Blobs from outer space. Amoebae in a tunnel. Three hours
waiting for ten minutes' worth of fireworks and that's all we have
to show for it. Bastille Day can't be what it was.

Rona
only Rona

drove back along the unlit road with Cassie asleep beside her in
the passenger seat. Next morning, Cassie could not remember
getting home but it was ok. She couldn't remember lots of times
getting home but she had always got there. The vague notion of
being put to bed and kissed goodnight. It was always Rona.

eleven

If you were the only girl in the world
And I were the only boy
Nothing else would matter in the world today
We would go on loving in the same old shit shit shit
                                        shit

The knife skidded, slicing the blunt blade under the surface of one stiff finger, the onion skiting off the table, trailing cloudy wet stuff that turned dark on the dry boards. Blunt to hell.

Shit shit shit.

Cassie put the knife down and checked. No blood. A thin wedge of skin opening into the meat of the second finger under the first knuckle joint. You could see muscle moving in there, exposed. The lifted skin would catch on things, open out a bit more every time. It tucked in on itself when she reached down for the fallen onion, refusing to help, stinging anyway. The onion looked chewed. Bloody knife. They were meant to care about such things, these people, the elegance and poetry of preparation. Sabatier my arse. Cassie threw the knife into the sink and closed her eyes. They nipped worse like that, sending out radio signals: the whiplash of acids eddying under the lid. Opening them again made water run all the way to her chin. At least Rona was out from under her feet. And there were plenty of onions. Nothing else but plenty of onions.

Cassie threw the first attempt into the pail and picked up a fresh, digging her nails into the paper skin. It whimpered. No it didn't it was something from outside. She let the onion sit for a minute and listened. A kind of whining noise. The odd whuffle and low-sonar howl. Like a dog dreaming. Cassie had heard that noise before. It was Rona. Rona singing. She did it clearing out filing cabinets, watering plants and knitting. Things she liked. Rona must be doing something nice out there. Cassie tilted up, stretching to see out the too-high window. All she got was a different square of sky. Dirty laughter. The invisible Rona scuffling, crunching gravel. An unclassifiable wet slurp.

Rona?
A muffled laugh and the sound of water.
Rona? What are you doing out there?
Splashes and gurgles. Cassie turned. The top half of the kitchenette door was open: a view of sunflowers and the goat's head, chewing. Whatever it was, the goat was not involved.
Rona?
Complete silence.
Rona?

Feet on gravel to flat soles on slab. Rona's face appeared over the top of the horsedoor, a smear of white high on one cheek.
Hello. Beatific. I'm doing the washing.
Question answered before asked. Trying to think of another, a reason for calling Rona away from her own devices, Cassie looked back at the chopping board. Soup, she said. I'm making soup

161

because there's nothing else you can make with the things we've left. We need more stuff, Rona. We need shopping.

Do you want me to make something then?

No I'm making it already but we need more stuff. We've only onions and carrots. And three mushrooms.

I could make carrot soup if you like.

I've already worked that one out, Rona. I'm on to it. The carrot soup is safe in my hands. I'm just saying we need more shopping. We'll have to go this afternoon sometime ok?

Rona dabbed a wet bit on her T-shirt, hands dripping. A new T-shirt. Scoop neckline and polka dots. Not Rona's usual.

Fine, she said. Ok. Want me to wash anything through, knickers or something?

No.

That Travelwash is good. I can put them through with mine.

No. There isn't anything, Rona.

Sure?

I'm sure.

It's no bother.

Rona away and give us peace for godsakes. What's that on the side of your nose anyway?

Rona dabbed at her nose with one damp hand, missing the white mark twice and catching a smear of it on the third go. She looked at her fingers and lied.

Don't know.

Yes you do. It's suntan stuff. You've been putting cream on. Cassie shook her head and made a tutting noise with her tongue.

Only a wee bit. Rona rubbed at the smear, redistributing smaller white over the same area. Only my face. To stop my nose going red.

There's no such thing as a wee bit with vanity, Rona. Thin end of the wedge. Rona sighed. Cassie sighed back. At least rub it in right. Now clear off. I'm creating.

Rona stuck two fingers up at Cassie and stayed put. Cassie opened the cutlery drawer, looking for a sharper knife. Rona kept where she was.

Away and wash your stuff. The goat'll eat it if you don't watch. Shoo. Out my kitchen.

Cassie pretended to shut over the top half of the horsedoor, hiding Rona's face. When she opened it the second time, Rona was gone. Halfway through another onion, Cassie heard the dirty laugh insinuate from the side of the house and settled the knife on the table, listening. No telling what she was doing out there. Whether she wanted carrot soup, whether they'd go shopping. Rona and her not-answers. Cassie thought about the day being young, the goat, the sunflowers, the sky that colour it was. Rona out in the middle of it, washing knickers and laughing all by herself. Next time Cassie would give her some. Serve her right. If Rona got that much fun out of washing knickers, she could get on with it. Outside, out of sight, Rona laughed again. Rona and her secrets. Cassie laughed back, lifted the knife to start afresh. Rona was off her bloody head.

> FONTEVRAUD L'ABBEYE, the largest monastic complex in France, has an architecture rich in Romanesque, Renaissance, Classical and Louis XVI period splendours. The church, with its wide nave and broad cupolas, restored this century when the nave was a converted prison, was finished in 1150. The tombs of Henry II, Count of Anjou and King of England, his son, Richard the Lionheart and Eleanor of Aquitaine are in the southern crossing.

This one
this one's the middle of Aya Sofia, a big church the Muslims

stripped and turned into something else. A mosque. Those things up on the columns there, the gold writing on them, like great big targes or something: huge. The whole thing is huge only without arches and buttresses and stuff getting in the way. Filleted. Anyway I'm up there, on the balcony with the big shields. I got dizzy just being so near that kind of drop so I stood back and just held the camera at arm's length so I could get the photo without having to look. He's in the middle there, the denims and the green shirt looking up. He's looking up to see if I'm there and I wasn't. I knew that's what he'd be doing though. I made myself go to the edge to wave but he'd shifted by that time. He has one of a hand waving across the parapet. My hand.

And this is one of

      one of

   this is one of

DAMN ALL

Cassie put the camera down. It made a sore noise on the flagstones, an echo round the wee room. Rona was taking ages. We should have gone shopping first, called in here on the way back. But we haven't. We've come here. My fault for finding it in the book, reading it out in an interesting way.

My fault.

Cassie shivered. The cardigan was in the car. Stone walls with paint flaking off. The place exuded a notion of damp though it couldn't be really: the paint wouldn't have lasted as long as this if it had been. The three tombs in a row at her feet had bald patches, red and blue rubbed away to show the pale stone beneath. Henry II, Richard the Lionheart and Eleanor of Aquitaine, each at a measured distance, fringed by chipped drapery. Cassie tried to think what she knew about Eleanor of Aquitaine and found nothing satisfactory. All she could come up with was Katharine Hepburn looking heart-broken and defiant in a film. The Lion in Winter. Nothing else. Films did that. They contained your imagination, packaged even real things up in wee parcels you couldn't get rid of. And that was a good film. Others didn't bear thinking about at all. Richard the Lionheart. He was only a jumble of Robin Hood costumes and chainmail with crowns, Herbert Lom corked up in an Arab costume, galloping across the dunes roaring Infidel and waving a scimitar at a man with a bucket on his head. Not even one-dimension fictions. The bones of three of the most powerful political forces in Medieval Europe were inside these stone shells at Cassie's feet, the bones of people who had directly affected the lives of thousands of people, whose own lives must have been written about and recorded hundreds of times. And Cassie knew damn all about them. Not anything real. That was a given, she supposed, the bulk of recorded history being oversimplified rubbish anyway. Even so, it didn't seem right. It didn't seem right at all. Mind you, she knew even less about what passed for Scottish history. Macbeth. St Columba. Your own country's medieval life restricted to an English play and a velcro shape off the felt table at Sunday school. Robert the Bruce. Kings and generals, Men of Letters. Of the mass of people, less than nothing. Women didn't come into the reckoning at all.

Mary Queen of Scots though. Rona knew lots about Mary Queen of Scots. None of it very comforting. They had been to Fotheringay and it was cold as hell. Fotheringay. Cemeteries, tombs and burial places. It's something a certain kind of person does on holiday. They visit death-haunts.

Me and Rona, Rona and me.

165

We've been to Corinth and Mycenae, Viking burial mounds, castle dungeons, crypts and vaults in umpteen churches and abbeys, the burning sites of witches. We have traced the names of plague dead in Eyam, seen grafitti on Karl Marx in Highgate and taken photos of Greyfriar's Bobby. Greyfriar's Bobby for christsake. Reluctant to eat our pre-packed sandwiches in the bus stop outside Dachau, oddly uncomfortable that the barracks had looked so clean. Pain, suffering, finished lives and tombstones.

Now here we are, doing it again.

Cassie stood looking down at the points of the chiselled hands. Eleanor looked up at the ceiling, eyes mean as blotting-paper. Giving nothing away.

Come and see.
A silhouette of Rona was standing at the door, light in an aura behind her head.
Cmon. You've been in here ages. Come and see.

Over flagstones that monks and prisoners, the rich, the poor and the sick who had been dead for centuries had worn hollow, over the grass, we walk towards a beehive. A round house with a hole at the top of the domed ceiling.

Inside, Rona leans back against the wall and says Bakehouse. They think but they don't know. It isn't the right shape for cooking or something. I can't translate the whole thing over there but that's the idea.
Cassie looked up.
They used to think it was a mortuary. The hole is to let smoke out. Weird. Rona stood back to take a photo of Cassie looking small against the pale plaster, gazing up. Weird.
Cassie imagines smoke escaping upward, drifting out over the cemetery outside and wants her cardigan. She wants out into the sun with food and light, the feeling of frying on her skin and Rona not

reading on the grass beside her. It is cold in this place. The hole in the ceiling lets in a draught. A piece of the sky passes overhead, distant and separate and Cassie shivers. Something about the hole in the bakehouse ceiling chills Cassie to the bone.

Car drivers should NOT MISS the opportunity of driving through the beautiful, winding roads of the Layon Valley, sampling the scenic vistas of the region to the full by stopping at one of the many signposted PANORAMAS you will be sure to see on the journey, sampling, if possible, the wines of Anjou as you go!

What kind of bloody irresponsible thing is that to put then? Invitation to drink while you drive? What kind of bloody stupid advice is that?

Cassie and Rona
Rona and Cassie

drove out along the side of the river. Cassie rolled down the window, held her arm outside till it stuck to the hot metal. Every junction, when the wind changed, she smelled something like roast pork. A PANORAMA sign appeared. Rona followed it. She thought Cassie didn't notice but Cassie did. At the top of a hill, the slope rolled down to the riverside, boats reflecting on glass, the car slowed to a halt.

Shopping Rona. We need to get stuff in.

I know, said Rona. I know.

We pull in anyway. Only one of us can drive.

The obvious place was under some trees. Cassie got out carefully, not touching the bodywork. Sweat ran in a line down her back, gluing at her thighs when she walked. She sat under the thickest part of the shade. No sunglasses. Rona sat too.

No personal stereo, no sweeties.

Rona, what do you know about Richard the Lionheart?
A long silence. Cassie thought Rona had fallen asleep. She looked over but couldn't tell any better.

Was he gay?
A reply took Cassie by surprise. She couldn't remember the question.
Or maybe that's the Knights Templar. Crusades and things. Raising taxes and generally giving the peasants gyp. Or maybe not. I don't know. We can look it up when we get back. Encyclopaedia Britannica. Or ask Social Work through the wall. They'd be only too keen to help out, I'm sure. Haha.

Another pause.

This time she had.

Across the bridge, Cassie could see half-naked men fishing. Wading up to their thighs in fresh running water: rapids moving like working muscle.

Mussel stall. They were dotted all along the banks of the river, places to eat out and watch the Blue Mosque and the domes of Aya Sofaya, gulls screaming through the flat gold lines of cloud. Chris was always starving. Smelt the place out before we saw it. Mussels fried in bread and batter, strung like washing on thin strips of wood, the ground meshed with cast-off skewers. Litter.

Chris eating. Delighted with himself. The man at the counter gave us the last one free because we'd been such good customers, teeth whiter than a Daz advert under the electric bulb. Three women in veils were drinking coke right next to the place, head to foot in black drapes. I tried to take their photo as well only they hid. After that, we went there every night, watched the same skyline and thought how remarkable it was, to come from where we'd come from and be able to see this kind of thing. Almost illegal. I just used to stand and watch. Holding the rail and staring out over the water. Wouldn't even have noticed he'd taken this. My profile against the Turkish sunset. Nose obscuring the view.

Me and Chris
Chris and Me

standing on the edge of the Bosphorus watching the skyline frazzle in the setting sun, the five minarets of the Blue Mosque striping the skyline. An American took it.

Fastest shopping on record. I'm not in the mood. Rona shows me a huge cheese split along the middle, holes stretched top to bottom of its rind. Like a juggernaut radiator grille. It perks me up momentarily then I look at my watch. Only four thirty. We've done three days' worth of stuff and there are deserts of day left to get through. You can't trust time on holidays.

Anyway.

Going home along the Loire I turn to Rona. She is there where she always is, in the driving seat beside me. And I open my mouth and say

Men. Do you like them Rona?

I never learn.

Do you like them Rona?
Rona looked.
I mean can you look me in the eye and say you actually like the way they are? As a sex, I mean?
Rona looked nonplussed. Well I don't like John Blackwood. But I always put that down to his being a complete bloody idiot.
But the quality of his idiocy Rona. D'you not think the quality of what you're content to call idiocy is quite different in the likes of John Blackwood than say . . . Cassie riffled an index in her head . . . Moira McCubbin?
Rona thought.
Well. Yes and no. They're both bloody idiots just different bloody idiots: one isn't any worse than the other. I wouldn't want to be stranded in a lift with either of them thanks.
Och Rona.
I wouldn't. I don't know what you're driving at.
Rona. You're just being obtuse. Cmon. If you had to be stuck with one of them what one would you hate it to be most? Be honest.

Rona looked hard out the windscreen, eyebrows meeting in the middle. Then they separated, her face relaxing. Cassie started nodding agreement before Rona even spoke.

You're right, she said. You're right.
Of course I'm right, Cassie said. John Blackwood every time. And you know why?
Because he'd spend ages telling me how he wasn't scared and showing off then expect me to rescue him and protect his vanity from knowing he's a useless big sumph.
Quite. Moira McCubbin might well drive you daft with her inane rantings about how they should bring back school uniforms but it's not the same. There's no taking it for granted you'll make

allowances for the rubbish she talks because your shape makes it your job to help her feel important. John Blackwood, on the other hand, is a man. Somewhere in that murky wee brain of his there's a major assumption that he's more *real* somehow, that we're there to look after his ego because we've got bumps in the fronts of our jerseys and he hasn't.

Also he's disgusting.

Well yes. Also he's disgusting. But the most disgusting thing is his belief we're there for his benefit. He thinks that being thought fascinating and competent and admired as a sexual entity are his entitlement as a man in an office of women and he's noticing we're not playing along. That's why he's such an irritating bastard. He thinks the only reason we don't collude is because we're twisted, not because there's anything wrong with his expectations. That's also why he called you – what was it he called you the last time?

A past-it lesbian.

A past-it lesbian. It's pathetic but it's also typical. It's totally bloody typical and what's worse is that it's not an individual malaise. He thinks he's right because most men think exactly the same bloody thing. They're all waiting for their bloody entitlement, Rona, expecting to be made feel they're the important thing off you being the not-important thing. That you're somehow ideally suited to doing things he's too selfish to do, all the shitty stuff and the compromising. And that you'll do it *without wanting anything back*. It is not a reciprocal arrangement. They're not interested in what we want, Rona. What really interests men is what interests John Blackwood ie themselves. Themselves and other men, the things that accrue to maleness. Bloody daft ball games and violence up to and including wars, chemical weapons and genocide, philosophical and political debate of the kind that reduces everything to a competition to prove who's RIGHT all the bloody time and backing winners and going to the dogs and bloody CARS and machines and things that don't talk back and are easy to control and who gets to boss who about and who's got the biggest dick and/or paypacket and/or voice and/or capacity for alcohol or whatever. Ok I know they're the products of their conditioning and they've been done out

171

of their emotional birthrights and all that stuff. But they're not exactly fighting very hard to get shot of these terrible disadvantages ARE THEY? Too bloody right they're not. There's no social power to be gained out of bloody emotional birthrights is there, and that's what matters. Power. What other powerful persons ie other men think – THAT'S what interests men. Women might as well not fucking exist. Heterosexuality is a complete farce, Rona. A CON. Because what men are REALLY in love with is men. And that's why John Blackwood is so awful. He's the naked truth, Rona. Just too stupid to mask reality with any charm or humour whatsoever.

Also he's an ugly pig, said Rona.

Also he's an ugly pig. And there you've hit the key to the whole thing. Sex. We let them away with it because there seems to be no alternative and it's so hard not to want

different skin, the way the hair thins out at the top of the thighs into perfect smoothness before the pubic hair begins to crowd in, thicker, deep and

Rona this isn't the right way.

Outside the window is not the way back. It isn't the right way.

Rona? Where are we going Rona?

Outside was just sunflowers. Squares of countryside choking with them: great yellow fireballs facing up to the sky.

Just thought I'd try another way back. Adventure.

The lower edge of the windshield permed with heathaze, the yellow waves behind. Cassie could feel heartbeat pulsing in her wrists, adrenalin trying to steady itself and failing. Her mouth was opening and closing, breath suddenly stuck in the gullet. Just commercial crops but still. They were flowers as well. Designed to attract. The open petals and the chests bursting out like that, all this raw sex in the middle of the French countryside. Literally dizzying.

172

Cassie turned to see if Rona saw it as well and saw Rona already looking back, holding the wheel.

Cassie, she said. I want my dinner outside tonight. Outside under that canopy thing. I've been wanting my dinner out there since we got here: I've got surprises. Cassie, can we have our dinner out?

Cassie looked at Rona's teeth, sliding back and forth over her lower lip.

You don't just want your dinner out at all, Rona.
No?
No. You want your dinner out with me don't you? Don't you?
Rona started to smile, easy as butter.
Beasts will rain from the skies, bats will fly into our coiffures and midgies will blow into the mashed potatoes but what the hell. Yes we can have dinner outside.

A windmill on the horizon was getting bigger, poking into the skyline.

Look at this place, Rona. Pure filth.

Rona didn't turn round but she laughed.
The dirtiest laugh in the world.

The dog was waiting, tail stump a blur.

She's lonely, I suppose, Rona said. Missing her pups or something.
Pups?
Pups.
Cassie laughed. The idea of a dog pining because it was missing

173

its chance of motherhood: the biological clock ticking away leading to manic displacement activity. Rona you're gaga. Pups.

No I'm not gaga. Look at her. Rona rolled the car slowly on to the red ash. On you go, look.

Cassie looked. What then?

Just LOOK.

The dog rolled on its side, waiting for the women to emerge. Teats. It was studded with two-inch long black teats. Rona switched off the ignition.

Cassie sat at the mesh with her hand out, watching the dog hyperventilate.

Rona unpacked the shopping and put it away. After a while she came back for Cassie.

I know she said. I know.

You are my sunshine, my only sunshine
You make me happy when skies are grey

Singing, trying to keep the hair from getting wet you push out your chest, tilt your neck back. The nipples snub when the water strikes, not knowing if they like the pressure. Even when you switch the water off there is not enough room, no chance to get even halfway dry. You try not to let it matter too much, wiping the walls down for Rona.

Back in the room, the dried flowers lift and fall in the draught from the cracked window. Taps scud. The sound of Rona stepping under water in another room, making awkward curtains in the downpour. Under the towel, your pubic hair regains its curl. A single drop of water worms between toes. You sit, dry your feet on the edge of the bed. A wet kiss mark is there on the sheet when you stand up again, unarguably female. Naked, you find slippers and the

174

red satin kimono Rona made Cassie for her birthday. Thirty-fifth birthday. Maybe thirty-sixth. Anyway. You can relax like this, sit with a mirror and a make-up bag, the way they do in films. Candle-lit dinner for two.

Guess what?
Rona looks about five years old. Holding a soup tureen at chest height. That meant it wasn't soup. Cassie tried to imagine something you got a lot of that were bulky and didn't weigh much.

Bet you can't guess.
It's mushrooms Rona.

It was mushrooms.

Two candles
a cover out of a spare quilt
a strawberry flan and a bowl of apricots. Surprises.

Rona and Cassie
Cassie and Rona

sit out under the canopy till the light is too low to allow the candles to be merely decorative. The night stays warm, thickening. Cassie's dressing-gown that Rona made on her sewing machine is blood-coloured at the collar, black-red with water from hair that still hasn't dried. Mascara, perfume, a poppy behind one ear, the drapes of the satin split to the thigh. At the side of the empty plates, near the apricot stones and patisserie box tissue, an empty bottle and a smaller one, half full. Rona pours liqueur, drizzling it on the side of the glass, through the green fuzz stripes of one sleeve.

175

We clink glasses and say cheers, teeth completely grey from cheap red wine, writing postcards. I write to the office staff, the woman across the landing who said she would feed the cat, Chris's mum and dad.

Weather is here, wish you were lovely, the place is full of fungi and foreigners love Cassie x.

Went to Topkapi this afternoon. Four hours with Chris trailing round the armoury and me trailing everything else. Saw the breakfast robe of Sultan Aziz. It said what he'd eaten the morning he wore it. AD434. Chris said they must have made it up, they couldn't possibly know what some guy had had for breakfast that long ago. I said just because we were jumping around covered in woad didn't mean other places weren't civilized. Just as well we never went to China. Chris' favourite thing was the display case of daggers with rubies the size of ox kidneys. I liked the mosaics love

Midgies frazzle themselves on the flames. Beasts with lean grey mandibles fall through the green mesh. A huge spider does knee bends in the corner of the overhanging vine, gestating silk.

Ahh. George. Man we met last night in Istanbul. Started blethering to me quite the thing while I was standing holding the rail and looking out, waiting for Chris to stop taking light readings. I didn't even see him till he spoke. English? he said. I looked into the distance, pretending to be entranced by the Blue Mosque and the water in the evening light. Topkapi? He knew I could hear him. It's beautiful, yes?

Yes I said. Beautiful. I figured monosyllabic was safest.

You have been there? Inside?

Thin with brown arms on the bridge rail, shirt buttons shining. All his teeth were gold. And though I knew it could

176

have meant anything, anything at all, I smiled back. I said we'd
been. Chris took a shot from the edge of the bridge, the flashgun
torching our skin. He was looking at the water when I could see
properly again. He said his favourite was the Harem. He went
to the Harem every day to see the mosaics. I said I hadn't
wanted to go there. Not the harem. I had this idea it would
depress me, that I'd keep thinking of wee girls not able to leave
and wanting their mothers, women locked away behind a
barrier of eunuch fat. I knew there was a room with a couch and
I didn't want to see it. I couldn't even think about the couch
never mind going to see it. My face must have been giving it all
away. He just kept shaking his head.

The harem is only women's quarters. Where the women
played music and sang, they talked. Harem. The special place
for women. They have the best mosaics.

Then I heard Chris' voice saying Did somebody mention
harems? in that Terry-and-June way and that was it. Turned
out the old guy had worked in Scotland for six years, an
engineer. George. He offered us cigarettes, laughed when I said
I didn't. Chris took one. He didn't smoke either but he took one
and the two of them talked about industrial processes. I stayed
put at the railings, keeping staring out at where the Harem
might be till the water was black. Keeping mum.

Her ankles hooked on to the table top so her knickers show, Rona
smiles at the card she is writing as though it has just proposed
marriage and she is willing to accept. The bitch paces on the other
side of the green wire, watching our candles gutter. The glitter of
mucus in her eyes.

twelve

COOEE

The carpark was thick with dust.

Two people herding a shapeless mass of weans, an ice-cream van coming and going behind the veil. A lost little girl surfaced near the grass, mouth unnaturally red, looking for an adult who might know who the hell she was. Then the cloud of stour rolled forward and claimed her too.

COOEE

Cassie put the chocolate in her pocket and looked up. Rona was waving from a turret.

The black hair, the shape of her shoulders. Before Rona was much older she'd have curvature of the spine. All those bloody bags. Her breasts would be hugging her belly by the time she was fifty.

178

Knowing none of this, Rona waved again, shouting IT'S LIKE
DISNEY OR SOMETHING. WALT DISNEY, waving some
more.

Cassie waved back, shielding her eyes. Rona laughed and stuck
one digit in the air, poking it vertically. She meant to come up.

I got us some chocolate, Cassie roared. Chocolate.

Rona stuck out her tongue and poked the air harder.

Chocolate, you daft bugger. Words spiralling up into nowhere,
not reaching at all at all at all.

she sees

God. The colour. I look like a peeled scab. An hour on the
beach before breakfast and that was what happened. I tan like
a bacon rasher. No, it's not hair gel, just wet. I had this idea
that water running down the back of my neck would help
soothe the sunburn. It didn't. Anyway it's a cafe in downtown
Antalya called UFUK. UFUK. No I don't know how you
pronounce it either. People tried to buy us breakfast every
morning, desperate to practise their English. Chris loved all
that, talking in a drawl about the Houses of Parliament and
London Our Capital. It's Edinburgh his bloody capital only he
didn't want to risk saying that and have them think he was less
important than they thought. I was all ready to do that for
him, to see their eyes blanking up when I said SCOTLAND
ACTUALLY but he got there first. Come on Cassie, for
christsake lighten up we're on our holidays, smiling like he was
going to bite. So that's me being supportive of Chris' notion of
holiday. Dayglo skin. Overtight shoestring straps from putting
on weight. I look like a bloody salami.

179

Her lungs were taking up too much room. The chest cavity bursting, filled with sore breath that still wasn't doing its job properly. Only halfway.

Halfway up the spiral steps, Cassie stopped. Careful breathing through the mouth, ignoring the saw edges digging in behind each breast. Totally unfit. Always had been. Cassie hated sport. Sport meant rules and discomfort, jumping up and down in front of other people with hardly any clothes on. Not that there hadn't been efforts. Twice to a badminton club with Rona, the swimming lessons. The sweat, though, the embarrassment and disgust, trying to care what wee lines you were meant to stay on one side of; the pool full of human debris, cattle troughs of disinfectant that had coated godknew how many verrucas yawning cold on the floor. Yoga had been better, the church hall annexe with no mirror had been almost reassuring. Till the relaxation period. The way they asked you to imagine waves on the beach while the sound of your own heartbeat washed in your ears, the gulp of blood in the jugular magnified to horror movie proportions. Since then, an adult acceptance of sport's intrinsic hellishness seemed best. Along with slow crumbling of the respiratory bits and pieces, rusty knee joints, creaky ankles, a stiff neck and roaming digestive organs. Ribs gradually burying under layers of flaccid skin. Breathing difficulties that were getting harder to conceal. Cassie had good pectorals though. Some exercises you could do drinking tea at the desk and nobody noticed. She could probably crush coke cans with her pelvic floor muscle. Some bits were fine fine fine.

Two big women squashed past, the cold plucked skin of their arms brushing her own. Ashamed not to, Cassie followed. At the top there were more steps. The faulty heart-valves spluttering, a red tide rising behind the eyes and the tongue getting thick. Not forty-one. It wasn't old for godsakes. Not even middle-aged. It should have been possible to go up four flights of stairs. Blood hurt her ears just thinking about it. Her face would be blotchy as well, livid with burst capillaries. Cassie forced her breathing slower and quieter, hoping no-one else would spot how diseased she was, how ruined. Looking upward in an unconcerned way, bluffing health. Rona was there, one level up. The pencil turrets with entire leads at the sharp end. It was. It was like bloody Disneyland. Frightening how pretty it looked, how charming. Cassie felt her shoulders steeling, getting on their guard. Cassie had not expected to feel charmed and didn't like it. She didn't like it at all. Charming went with words like plausible and bastard and was better not trusted. Rona leaned over the side of the stairwell, looking down. She had taken her bra off. She did that sometimes, driven mad by nylon in hot conditions. Cassie could see the changed shape, Rona's nipples tenting under the soft material like radio tuning buttons.

Rona was shouting something.

Cassie was squinting without looking up. She could feel it. Her own pulse thrashing like a beached fish behind the temples. Rona hanging over the safety rail, damning her breasts to hell for all eternity. Squeaking like Minnie Mouse.

I can't hear a bloody word.

We walk round the outside of the château then the inside, trying to generate interest in paintings of dead rich people, bits of china they might have eaten off but can't be sure. The wee cards that usually explain are missing. We are supposed to take it on trust these things matter. Every so often a tour group with an English-speaking guide goes past and we listen, clandestine. They are all white haired, experiencing different degrees of fear we are stealing something off them. After all, they paid good money for this tour and we didn't. We hang around anyway, refusing to pick up signals on purpose. The guide gathers them together, a hen with chicks, glares to let us know we are not nice. We attach to a passing French group instead. Their guide belongs to the château, kitted out like the Park Ranger in a Yogi Bear cartoon. He talks far too fast, his voice all one colour: no up or down beats and no pitch clues. Like a machine. Like one time, one time in Orkney, we went to this Viking burial mound. Maes Howe. We bought tickets. We paid for the tickets to see Maes Howe and the man in the booth told us to wait. We waited five minutes and nothing happened. Rona was just on the verge of asking why not when she arrived. A woman on an antique bike, bits all falling off it and brick-red with rust. Catrinyourguide she said, throwing the bike into a corner. She was off down the entrance tunnel like a late rabbit before we knew what was going on. By the time we'd caught up she was already waiting in the underground hole where Vikings had been buried, holding a torch under her face. Like a vampire, all the shadows dragging upward. She switched it off then back on as a kind of signal. And started. It was all one word. The eerie face and one white hand pointing at drawings etched into the stone but between the drawings and what she said, between one word and the next: nothing. Her mouth was just covering ground, going through the motions of something she had learned a long time ago and from which all meaning had been lost. Us getting anything from it seemed to be entirely up to ourselves and incidental. Immaterial, even. She pointed up at a hole in the top of the dome, looking at her watch and the mouth just keeping going. Like it had never occurred to her we might care or be trying to make sense of it. Rona asked some questions after and she offered to sell us a wee book. It'sallinthat, she said. Cheerio. I had to walk for a bit on my own afterwards, breathe deep and count. I had to force myself out of a raging need to weep. Panic attack or something. I just needed to get her out of my ears. Anyhow.

Anyhow.

The French guide isn't really like that at all. The French guide is just boring. He points at nothing except a collection plate as we file to leave the last room. I give him damn all. Rona puts something in and smiles till she sees me watching her and the smile just wipes off. One minute it's there, the next, gone: the guilty hand seeking sanctuary in the shorts' pocket. Christ. I wonder what on earth it was my face did to be able to do that, what it was I did that made her feel so judged. It's a terrible feeling: knowing you can force somebody's pleasure off beam just like that without even trying. I can't even touch her to let her know I'm sorry because there are people in the way and besides I feel too shocked. Or is it ashamed. Whatever it is it's terrible. But I try to think of something nice I could maybe say or do once we get back over the threshold again and outside. I keep thinking it as we step through the door, the sun wrinkling up my eyes again and something stops me. It stops me cold. The cool voice, the one that acknowledges nothing, says

Well, what did you think then?

Rona looks at me and says Sorry? Sorry? and it says it again. Well, what did you think?

And all the warmth, all the wanting to make her feel ok again is icing over, my stomach tightening from the inside. I watch Rona smile, wondering if it's a trick, if I'm setting her up in some way. Maybe I am.
Aha, she says, You tell me what YOU thought first, trying to keep things light and wondering where it's all leading. You tell me what YOU think. And I feel nauseous. Something is rising in my gullet. I watch my feet walk one after the other to the middle of the slabbed walkway and stop.

Cassie stops.

Cassie stopped.

She stopped in the middle of walking forwards, breathed deep and looked down at her château ticket. She shook her head and kept standing till Rona stopped too. Rona, Cassie said.

Rona waited.

Rona did you understand any of that in there?
A dark voice. Not to be trifled with. Rona didn't know. She just

183

thought it was Cassie asking a question. She stood cagey for a moment, doing a face from a book of eighteenth-century attitudes marked THOUGHTFUL.

Rona tell me the truth. Did you?

Rona bit her lower lip. No she said. No.

No. Neither did I.

The heat almost choking. Cassie raised her head and looked Rona right in the eye. A terrifying and necessary thing, to look another human being straight in the eye.

What is it about, Rona? What are we doing?

Rona breathed in, puncturing the stillness. Well I got bits of it but he was talking too fast. He said something about clocks and Louis XIV and –

I don't mean that stuff. I mean the whole thing, Rona, the *thing*. Us walking round that place in there. Why we did it. What was it for?

Rona said nothing.

I mean does it matter who lived in there and what they drank their tea out of? What their chairs looked like?

Blank.

What d'you think it's *for*? People going round looking in places like this. It's just old stuff. It doesn't actually have any bearing on anything, any meaning.

The air round Cassie's head seemed to have become very still. She could hear nothing but the echo of her own voice, a distant car horn repeating the same phrase. Rona looked bleachy under the strong sunlight. Clueless.

Looking at furniture for godsakes. What are we under the impression we're looking at? It's just OLD STUFF, Rona. People toing and froing round an old house looking at furniture. So what I want to know is what do folk think they're doing? No, what do WE think we're doing? What are we looking at it FOR Rona is what I'm

184

asking you. What investment do we think we're making here? What's it meant to MEAN?

I don't know what you're asking me, Rona said. Her face looked very small and earnest. Cassie breathed in deep in case the next sentence was a very long one.

I mean, she said, I mean this is our only crack at – what date is it? The sixteenth, Rona said. Ok our only crack at the sixteenth of July nineteen christnose and we spend it looking at all that OLD STUFF in there. We do it all the time and I want to know why Rona. I want to know what the plan is between us here or whether it's just not thought through at all and just a TOTAL WASTE OF TIME. My time and your time. Whether this is something we have actually chosen to do, whether this is what we're always going to do or whether we're just – the thing in her gullet was getting bigger – killing time. I'd like us to know, that's all. I'd quite like to know what it is we've elected to do with our time. If it's thought through. If we have any choice.

Rona looked at Cassie being out of breath. Cassie could see her doing it. She waited, knowing something was wrong. Cassie knew Rona knew something was wrong. It radioed out of her, out of the benign look that was making Cassie feel murderous. Desperate. Rona knew that too.

Well, she said, stretching the word out like an accordion, Well. Maybe it is. Maybe it *is* a waste of time. We don't need to come to places like this if you don't want. If it makes you feel any better.

Cassie looked at her.

But some of the stuff was all right, Cassie. You said so. It was nice to look at. Did you not think it was nice to look at?

Cassie looked at Rona. Rona rubbed her neck with one finger.

It's ok not to know what it's for. Just like it while you're doing it: let yourself enjoy looking at nice things. It's ok to not give yourself a hard time every so often. It's called relaxing, Cassie. You might as well ask what's a bee for. It's not for anything: it's just there. Just allow yourself to let it be there. Try to enjoy it. Ok?

She was picking at a stain on her shorts now, walking away.

I thought it was ok. I liked it.

Cassie watches Rona getting further away. Drifting to the other side of the square of yellow dust to the parapet leaving Cassie behind.

I want to shout after her RONA ARGUE WITH ME TALK TO ME FIGHT ME FOR GODSAKES RONA, TURN ROUND AND FIGHT ME LIKE A MAN but I don't. I feel I am going to implode. And Rona turns round.
Rona turns round.
She turns round, the light behind her making her hair sheer, the round shape of the pink scalp visible through the black mesh and she points one foot, flexing the ankle into a flat, clean slope and says See. Come and see this.

And because I can't think why not I come. I come, letting my eye follow the length of her sandal to the toes sticking out the end. For a minute, I can't see a bloody thing. Just the tips of Rona's toes. And Rona catching nothing in my voice maybe knowing she has nothing to be afraid of maybe Rona is not afraid of me at all she just tilts her foot over the edge of the parapet to help me work out what to look for, brushing a lump of gold-coloured stone with her toetips. And I let my eyes stroke over the surface of the stone before I focus, worrying, knowing it must be a gargoyle or something monstrous and it is

186

beautiful.

A pup.

A labrador pup looking like flesh and bone, sitting so its huge paws drop off the thin ledge of stone where it overhangs nothing. Just the sheer drop down to the well where I had stood earlier, waving up to Rona.

Look, she says, look at its feet.

She kneels down, leaning to touch the crumbly forepaws, too close to the precipice, looking up at me. Knowing nothing of the danger she is in / I am in / we both

Inside her pocket, Cassie's hand closed round a ribbon of luke-warm pus. Something warm slithering under a thin cover. The chocolate. Far below, round the distant ice-cream van, KIM FUZZ and NELLY wrappers chased each other in circles, smaller every time.

The castle's profusion of conical roofs heightens its air of medieval fantasy. Though now minus a wing and somewhat mellowed with time, it maintains the look of the elegant residence of the Duc de Berry. A wonderful view from the terrace shows the Church of Saint Pierre, the Loire and her two bridges and the birthplace of Coco Chanel.

Museum of the Horse, Cassie said. She shuffled through the book forwards then back again. I read it somewhere.
Eh?
Horse, Rona. It said somewhere in here. Maybe the man said it

in the château but I've got the idea from somewhere. Musée des Cheveux.

A crease appeared between Rona's eyebrows. That's hair, Cassie. That's Museum of the Hairs.

Cassie looked at her.

Cheveux. That's Hair. It's chevaux that's horses. Anyway it would be Musée du Cheval, Museum of the Horse. Singular.

Pedantry, Rona, thin end of the wedge.

The sign was round the corner of the bus park, pointing back up towards the château. White line drawing of a pony. Someone had added a huge penis with a green felt-tip pen. And a smile. Musée du Cheval.

Cases of stuffed dead things, bridles, bits and brasses and lots of pictures. Pictures of horses with farmers, members of the aristocracy, robbers, watchmen, miners, carters, blacksmiths, soldiers and godknows. Men and horses. A horse-drawn cannon. Rona found a Clydesdale-size skeleton in a glass box.

Enough.

We've both had enough.

Second last day in Antalya. Bus at the terminus. We were trying to find a place called Pamukale somebody told Chris about then just got on the first one that came. Outside the town the road turned into track, the bus kicking up dust in the middle of nowhere, sounding the horn for what looked like no reason till we saw the camels. Some of them shift and some of them don't. If they don't, the bus bumps off the track onto the fields and goes round them. No choice. More people got on. Some of them with chickens. It got very very hot. A young woman posted a baby through an open window to whoever would take it before she squeezed in through the door, looking for him inside. A big woman stared at Chris till he got up and went to stand near the driver, where the other men were. I stayed put, jammed in with big middle-aged women, chickens and stour. Every so often a man squirted lemon-scented stuff from a plant spray to keep us cool. It was wonderful. Off the hook for the whole day, a mystery tour over the brows of higher and higher hills till my ears popped. We ended up on the edge of something like a volcano crater full of scrubby little trees and goats, skinny boys with bare legs and close-cut hair driving sheep along with sticks in their hands, the occasional girl with a black scarf over her mouth turning to watch us watching her going past. As the climb got steeper, the bus clanked down another gear till eventually it was in the lowest and still failing. So the driver put on a tape. Turkish popsongs. And people started joining in, ones and two till the whole busload were singing along with it, the soft under-the-voice singing you do when you can't help it. Outside, another twelve yards of hill left to go, the side of the cliff edge all dried out vegetation and dusty goats and inside, singing. Three men jumped off and gave the bus an extra push. Everybody applauded when they got back on: the bus was going down the other side. I really thought I was seeing an ancient race going about its life, babies going hand to hand, the singing and the squirts of lemon. And at the other end, through the grey chicken dust, was Chris, scowling and clutching his beach bag. An anachronism. It was then I realised. I didn't want to be with him a minute longer. Simple as that. Down there at the end of the bus, separate to me: it just dawned on me that's where he would always be. Not Mr Right after all.

Rona stays out while I cook, clearing the inside of the car.

I wash dishes, put things away, brush my hand over the kitchen table as though I'm memorising the grain. The roughcast on the sides of the doorframe. Learning the house by feel for when it is no longer there.

The Last Supper.

Two bowls
soup tureen
poppies in a jar
mint leaves
salt in a thing that was probably an ashtray
anything else left in a salad
one and a half bottles of wine.

Butter knife diagonally poised on the plate.

Still Life.

Rona comes in when I shout, two bags of rubbish cleaned out the car and a final washing. Socks and two pairs of knickers drip between her fingers on to the brushed boards. We hang them up on the mantelpiece and I tell her they won't be dry. Not in time.
Cassie, she says, Shut up.

I straighten for a moment, not sure I like it. Then decide.
I know, I say. I bring you in then give you a row for doing it even though I've been pining for your company for the past hour. I know. The kind of thing I do. I'd be hell to live with, I say. Think yourself lucky this is just for holidays.

Rona just laughs. I weigh and measure the laugh, looking for clues. There aren't any.

Rona said, That's enough.

    It's plenty. The place is fine.

    You'll just keep dusting things all night. Cmon.

We're going for a drive.

We drive for miles.

Rona did you like Chris? I mean really like him? Or what?

Rona pulled her mouth down at the corners. He was ok. Her face getting more definite. He was fine actually. A bit assumptive but fine.

Assumptive?

That time you had the party at the flat. He was giving out cigars and missed me out.

Cassie looked. You don't smoke Rona.

What's that got to do with it? You don't just decide for people. It's not right. It doesn't give them the chance to do something unexpected if they want, does it? It's assumptive.

Cassie said nothing.

Rona rounded the next bend, switched off the indicator. Och Chris was ok. Whatever he's doing, he'll be fine. You don't need to worry about Chris. You know who I didn't like though? That bloody Tom you took up with. Richard was a bit of a nonentity but Tom was a complete waste of time, Cassie. I don't know what you saw in him.

Water squirted unexpectedly on to the windscreen, the wipers waving back and forth. Cassie laughed. Rona just shook her head. A complete arse.

We drive

191

through the narrow sideroads full of overhanging trees

the lights in the tufa houses drilling the dark with yellow holes

then

complete extinction of light. Black dustsheets cover everything except the slim slice of road caught in the headlights. It goes on for a longer time than begins to feel comfortable then I hear Rona breathe in sharply, start pulling over. She looks outside, back at me, then steps out into the nothingness out there. Cassie, she says. A half voice. She clicks the switch to full so the beam cuts across the verge, unrolling a swathe of visibility through the murk. Inside, a field of luminous yellow roses appears. I step out and they are there for me too. The light bursts petals: their scent fills the road. We stand on either side of this car I cannot drive, Rona and Cassie, without cameras, not knowing our place on the landscape, looking out over this field brim full with unexpected roses. And find it bearable. Bearable. Fine fine fine.

Back from Turkey. Home and not sure I had the right to call it that any more. Chris wanted a picture at the door before we went in, knowing nothing of the treachery staring him in the face. He thought it had been a raging success, going to Turkey. He was full of it. It took me a week to say I was leaving after that. Guilt. Sorting the photos was the worst, the custody allocation. Sifting through the accumulated junk of thirteen years, thinking the best thing might be to throw it all away before it all became whatever it is these things become after the event. You can only throw away objects, though. Things. It was desperate anyway. Rona came to help, carrying boxes down the steps from the flat to the car. Tea-chests that nearly wouldn't go through the door. She found the photo of my

192

mother and father on top of stuff waiting to be shifted. Who's that, she said. He looks like an identikit picture of a waste of time. That woman's lovely but he looks like a complete chancer. I couldn't help myself. Bawled like a wean all the way downstairs. Two tea-chests and seven albums of pictures. I never want to have to do anything like that again.

No dog. No lights on in the farmhouse.

We finish what is left of the Grand Marnier, a bottle of wine, the dregs of two bottles of red that went into cooking and pack up more rubbish. Two big bagfuls.

Rona how do two people manage to make this amount of pollution?
Life, Cassie. Life.

The cleaned living room, brandy, silence. Routes, Rona said. She yawned. We could go back via Blois. Amboise or something. We need to work out routes.

Rona lay on her belly with the map opened out flat like a keeled-over butterfly, pinned with highlighter pens and bits of yellow sticky paper covered with Rona's writing. Cassie looked at the map but it was no good. All the lines were joining up.

Not tonight eh? Tomorrow, Cassie said. We'll do it tomorrow, and heard the click of the pre-record button in Rona's head.

A promise.
A vow.

Tomorrow we will have to mark out routes that will make me hot and desperate because they tie me down and make me think about what must be left behind. Confrontation with limitation. Saying we'll come back and do those other things another time knowing it's hogwash. You may never be back. You may never have other chances.

Flat on her belly, you watch Rona computing the discussion of our narrowing time and see something radiant in there. Saint Rona of the Computation: limitless, fearless of mortality. Boundless as a cracked egg, as molten wax, the sea.

Cassie says,
I'll go last in bed.

I'll put out the light and check the door is locked and the bathroom window bolted down.

You go on through and get some sleep: there's a lot of driving to do tomorrow.

Two minutes after I pull up the top sheet, I hear the clank of the toilet. A rustling noise as she walks into one of the rubbish bags, forgetting it's there in the dark. The sound of Rona growling Shit and something thudding on to the floor. Shit. Rona reclaiming her territory, rattling the lock and the windows in turn. Making sure.

Sometimes I think it is not possible to do anything meaningful for Rona. Not a bloody thing.

Two minutes pass.
Cassie puts out the light.

Bedsprings. Rona turning over and sighing like something lost.

Alone in the dark, Cassie pictured Rona alone in hers. A tumulus under different bedsheets, turning to find a better way to induce unconsciousness. Snorting like a buffalo, probably, like a hog on a truffle hunt. The night they'd spent in that B&B in Dorset where they'd had to share the same bed, ending up fighting at 3 am over whether it was worse lying next to someone who grunted all night or someone who lay so still they could easily pass for dead. Haha. Alone in the dark, Cassie laughed, tapping the headboard against the wall. Hahahahaha. Knocking. After a moment, knocking came back. A pattern with the end missing. The daft bugger was through in her room, listening. The opening phrase came again, waiting. Cassie crooked her arm at ear level, knocking with one knuckle. Twice. A reply.

The sound of Rona muffled through two thicknesses of wall.

Dirty as hell.

thirteen

The cottage. Just before we left. That's me in the mirror over the fireplace. You have to look hard but I'm definitely there, taking this. I tried to get one of the goat as well but it wouldn't co-operate. The last sight of the place was the boxer, held at the neck by the collar, rearing like Champion the Wonderhorse as we drove away. Rona waved. I tried to take a picture of that but we went over a bump at the wrong minute and I got this instead. Row of socks over the back seats, steaming.

Cassie wound the window down, roaring at the car roof. LOOK AT THE COLOUR OF THE SKY RONA LOOK AT THE BLOODY SKY. Rona gripped the wheel and said nothing at all.

> SAUMUR, the "pearl of Anjou", the grey pencil tips
> of the château's

Nah we did that bit. This is it.

Touristic SAUMUR is upstream from the bridges towards the castle, the Town Hall and Saint-Pierre. But to view the place as a whole, it is essential to balance tourist sights with the western side of the city where over 3000 military personnel live with their families. Do take the time to look here and at SAUMUR's famous Cadets Museum, the Museum of the Saddle, the Museum of Cavalry and Tank Museum.

Two choices. Choice One: we can go and look at swords and sabres, helmets and breastplates, panzers and the lorry that carried the corpse of General de Gaulle. Choice Two: we can get the buggery out of Saumur. I say to hell with military hardware this time. To hell with the complicity of watching tanks and bloody guns and helmets with bullet holes in. To hell with the memorabilia of men knocking lumps out of each other. It has nothing to do with us, Rona. Nothing at all. To hell with the lot of them.

I feel funny immediately after I say it though. A stillness with my voice ringing in it, a perceptible change of atmosphere has occurred between the start of me speaking and the end. So I turn looking, trying to work out if it's me or whether there's something wrong and she's right there at my elbow. Rona. Her specs are full of cakes.

Look can we stick with the point? she says. Do we want these lemon things or a couple with the redcurrants or whatever they are? What do we want?

Apricot halves bulging like buttocks out of pastry cases. A window full of glutinous flan, grapes in aspic rimming kiwi-fruit slices and bleeding strawberry pyres. In the middle, a horn of plenty spills marzipan vegetables.

Cmon, we haven't got all day.

Cassie watched Rona go in. On the other side of the glass, her eyes looked smaller than usual. Maybe she was feeling sick: all those bits out of different bottles last night. Maybe she was preoccupied. Or tired. Rona always said she liked driving but there was no guarantee it was true. She didn't have a choice. She might just be making the best of a bad job only not managing this morning. Maybe she resented it and this was a sign. On the other hand maybe there was nothing wrong with her face at all and Cassie was imagining it. She was imagining it because she was embarrassed: saying all those things about the Tank Museum before she remembered about Rona's grandad. That could be it as well. Rona might have been wanting to go to the Tank Museum for all Cassie knew, keen to see the tin hats with bullet holes and bayonets with rusty edges. She might have though. You could never tell with Rona.

A pair of lemon tarts levitated behind the sheened-out glass into a place Cassie could no longer see. Rona was in there, in the middle of the too-bright bit. Cassie imagined Rona hauling out the purse, remembering there was no change. She would sigh, dump a bigger note on the counter than anybody had any right to expect a shop to deal with at that time in the morning and not explain. She would just dump it, do one of the steely stares. The woman behind the counter would stare back but she wouldn't win. Rona stared out like the gorgon. She'd be in there doing it now. Winning. Rona just didn't explain much. Even in a good mood, she didn't let you in on what the hell was going on in her head. Which meant you were supposed to guess, which gave you plenty of scope for error and her plenty for disappointment if she was ever needing any. Plenty of scope for blame. Rona didn't come clean. She didn't fight her corner and say what she thought. Sometimes you forgot and then the bloody thing hit you when you least expected it. Like the time in the canteen queue, head down and trufflehunting through a rack of sandwiches, hearing Rona's voice from deeper down the line: I would have but Cassie wouldn't let me. You know what she's like. The shock of the familiar inflections being seditious, separate and underhand. Cassie remembered keeping her head low, feeling too

198

hot, trying to look absent and deaf, saving Rona embarrassment. She could feel it again now. Rona and her bloody Not Saying. That she had wanted to go to the Tank Museum then taken the huff because Cassie hadn't was entirely possible. It was also irritating and typical. You woke up in a decent mood, keen to get on the road and somehow this kind of thing happened. Rona ground you down. She stifled your enthusiasm and refused to make decisions for herself. She was untrustworthy and deceitful even to herself because she didn't just open her mouth and Say. Because she just wouldn't act. She denied responsibility for her own life and

Two leek tarts and some lemon things ok?

Rona in the doorway. A box dangled from one treacherous knuckle joint on a loop of white ribbon, a double bow fankled into the roots of her fingers. Cassie looked at the box.
They put them in this for me.
Something stuck in Cassie's chest made her not able to speak.
I can carry them for a bit. Get the use out the thing.
Rona already moving away, not waiting for a response.
I don't mind.

Cassie looked at Rona and thought about the office drawer they were supposed to share. Full of bubble-wrap and bits of string. Old envelopes and loose paper clips, broken pencils. One drawer was full of bits of corrugated cardboard. The fight to try and get her to throw anything away. Some things she was absolutely clear about and others, godknew. Mysteries. She would probably have loved the fucking Tank Museum. Cassie felt her eyes narrow, glaring at Rona's shoulder. She glared at Rona's shoulder so hard it felt like it ought to catch fire.

Look are you wanting to go or not?
Sorry?
I said are you wanting to go to the bloody Tank Place or not. Make up your mind.

Rona had stopped, turned to look back at Cassie, the box descending as her arm sagged at her side.

I thought you didn't want to go.

Never mind what I want, just answer the question given. I said are *you* wanting to go or not?

Rona shrugged. If you've changed your mind. If you want.

No do *you* want to Rona I said do *you* want to?

Rona looked left and right as though something might be driving up on the pavement towards her. She looked back at Cassie.

Is no the right answer?

Cassie said nothing.

No then. No. She shrugged again. Look, let's go for coffee and a sit in the shade somewhere. That'll be nice: a wee sit down.

Don't patronise me Rona.

O for crying out loud.

I said don't. Just bloody don't. I'm fed up with it.

I just said we could go for a coffee, that's all. Sigh. I don't know what's the matter with you sometimes.

It's not me, Rona, so you can just forget that tactic. It's not me, chum. And I don't want a coffee. What I want is exactly the same as what I wanted this morning when I got up ie to get on the road. To get shifting and out of this place, all right?

Rona looked. She turned and started walking.

They walked the distance of three shop fronts, not speaking. They crossed the road and started down the edge of a bit of wasteground, the Not Speaking getting bigger. Becoming Huff. The horrible speed with which it did that, growing like a plant from a space-pod: not assailable by reason or logic, merely of and for itself. Huffiness was a disease, a paralysis. A pain in the neck, chest, jaw and shoulders. Cassie could feel her forehead crushed up, the whole upper body tensed through not knowing what the hell was going on. It was not meant to happen like this. They were meant to have gotten up, eaten whatever food was left, put the bags in the car, had a touching parting with the nursing mother and disappeared behind a screen of pink gravel dust. But Rona had wanted to come back in.

200

We need to buy lunch, she said. Last look. The need to hedge bets and have things mapped out. Just when you thought you had things stitched up, when you thought you had grasped a Vital Truth about Human Happiness and it consisting in knowing when to Move On; just when you thought you were doing fine, things like this happened. You ended up walking along the road, the possibility you had woken up with stuck in your gullet like cold dumpling skin. Wedged. Rona and the starts of journeys. Always the fucking same.

Further along the road, Rona stopped, looking in a fresh window.
Chess set, she said. Out of bits of tufa cave.
Cassie drew level.
It's mushrooms.

Face flat as a fish. Cassie looked but didn't feel any better. She didn't feel any better at all.

Rona went round the one-way system three times before we were finally on the road
        the road
        the road.

Capri in the sun.
Reeking of melting plastic and turned cheese. The wee christmas tree air freshener making no impact at all. Company car. He was proud of having a car like everybody else's, off the assembly line. Tom with the Capri. Makes me feel sick just looking at it.

Panorama. Montsoreau.

Panorama. Candes St Martin.

Panorama. Usée

and these.

Sunflowers. Millions of sunflowers. Rona's in there somewhere. I wouldn't have taken it otherwise. That lump off to the side there is her folded double. Taking pictures of more of the bloody things. Sunflowers.

Is it not time we were shifting, Rona?

Rona. The time. I'm starving.

Rona rolled like a seal and repositioned, peering through the lens at the place where the leaf joined onto the stem. Ok she said. Last one. She angled the camera afresh, pulled her head back to refocus. Not meaning a word.

Cassie had been for a walk down the road at the side of the field for a look at the windmill wearing her hat, pretending to be in a French film. Then she came back and did it again. Twice. Rona was still in the same place. With the same flower.

Cassie watched Rona taking pictures of the same flower and knew Rona was doing it on purpose. Wasting time to drive Cassie gaga, using the pictures as an excuse. Rona took lots of pictures. Pictures of things. It was one of the things Rona did. Pictures of disconnected, non-human things like mountains, waterfalls and godknows. The first time Cassie had seen an album of Rona's, she had looked at it for a good five minutes or so before she knew what it was that was bothering her about it. Rocks, the sea, skies. Trees and fields. There were no people. Cassie had some like that as well, grass with feet and sawn-off legs, heads floating like UFOs in the corner of vast skies, extremities dangling in time and space. Rona's weren't mistakes though. Cassie couldn't work that out. Except for the accidents, Cassie's were all people. People and animals but mostly people, smiling and telling lies. Her mother at some cousin's wedding smiling like Betty Grable in a yellow suit out of Arnott's sitting next to the sister she wouldn't have put out if she was on fire, that kind of thing. Desperate. Faces crumpling to find appealing attitudes, trying to leave recorded evidence of how they had been before they started all that sliding about, melting and shifting like sand dunes that faces inevitably did. People were supposed to smile in photos. Even the one photo Cassie had of her mother and father together, even in that one, they smiled. Well, her father's was more a kind of grimace, probably because he was drunk. He'd never been anything else. Her mother's, on the other hand, was so like the real thing you couldn't tell. Cassie's mother's smile was radiant, wholesome, unstinting. It was also a rabid whopper. Plenty of folk did it though; they did it all the time. That kind of mendacity was, in some circles, regarded as a duty. You were supposed to smile in photos pour encourager les autres. You were supposed to smile in photos as proof. Proof a) that you really had been there and b) it wasn't awful all the time. It was evidence. In case. Cassie couldn't think what the case might be but the photos were proof against it anyway. Rona's were the first she'd seen that didn't join in. Photographs of flowers and hay stubble. Cassie wasn't sure what she was being drawn into looking at them. She hadn't known what they meant at all at all.

Rona lay flat against the bitten earth. Her shorts would be getting all stour and she didn't care. Her eyes all crushed up, scores into the temple like slashes in wet cement. She wasted her face, Rona. The hook nose and blue eyes and the black hair with the grey that had never been there once and Cassie sometimes couldn't remember without looking at a photo what it had been like before. Though she had plenty. Most of Chris but Rona next. Nearly more of Rona than anybody else. Rona halfway over the Auld Brig in Ayr wrapped in a headscarf, shouting Ochone Ochone in clouds over the frozen water and her face all pink with cold like a wee girl and laughing

on top of a ruined tower somewhere in darkest England waving with nine and a half fingers and shouting COOEE and laughing

with a box covered in polar bear wrapping-paper, wearing a green crèpe paper hat and laughing

pointing at something out of shot and you couldn't even remember what it was any more and laughing so hard she was a blur, pointing at something in the sky and

fill in the blank.

The thing is, you could never be too sure what about. What was so bloody funny. Cassie had thought, once or twice of taking Rona to one side and pointing out that unexplained and non-specific mirth could seem like idiocy. It could also seem complacent, gratuitous and fucking smug.

Other times though
other times

Rona was still lying on the ground. Making sure she got the stamens just right. Rona taking photos. Flowers. Flowers for godsakes. At least rabbits moved about. Cows took grass if you stood there long enough holding it out. Flowers did bugger all. But Rona took pictures of them anyway, completely absorbed. There were times you looked at Rona and wondered what the hell it was she thought she was making a record of, what she thought the sum of all her activity was for. She was completely off her head. Other times, though, you knew it wasn't Rona.

It wasn't Rona.

Rona had come out from behind the lens now and was staring up at the sky. Cassie looked at Rona, feeling a dim anger somewhere. A jealousy. Whatever it was, she wanted to see it too. She wanted to look and see what it was Rona saw, what the hell was so bloody interesting up there. Cassie turned her head, tilted her neck and looked. Hard. Too bright to be blue. It hurt. But she stood it. Cassie stood looking at the sky for a full minute before admitting it. There was nothing there.

There was nothing there.

Cassie turned back, refocusing through newly-bleached colour and sunspot blotches, rubbing her eyelids. And she reached for the camera. She reached and took the camera from Rona's hand, raised it to one eye, looked into the viewfinder. At the other side, a bee hovered much too near Rona's ear. Rona sat perfectly still in a haze of dizzy light particles that refused to settle down, waiting. Keeping her eyes on the sky.

We eat tarts at the side of the field listening to the car bonnet crack like a tray in the oven, searing our arms on the plastic seats. Rona puts the radio on and we listen to hellish French rock music, slewed to sound American. When Snow White singing Some day My Prince will Come comes on in the original, Rona puts the radio off and turns the ignition. Even on the road there is no air. We drive along the side of the river with no breeze, through miles of grey dust thrown up off the sideroads, on to the runnel of hot tar. My back running like glue, sticking to the seat. Arm blistering on the windowframe.

Tom. Happy as a pig in shit. Rows of compact arses turning their cheeks up to the sun in the guinness-coloured ovals of his shades. Not many beaches like that in Albania but Tom found one. His nose flexed at the sight of some kinds of woman. What he called a good handful, his eyes following cup-weights of unfamiliar flesh up the beach. Always put his palms on my buttocks when he danced. I stopped going with him to the disco after a couple of nights: thirty-two with a man glued to my bum for godsakes – I thought it was degrading. I thought the disco was degrading never mind anything else. I think I joined in to join in: I thought that was probably what most men expected to do on holiday with a new woman friend. I thought I'd better give it a go, not be stand-offish. Used to stand at the bar with him, feeling that big hairy arm round my shoulders. I thought I'm too old for this carry-on but I didn't say it. I thought maybe I was wrong. Hairiest arms I ever saw. Alien things, Tom's arms. In the mornings we waited for the bus against white walls slack with flowers, headed for the tourist beach: code-name for a place the police turned a blind eye to nudity provided it was the kind they liked looking at. Grass also a code name: it meant five foot high dune rushes. This yellow dust ribbon that passed for a road. If nobody was looking, I would wrap his hairy arms round me to hide from the sun, remembering what we had done before breakfast, after breakfast, putting on our things ready to leave. Tom's beautiful arms and what he could do with his mouth. I could feel the push of his tongue melting against me inside my jeans all day. I got a thrill just sitting down, walking with that aftermath: anything that noticed the extra lubricity. Sheltering in his arms waiting for the bus, trapped in the smell of that coarse black hair. He didn't always like me doing it, though. Not if the three men he found in the hotel who were also Aberdeen supporters turned up at the stop as well. Other things to do then. Anyway. Tom.

This is him again coming out of a toilet saying fuck off wittily. Serves me right. Finished right after the holiday and felt inexplicably terrible. I don't know what made me go anywhere with him at all. Och yes I do. I know fine. I've got one of him sticking his tongue out that still makes me break sweat.

Weakness. Same weakness every bloody time.

Bugs on the windscreen. The bloody thing needed cleaning. Again.

Rona d'you think we should have bought souvenirs?

Sorry?

Souvenirs before we left Saumur. Presents or something. We were there longest. Maybe we should have bought something to remember it by.

Rona rummaged in the glove compartment for a moment, threw a paper bag on to Cassie's lap. Cassie looked at it.

Open it. I wasn't going to give you it but you might as well. I bought it for you.

Cassie put her hand between the brown paper leaves, her fingers tipping something neither hard nor soft. She looked at Rona peering to see through the glass, flipping the indicator right.

On you go.

Slim white shaft, bulbous green tip. It was a marzipan penis, septic colour glittering faintly with icing sugar. Cassie looked at it hard. Then she looked at Rona.

Rona why did you buy me this?

Souvenir, she said. I nearly got you an artichoke but they were too dear. That was nicer anyway. I bet you thought it was a bluebell but it's not. Asparagus.

Cassie looked back down, watching the penis metamorphose. Not completely but enough. Asparagus. She shrugged her eyebrows, bit the tip off the sweet and rolled it in her mouth, offered the remaining piece to Rona.

207

Good?

Fine, Cassie says. Short-lived kind of souvenir but you can't have everything in this life.

Rona took a piece. She still didn't smile but there was more of a chance she might later. The lights changed. Something exploded on the windscreen, scattering legs over its whole breadth.

Cassie and Rona
Rona and Cassie

pulled away with the wipers clicking, waterless, fragments of shattered vitality shimmering before their eyes.

AMBOISE, erstwhile haunt of Charles VIII, Abd-el-Kader and Leonardo, is dominated by a château terraced high above the river, flanked by two stout towers. DON'T MISS the chapel of St Hubert (which purports to be the burial place of the great painter and inventor), the Logis do Roi (built by Charles VIII who died there) and the Manor of Le Clos Luce where da Vinci spent his last few years, now housing models of his inventions put together by IBM. Excellent local specialities like rillettes, goat's cheese and pastries will tempt jaded appetites.

Cassie saw Rona appear momentarily, disappear. Still looking the wrong way. Cassie waved and shouted again, knowing there was no point. Rona would not hear. Not all the way from the other side of the road. It was Cassie's fault. She had said she would wait by the bakery till Rona came back from parking the car then she hadn't done anything of the sort. She had crossed over, deliberately, nursing some kind of notion Rona would come back the same way she had left: it was meant to be helpful. Only she hadn't and it wasn't. Cassie saw Rona's head come and go again between too many people, the endless slow current of cars: blank and getting blanker. And it was entirely Cassie's fault. She was not where she said she would be.

Cassie pulled back the foot that had been hovering off the kerb just in time. A too-close bonnet tipped her arm on the way past, stinging like an iron burn. They couldn't have cared less these buggers. The foot could have been off: bone and minced muscle oozing out through the canvas straps and he still wouldn't have stopped. Taking her eyes off Rona for a second had lost her again though. Not so much as a single black hair still visible. Maybe she had turned the corner at the side of the patisserie, be headed off to godknows by this time. Clueless. There was no option. As Cassie tilted forwards, pushing away from the pavement into congealing traffic, she had a notion they jailed jaywalkers in France. Somebody's horn blasted the first two bars of Colonel Bogey but she was there, home and dry on the other side, moving through the crowd. And there was Rona, surfacing from the patisserie corner. Cassie shouted RONA, waving both arms in X shapes above her head. And Rona's head began to turn.

The split second before their eyes met, Cassie knew she had two choices. She could run towards Rona, smiling fit to bust, arms reaching till they merged, skirts swirling and rippling in slow motion, embracing in a dance of welcome, all blame and false starts forgotten, laughing soundlessly through a peal of church bells. Or she could shout RONA YOU DAFT BUGGER I'M OVER HERE.

Watching Rona, her face opening up like the sun, knowing She who was Lost had been Found and that Rona knew it too, Cassie made up her mind.

After all it's the same thing. Exactly the same thing.

Best Madeira Cake stall. Ayr. Richard. Smiling in the rain. I've only got this one and it's always a surprise. Used to come into the office from the Social Work place over the road and we got talking, coffees and theatre a couple of times kind of thing. Then he invited me to stay over at his place for the weekend. I thought about gift horses and widening your circle of possibilities the way I'd read in Being Single and Loving It. I tried to think constructively. Ok he was boring in the office but he might loosen up given the chance. He might be Lord Byron between the sheets. Not that I wanted to presume but he had invited me to stay over. Maybe I just thought he was boring because I had a masochistic fix on rotten men or something. He was a perfectly nice guy and maybe it was me that hadn't seen a way to appreciate that yet. Godknows. Condoms in the overnight bag anyway. Six. Just in case.

He'd bought tickets to the Ayr Flower Show. I took lots of pictures of leeks and dahlias. Then we went to Brief Encounter at an arty cinema he went to all the time: only foreign films and black and white, Cassie. They're the only ones worth watching these days. You got the feeling he'd read it somewhere. The worst was at his place, though, not knowing how to pitch anything: listening to CDs and drinking wine in separate chairs. Like teenagers gone wrong. I tried to make a joke of it but I only made him uncomfortable. He put his arm round me showing me where I could sleep, goodnight kiss at the bedroom door. Called me dear. Two different planes entirely. Nice enough big soul just och I don't know. Yes I do. Richard. Oh well.

BONJOUR.

A woman with two sets of lips opened the door.
She had pencilled-on eyebrows, hair red at the tips with white

210

roots like a sheep on fire and a single curler over one ear. Pink. The mouth that wasn't lipstick opened again, pursed itself round another BONJOUR so slow it came out as three separate words.

When Rona asked for a room, her face creased like an accordion, the scarlet nail of one finger beckoning us inside. The CHAMBRES 100F sign flipped over in the window. The back said COMPLET.

Ici.
A light switched on somewhere in front. Crimson flock wallpaper, green velvet curtains with tassels, two oval mirrors set in carved wood with big cracks and a four-poster covered with purple taffeta.

Lovely, Rona said. We'll take it.
She held out the money. The old woman took the note in one hand, held it up to the bulb and folded it away inside her palm in one movement. The key was offered in the other, poking between thumb and finger joint. She held on when Rona tried to take it from her, making Rona look up.

Aha, mes petites. You are English?
She waggled a finger at Rona's eyes. The thick whiff of incense gusted up from somewhere when she moved, incense and cough sweetie. Rona nodded hard, keeping a grip on her end of the key she'd payed for. Oui. Yes. Scottish.
Yes, beautiful English skin. She stroked Rona's cheek, the hand still holding half of a key. Beautiful English rose. And you are friends? The finger waggled again, the eyes slithering towards Cassie. Very good friends.
Yes, Rona said. Very good Scottish friends.
Ah. The woman fluttered her eyelids, pushing out both sets of lips. How beautiful. Beautiful. She stroked Rona's cheek again. Mes enfants, she inhaled, looking me straight in the eye behind a grin like a fish skeleton, Vous ne regretterez pas d'être venu en bel Amboise!

211

fourteen

Barry. Passport photo. Full lips the colour of fingernails and little white teeth, a mole on his neck that made me salivate, aching to suck. Barry christ Barry. I went in to use the phone in this bar and he just walked over, more or less invited himself home. It didn't seem outrageous, not even mildly cheeky. Just the calm expectation of someone who expected to be given things because he was beautiful. By and large he was right. Twenty-four he said. I lied. Undressed more elegantly than anyone I'd ever seen. Like he was in an advert. Four times later he suggested I come on a work trip with him, translating in Italy for a German company. He didn't give much away. I didn't let it worry me: maybe more could be less, I thought. Force me to keep my emotions to myself. Besides, that mouth. The way he slid from one language to another, unwilling to be explicable in any of them. Listening to him talk German on the phone made my entire lower half turn runny.

212

Italy was a precast concrete Riviera estate with stalls that sold inflatable pink horses with yellow spots and sunhats. Oldfashioned buckets and spades. Like Saltcoats only warmer. Actually I liked it. While he was out at work I would go along the shore front watching the people in their bathing costumes, knowing they weren't watching me; nipping into Spar for cheese and biscuits, the odd bar of Vanish to wash things through. In the afternoons, sleep; early evenings, another walk then back for a bath, waiting. Thinking about him coming back, sweaty and tie-slack, ripe for loosening off, completely consumed by lust. Eleven years younger than me and liked me to know it. You're my older woman, Cassie, leading me astray. Cold as a surgical glove. Skeletal hands and blue eyes, almost like a human's. That beautiful mouth he would not use to kiss. Turned out he saved that for another. Anyway. The shore front outside the hotel. What did I tell you?

Blackpool. Well nearly. Downtown Amboise. Admittedly I was feeling a bit funny when I took these but it was. Exactly like Blackpool.

⁂

A queue went twice round the Tourist Information place, past a shop with wee plastic dolls in costumes and hats with I ♡ AMBOISE written on. Posters for the Son et Lumière flaked off every visible wall, bunches of tickets for same begging from news-agent kiosks. Cassie and Rona stood on the patisserie steps ignoring a big cake with LULU and a wobbly stork in livid pink icing.

Rona had never been. Not Blackpool, not Alton Towers. If she was missing the allusion she didn't complain. She stopped looking at the cake and walked to the delicatessen next door.

Carottes râpées. What about those?
Whatever.

Rona rubbed her nose and looked. You said that the past two places as well.
I know. I'm tired. Just you get what you like and it'll be fine. I'm just tired.
Rona tilted her head to one side.
I'll be quite the thing. Get what you want.
Rona kept hovering at the doorway, one hand over the top of her bag where the purse was.
Look I'll just wait out here a wee while. On you go.
Rona went in. She disappeared behind the polarised glass then popped her head out again.

Cassie looked at her. Rona. Get the tea.

The whole of Rona disappeared.

Cassie leaned back against the roughcast, breathing out. Nearly four and the sun still belting you over the head that way it did here, pressing the sides of your skull together: spots in the dark when you closed and squeezed, closed and squeezed. The eyeball so dry it creaked. Cassie thought about what kind of drink might make the inside of her mouth feel better and came up with nothing. Nothing at all. She walked under the next awning, the next. Postcards with kittens on pastel-coloured grounds, tanned buttocks oozing from the sides of tiny slivers of coloured cloth. A copy of The Daily Express. No it wasn't. Yes it was. The Daily Express. Headline flapping back and forth in the draught from the main road DIANA ON SOLO HOLIDAY: CHARLES TOURS WALES.

Cooee.
Rona had emerged from the shop, a smart polythene bag over the crook of her arm. Holding an ice-lolly. I've got the tea then. You better like it. Peeling back the rocket wrapper like a stripper's glove

214

and drawing you a look. Her face changing. Are you ok?

Tired. You tell her you're tired. That you'll be fine in a minute.
You'll be fine after a walk.

Rona walks beside you, her mouth on an awkward bend where
the fuselage would be. Every so often she slips from three dimensions
into two, the sucking sound seems more distant. But you don't want
to worry her. You don't want to worry anyone at all.

Le Clos Lucé. This is a helicopter model. A cold air fan. Some
kind of war machine, I forget what. The room where da Vinci
died. The beams are artificial. Trompe l'Oeil. I can't
remember taking these at all. Can't remember anything about
that place really except I had to go and sit outside because it
was too hot. And on the way out I saw the wee handwritten
sign. **Exhibition: Service de Psychiatrie Infantile
d'Amboise**, an arrow through to a big white space, not
another soul inside. It was full of A4 paintings, collages of
peas and beans, grains and kernels that didn't look too
identifiable glued on polystyrene and stacked so they looked
like city skylines. Right in the middle, a table with a shadow
box, a wooden frame full of wee boxes like the kind that might
have contained baby shoes, sellotaped together, all filled with
something different. Pine cones, pebbles, macaroni in animal
shapes, plastic beads, raffia, dried grass, sand, earth, salt, soda
crystals and human hair. I looked at that one for a long time,
trying to make it look like something else but it wouldn't
co-operate. It was definitely human hair, sprouting from what
looked like a piece of hide. On the way out I took a closer look
at the paintings. That was when I saw this. Almost missed it
but I looked back at the last minute. Through the poster paint
sheep and cows, skeletons and roses, blobs and melting cakes,
all the way from the other side of the room. My mother. Some

little child with a sick head had painted a picture of my mother and it looked more like her than she did. She watched me all the way to the top of the stairs, big red eyes and this gentle purple smile. It took me a moment to realise I was doing it back. Thank god nobody else was down there. Anyhow there she is. You can't really see it properly but I wanted to take it anyway. One day I'm going to get it framed. The best photo of her I've got.

In the front-green size garden of Le Clos-Lucé, Cassie put her watch up to her ear then put it down again. It wasn't that sort of watch, the sort that ticked. She kept forgetting. The pain in her head was getting worse. Rona came out, a guide to what they had just seen in one hand.

You ok?
Cassie looked up at her hard. Rona's face blocked out the sun, the hard white light. On its own that felt good. Maybe she had sunstroke or something. Maybe that's why she was feeling dizzy. I'm fine, she said, knowing she didn't sound it. Knowing Rona would know she wasn't. Rona touched her arm. Cassie didn't move, just kept sitting, watching people queuing up to go into the house. If she moved she felt her head would just burst. It would just

ah god.

Rona kept standing. After a while she put her arm round Cassie's shoulder. Cassie didn't pull away.

You're roasting.

Palm on her forehead, cool and flat.
Cmon, we're going back. Let's go back and have our tea. You need a lie down. Ok?

Cassie giggled without wanting to and stared up at Rona.
Ok she said. Her teeth chattering. Ok.

Cassie saw it first. It was a cat. Huge ginger brute, white bits on the paws, plumb centre of the cobbled walkway. And it was moving. Very slowly. You knew it was moving because one of the white bits shifted position though the whole cat did not seem to be any further forward. Cassie stopped and watched. In the space of a whole minute, the cat moved from one paving stone to the next and sat down twice.

Mibby it's had a stroke, she said. Old, it could be very old.

The cat gave nothing away.

Mibby it's been run over and its internal organs are packing in. Mibby it's arthritic.

The cat was looking back now, a low growl beginning in the base of its throat.

It could have had an accident or something, it legs mibby broken and you can't tell under all that fur. It could be trying to get home and can't. Mibby it's stuck here.

The cat raised its bulk on to the four legs. It was so fat its belly reached down to the pavement even when it was fully upright; so fat you wondered how the thing moved at all. Maybe it was pregnant. Then it rolled onto its side, offering itself to be stroked and the swelling showed for what it really was. The belly wasn't belly at all. It was a tumour. A spongy, swollen growth ballooning half the beast's underside, the fur patchy. As though it had been grated away. In the gaps, the greyish leather of the cat's skin showed through, cracked as a dried mudbank. Hairline cuts fringed the edges of the main sore, bleeding watery fluid. The cat tried to arch its back in an effort to appeal again and wasn't able.

I know, Rona said. I know.

A crumpled paper hankie in her open palm. Here.
Cmon. We can't stand here all day.

Eventually Rona leads us both forward. We keep walking.

Rona pulled the curtains and turned round. Now then, she said,
breathing out in a decisive way. Her hands came together, fingers
interweaving as she raised one eyebrow. Now then.

The Nurse Routine.
Even through the haze, the tourniquet winding tighter behind
one eye and the dull hammering inside the skull, I recognise Rona's
Nurse Routine. I've seen her do this in Antwerp, Copenhagen,
Warsaw, Brodick and godknows where all. Now she does it here too.
I watch her lay out a dressing-gown, soap, a squeezy tube of
shampoo, two towels, three herbal teabags, two sachets of sugar, a
plastic spoon and a pack of two shortbread fingers. I watch her
plump up unplumpable bolsters, produce Healthy Living 40+ and
shove the opened cases under the bed with one foot. Behind closed
lids I hear her rummage behind the shower curtain, turn on the taps
and let the water run so it heats, dig the travel kettle out from the
brown bag and fill it at the wash-hand basin, tour the skirting,
follow the cable from the bedside lamp and burrow behind the
headboard to plug it in then emerge, dusting down, triumphant.

Right, she says. Shower, lie down, sleep. The food is there if you
get hungry. Two cups of tea before a sleep ok? Dehydration is no
good. You don't drink enough. I'll go out and get more mineral
water, maybe a couple of tickets for the Son et Lumière and you can
decide later ok? Ok?

Rona reaches towards Cassie, unbuckling her belt with one hand.

I told you that travel kettle was going to be useful. Did I lie?

The shower scudds against the plastic curtain, washing up spray. I acquiesce, docile as overcooked spaghetti. Que sera.

Prom front with big advert for babies' nappies. View every morning from the breakfast bar. He started at some hellish time in the morning so I always went on my own. Cappuccino and succo d'albicocca. Apricot juice. I didn't know the words for anything else and anyway I was never hungry. Waking up somewhere hot gets me like that. Then I was on my own, killing time while he went for two days down the coast, translating machine components and points of policy for German engineers. Heard him get out his side of the bed at seven and didn't even get up to wave him goodbye.

Picture of the waiter. No it isn't like me to take pictures of total strangers but I wasn't myself. Defying repression, or something. I thought I was being self-sufficient taking a photo of the waiter: being brave, challenging the boundaries. Thirty-five years old and that was the best I could come up with. That and lots of walks along the shore front. I remember everything about that holiday. The steepness of the kerb down to the road guttering, the precise colour of German beer cans and douts. Sharp red corners of empty cigarette boxes. No crisp pokes though. You could look along the sand for miles: there were definitely no crisp pokes or greasy papers. That made me think about being wee again, maybe as far back as being four or so: walking along the prom wall looking through the dunes at Glasgow folk who came and sat there on sand billowing with larded newsprint and blue Golden Wonder wrappers and cast-off ice lolly sticks. Folk sitting out on the shale hungry for sea and getting rain, half-stripped among the limpets and mouldering, limbless starfish, determinedly going about the summer. And here I was doing it again. Only it was an Italian beach. And it was me that was the tourist this time, kidding on I wasn't, sitting apart and watching people on the thin strip of buff sand. Even behind the dark glasses I thought people would notice: someone covered head to foot staring at strangers' crotches and bellies, their varicose veins, the weathered leather of middle-aged ankles opaque as snake skin. Beautiful pubescent girls lying out on towels, their legs wide part to tan the inside of their thighs and not caring, not giving a damn who looked. A generosity I couldn't match. I just stayed back on the shore wall, making mental lists of rubbish and driftwood, my own toenails. The skin of my ankles was thickening too. I thought about Barry elsewhere at some unspecified trades conference, translating from one language into another while I sat dumb on the side of the sand watching folk I didn't know, listening to the sea keeping coming. Shutting my eyes just made it worse. I was on the verge of hyperventilating when a kitten came out. A black and white kitten diving at something under the railing along the edge of the shore wall then chewing. It took a minute for me to work out what it was. A tomato. Pretty flattened out and sort of disembowelled but definitely a tomato. I watched it chewing till a child ran up and scared the thing away but it had been there, eating this unlikely thing, something that was not real sustenance but maybe enough. It made me feel so good I thought I was going to cry but I walked back to the hotel bar instead.

It was still open. It was open all the time. Different waiter, thank christ. I ordered a glass of something yellow that tasted of coconuts then sat down. Stuck. I'd finished the novel and didn't like to stare at people when I was on my own. So I drank the drink fast and went back out again, keeping under the trees. I walked back to where I had seen the kitten and found a piece of cold meat where the tomato had been. For some reason finding that cold meat made me feel terrible. Like I'd fallen off the edge

of the world. Maybe it wasn't the same place at all but I'd lost
all certainty. That's what it was. Confusion. I felt so confused I
wasn't sure I could remember the way back to the hotel. I
looked back and forward and they both looked equally
unwelcoming, equally unkent. I can't remember how I got back
but I did. Of course I did. I went straight back to the room and
lay flat out on the bed. I must have fell asleep and dreamed
something nice because I remember being disappointed when I
woke up. So I just lay on, watching it get darker outside, the
lights of the bay going on outside. Red furthest off, white closest
to. The heat getting no less. Eventually I managed to get up and
stood out on the balcony where there wasn't enough room for a
chair till I felt cool enough to sleep. I didn't even want to brush
my teeth in case it made me hot again. Just lay there, waiting for
inertia to become more complete. At least night removes the
guilt you should be doing something. It's ok to lie in the dark
and wait.

I thought a lot about the kitten and the tomato.
It gave me great hope.

When Barry came back we fucked for hours but didn't laugh
much. It wasn't till we were on the flight back he did the I've
Been Thinking speech. What he'd been thinking about was his
boyfriend: a man he'd been involved with for two years on and
off, soldier in a UN pe.. :ekeeping force: a worry, a heartache
and, most of the time, an absence. Barry had needed time to
work out his feelings and now he'd decided. Despite the
problems, Tim was what he wanted. I'd been very nice and very
kind but you couldn't help who you loved. He realised he'd been
using me and he was sorry but he was going back to Tim. Sorry,
he said, and thanks for everything. Sorry.

Sorry.

It knocked the stuffing out of me for a long while. Even asking /

for that little from someone had proved too much. When I look back I realise of course he didn't know what I'd been investing in the thing. I only had the vaguest notion of that myself. Just a young thing. He phoned on my birthday and sent a card. With love on your thirty-sixth, Barry and Tim XXXX.

I can't wear this thing.

Rona looked. I don't see why not.

Rona. Cassie tried to sound exasperated. It came out pathetic. Look at me.

Cassie held her arms out, raising the quilt like batwings to make it look worse.

What's wrong with you?

Rona I'm wearing a piece of bedding for christsake. Kidding on it's normal isn't going to work. Look at me.

Rona finished a mouthful of carrot and smiled.

Well?

Well nothing, she said, still chewing. If you're going, you're wearing that. I'm not presenting you with an option.

I'm feeling better after that sleep though. It was just a touch of sunstroke or something. I'm feeling a lot better.

Good. Let's keep it that way.

Cassie looked at Rona and Rona meant it.

What if the woman sees it? She'll think we're pinching the bloody thing.

Cassie knew as soon as she said it, though. She knew Rona had won.

Look who's got the Guide badge for First Aid? Rona said, knowing fine.

Cassie dropped her arms where they belonged and looked back in one of the mirrors. Maybe Rona was right. Maybe anybody in their right mind would go out wearing a quilt if they weren't feeling great.

Anyway, it's lovely. They'll think you're part of the show.
Cassie looked. They'll think I'm your mother.
Rona opened the door laughing. They won't be far wrong then, will they?

Cassie couldn't think what she meant by it.

I just couldn't get a handle on what that meant at all.

I said we were too far away but she took them anyway. The yellow blobs on a black ground are knights on horseback carrying torches. This broken telly effect is meant to be jugglers. This is a lot of the backs of people's heads in front and this och this was a woman dangling a lot of blonde wig out of a tower window. Damsel in distress. You'll need to take my word for it. The tannoy was terrible: neither of the two of us had a clue what was going on. Halfway through, three pages came right up to where we were sitting and changed costume. The noise of velcro drowned everything else out. Anyway it was very pretty. Childlike and harmless, eager to please. I didn't take any pictures of my own because I was wearing a quilt and the logistics were too complicated but Rona took plenty. This was a procession of ducks. My favourite bit. You can't see a thing of course. But I remember the quality of dark. You can feel the ducks even if you can't see them. That picture's got atmosphere.

A candle lit in the room when we got back late, Rona's travel kettle switching itself off and on in the corner, boiled dry. The corner of the blanket was turned back at one corner, towels folded again at the bottom of the bed. A trail of chypre and cough sweetie ghosting the threadbare rug.

Tree in Hyde Park. The year Rona went to Lincolnshire for a wedding and I was on my own. Whitehall, changing the guard just to see. Like another planet. I couldn't work out what was meant to be interesting about it. Went twice to check and it wasn't any better. It wasn't any worse but it wasn't any better. Spent the rest of the time in the Tate, dotting from Blake to Bacon, pottering about in bookshops, watching telly late in my room. Teamaking facilities. Godsend. I went looking for the place we'd stayed in all those years before but it wasn't there. Toby Inn instead. Didn't know what to do with the camera at all. So. Tree in Hyde Park. All I've got to show.

Cassie's head was clear.

It might not have wanted to be awake very much but it didn't hurt. She drank two cups of herb tea made with mineral water boiled in the travel kettle then asked if she could stop now.

Rona, enough's enough eh? No more herb tea.

Rona held Cassie's chin in one hand, looked into her eyes.

Seen better, she said, but you're ok. You'll do.

The patronne, in lace and plum-coloured satin, is sad. One night only, she says. It is too soon. She embraces me. Rona hauls luggage about, keeping clear. When I can, I pull away, aware of a lipstick smear on my cheek. The patronne waits at the doorway, arms hugging her own shoulders. Getting smaller. Vous reviendrez, n'est ce pas?

Rona stops at the end of the road, waves.

Wave, Cassie. Don't you want to wave?

I keep walking. Forwards.

The car was in full sun and jammed. Wedged between the one in front and one behind, less than inches between. Rona stared at the too-small gaps, the rub mark on the rubber bumper.

It's what we get for sleeping in, said Cassie. Hedonism doesn't pay.

Rona paced the bit of pavement next to the car, getting pinker, dark centres forming on her cheeks.

Look, it's probably just a temporary thing, maybe somebody parking fast to get somewhere in a hurry and coming right back. They could be back any second. We'll have our breakfast and think of something, ok? We'll think of something.

My appetite is back. I have breakfast in the pink cake shop while Rona glares at everyone and everything, searching out a culprit. She says only one word. BASTARDS. Then goes back inside herself, unreachable. A machine makes her lose her appetite and wear her heart on her sleeve. She goes to the toilet, sullen. I shout after her: Nobody's dead, Rona. Look on the bright side for christsake: nobody's dead. I couldn't give a shit who looks. When we go out, both cars have gone. Clear space front and back, miles if we want it.

I say nothing. Nothing at all.

fifteen

CHENENCEAU château 1515 no guides boat trips guardroom chapel bedrooms furniture kitchens waxworks walk in the park children's facilities selfservice restaurant

The queue goes round the wall. Colour stills of hamburger, frites and steack haché hang at ear level, close-ups of sauce bottles tilting red goo over the heads of those under five foot one. There are cakes, pastries with yellow icing, sachets of salt and vinegar, a Littlewoods cafe doocot of perspex cages. Rona waves her tray to let me know where she is, the progress she has made. Cassie leans forward to wave back, feels something cold sucking her elbow. Puddle of spilled tea. It runs in a narrow stream down to a wrist, drips three brown drops onto the overpolished boards. Perfect circles. Sugar crystals make prisms under the table near a splat of gateau. Cassie scans other tables for a cloth, already imagining stacking cups, carrying them off elsewhere. On the other side of the room, Rona taps the cover of a polythene-wrapped bread roll, replaces it behind the screen. Choosing for two. The least Cassie can do is tidy up. Clothless, she shoves spilled crumbs with the edge of one hand into the cup of the other, gathers cutlery dirtied by previous unknown persons and notices herself singing. Blueberry Hill. Bugger the waxworks and the kitchens and the walk in the park. We want food, drink, a wee sit down. Rest. We can make the place ok and be lazy if we like and it aint nobody's business but our own.

Rona waves and shouts, There's Bovril. I could get you Bovril if you fancy it.

We can do anything we bloody well like. We're on our holidays.

Five people make a crowd. I sit in one of the front pews to get out the way, not rushing. A German trio look at the chapel walls, saying *ach wie schon* to no-one, go out to make way for another trio from the same tour bus. The next three begin with the boards at the doorway, a big white sandwich in four languages. The board tells them to look for grafitti scratched into the wall hundreds of years ago by the Scots guards of Mary Stuart with a wee drawing in case you can't find it. Antique Ts and Ds, the odd H hollowed out by stranded soldiers. The Germans peer at the stone wall, screwing up their eyes to make out the single letters surfacing through the blond blocks. They look at the ceiling, the font, the carpet covering the aisle and repeat themselves. *Ach wie shon*. They leave not seeing the best. Because the best is not so well publicised. What it is is here: behind a plastic panel at my elbow, a whole word a dead man took the time to chip into resistant masonry, four-lettered, legible, clear.

HAME.

Ouques is nothing special. The map shows no windmills or castles or crosses, free of coloured threads, the blue bisections of representational water and dot-to-dot towns: no promises. Rona and Cassie point the car in its direction and keep driving.

Do you mind getting older Rona?

Rona's arm settled on the open window frame, wee blisters of peeled skin open on the wrist.

Getting older, Rona. Do you mind it?

Rona didn't turn or look. What's that apropos of?

It's not apropos of anything, just a question. An attempt at engagement.

Ok ok she said. The car tilted round a corner, sides of the old road vanishing, the new one opening up. Rona checked the rear mirror again. Ok. Do I want to get old?

Cassie sighed. I didn't say do you want to get old. I said do you mind getting older.

Same thing.

No it isn't.

How isn't it?

Because it isn't, that's how. Of course it isn't. There wouldn't be any point asking you if you want to get old: you'll get it anyway. You get old whether you want to or not. Getting old is not an option, it isn't something you've any say in at all. I said do you *mind* getting older as in what are your thoughts on the process.

Look, she said. I still don't see a difference. There isn't any say about the process either is there? Not much point in minding when that's inevitable as well.

This was either an interesting point or nothing to do with anything. Cassie chose.

Yes there is. Just because something's inevitable doesn't mean you don't have feelings about it. They're maybe not feelings that

228

make any difference to the facts of the matter but you can have them all the same. You don't not think about inevitabilities. In fact inevitabilities are the very things you get feelings about for the very reason that's what they are ie inevitable. Whereas to ask if you want something is to suggest you have a degree of control over getting it or not which is redundant. It is a daft assumption ergo I wouldn't bother making it. And I didn't.

Rona's face was flat as Normandy. Oh? she said. Oh?
What d'you mean Oh? There's no Oh? about it.
Rubbish.

Cassie said nothing. No point arguing with a closed statement. There was just no point. It didn't matter a damn what you thought might be worth sharing with another human being if they refused to co-operate. You couldn't *make* people be reasonable. They either were or they weren't and this time, maybe Rona wasn't. Closed statements. They were the last refuge of the moral coward, a cheat and an insult but there was no point in saying or Rona would just say it again.

Cassie sucked in, blew out, waiting. After a decent interval, she tried again.

Well? Have you?
Have I what?
Any feelings about the fact that you're withering on the stem as we sit here driving through the ageless French countryside? The fact you're getting older, Rona.
You've asked me this before.
Well this is me asking you again.
You do though. You ask this periodically. You've got a thing about it.
Are you not answering then? You're not answering because I've asked you this before?
No, just I'm saying. You have. Every so often you do. You ask

me about Getting Older. That and telling me you've discovered The Meaning of Life for the umpteenth time. She laughed. The time we went to the Rijksmuseum, remember? I had to haul you out the gallery where you'd been to see the Sunflowers and that other picture, whatever it was. Potato Eaters. After we saw the Potato Eaters in that wee Van Gogh room?

Something was tightening in Cassie's insides. She could feel it.

We walked the whole length of two streets with you telling me about The Meaning of Life and the same night we went to see Amadeus and it happened again. Amadeus with subtitles. You were roaring all the way back to the hostel about Life, the Universe and Everything. You finally had it sussed. Twice in the one day. Neither of us was allowed any sleep that night for you talking about it and writing things down in a wee notebook so you wouldn't forget. Remember?

Rona's arm lolling on the rolled down window ledge.

Remember?

Rona didn't speak for a minute. Her voice was softer when it came back. I mean it's just one of those things you do every so often. That and asking me what I think about things.

I'm just saying. Just remarking. Cassie?
Rona looked over, her face studious with concern.
Are you ok?

Cassie didn't know. She didn't know the name for what she was feeling. It was more like scared than anything else. Or confused. Threatened. There was no telling if Rona knew she was doing it either, if she meant to make Cassie feel such an observed thing. An object. A kind of ridiculous object at that. Whatever, Cassie could think of nothing to push it away. There was no denying it. She really had done these things. The notebook existed. It not only existed it was in the case, here with her. It was in the boot of the bloody car: full of homilies and maxims ready for when the going got rough, things written down and waiting, ready for

Cassie couldn't think what they were ready for but she knew she was glad they were there. Now she wondered what Rona saw. What Rona had been making of her all this time. What shift might be occurring. Dealing with the sickening notion that Rona might not have been on the same side after all this time was making the root of Cassie's tongue taste of sour. Of incipient sick.

Look.
From far away, Cassie saw Rona pointing. She was pointing out of the opened window, slowing down.
Look.

OUQUES with a slat through the sign. It meant Ouques was finished. They had driven through and not even noticed they had been anywhere. The slatted signpost slipped under the dip on the underside of Rona's elbow before she pulled on the brake.

Cake shop, she said. Place open a wee bit further back. I don't think you saw it though, you were miles away. Have a wee walk or something. Fresh air. I'll go and get us something in the shop. Cakes or something. Rona patted Cassie's knee. Treat, ok? I'll get them.

Cassie watches Rona stroll the car down the deserted street that might well be the only street just beyond the pinpoint of Ouques. The way she waits on the kerb, looking left and right right and left like a Tufty Club devotee, the way she gets herself across the road, almost able to be called skipping. Free of malice after all, after all.

Rona off to buy cakes. Light and free.

Cassie sighed out, letting her whole ribcage off the brake. A remarkable woman, Rona. How the bugger managed it. The way she could caw the feet from under you along with any certitude about who was asking whom what: how she managed every time to get out of commitment. Cassie shook her head, miming I AM DUMBFOUNDED for nobody. Her neck weighing back against the headrest, mouth curling at the edges. Somebody needed to write it down. How the bugger did it. Every time. Every bloody time.

Light rain on the roof, broken scars on the side window.

On the other side of the road, Rona waits in the shop doorway with the box in one hand, angling herself over to save it getting wet before she is ready to move. I watch Rona, the Protectress of Cakes, Avoider of Decisions, Angel and Devil hover at the beginning of the assault on the crossing again and wind down the window to shout.

Decisions Rona. I'm making the decisions round here. Now get your arse over here with the grub.

Rona laughing, not making out a word. Not knowing we are going back to Chartres. We said we would and we are. Somebody has to be definite and it might as well be me. It's what Cassie does: she decides. We're going back to Chartres.

Cathedral towers over the fields. Rotten photo. It's not fog, just time of night. And filth. I took it through the car window after we'd been driving all day, the car still moving. I've only kept it because I remember taking it, remember the feeling of coming in over the fields and towards somewhere I sort of knew. It doesn't actually matter you can't see the towers, I know they're there. That's what I like about this one. That I took it for me. Just for me.

A room in a small hotel right in the old quarter costs only 20F more than the place we stayed in last time. I look at Rona and she looks at me. There all the time and we didn't know.

We didn't know because we didn't look, Rona says. Sunglasses fall from her case. You're never done laughing at me for doing research but it pays off. Impatience, Cassie. Impatience is the downfall of more women than strong drink shit.

A brown ball made of popsocks rolls under the bed. Cassie retrieves it, hands it across without letting go.

There's no time like the present though. A stitch in time saves nine. A rolling stone gathers no –

Rona's mouth withers. Never mind being smart. Anyway. She looks round the room, the painted rose on the ceiling flaking like dandruff. This is nice, isn't it?

Rona leans on the bidet tap, shooting cold water on to her front.

Cassie raises an eyebrow. Look before you leap. Anyway hurry up. I'm starving.

Rona tilts like a puppet, hands dripping. Cassie's stomach changes gear: squirting caustic juices and grinding its cogs. Ready.

The black dog is out on the balcony, carved saints visible from the corner of the street. Old times. I order two more drinks and make it four. We sit in opposite chairs, Rona writing messages on cards she has already stamped and will forget to post. I watch Rona writing, drink getting warmer inside my gut. Out late with Pernod and chips. Just like old times.

One time after we had the separate holidays and it was terrible, back at work with the whole two weeks finished, the two weeks I get through the screaming mundanity of work thinking about then we were back with me thinking I'd wasted the whole lot and had to take a week off work because I thought I was going to implode and Rona took the same week off for moral support the two of us kidding on we both had summer flu anyway that time

there was a whole week to play with and all I did was sleep. I mean right through. Rona thought I had glandular fever. Or ME. Office workers get it, she said; it's the stress and boredom. It's overwork. It's frustration at doing repetitive tasks. She came up with lots of ideas but none of them woke me up. She took me out instead. For five days she came round in the morning, checked my buttons were done up then walked me down the close stairs. Every day for five days. Inside the car she did up the seatbelt and said Right we can go anywhere we like only I could never think of anywhere I liked. I couldn't think at all. By the last day she was fed-up with that tactic and said this time it was a surprise. I slept all the way. I recall the car stopping and opening my eyes in a kind of rolling motion, hoping the lids would stay up long enough for me to be able to see more than dots and dashes of light but it didn't work. They closed again. She got out, opened the door at my side and said We're here and I moaned. Couldn't be shifted. I slept in the car while she went for a walk. Then she came back and had another go. We could get coffee in the Visitor Centre, she said. That didn't work either. I slept till she came back with two National Trust teatowels and Edinburgh Rock and she drove us back. I still can't remember where the hell it was even from repeated telling. Bannockburn maybe. I think it was Bannockburn. Anyway, it was terrible. Not that it hadn't happened before. I've sleep-walked round Ephesus and taken photos in the hope of remembering what the Blue Mosque might look like when I'd be more able to focus: I've started out of a stupor nearly falling off the steps of the Duomo in Milan and wished I were prone on top of Goat Fell. I don't remember when it started but I did know it had been going on for a while. It had certainly happened before all right only that was the worst. It was the worst partly because it happened with Rona. The awaydays and weekend trips, the breaks and nights out with Rona that I'd never counted as main events, the pieces that had always been there no matter who else wasn't, I never thought it would happen with Rona. Somehow Rona didn't count. Now she did and I thought it was the beginning of the end. I thought I might stay like that forever.

Anyhow.

I look at the other side of the table and Rona looks back. I see her doing it. She smiles, goes back to writing postcards with a purple felt-tip, the glass creaking with ice behind the fold of her knuckles, fitting wee words into a wee space. Rona. You turn round sometimes and she catches you unawares by being beautiful. Not in a way that is like everyday beauty but more like something beautiful in a painting, to do with the way it moves into the light or the set of how the features lie at particular moments. Because Rona is not beautiful in the magazine sense. She has this big hooter for a start, dry skin so her cheeks sometimes look like floured dough and sometimes you see something awful like sleep in at the roots of the lashes, sleep like grit where the lashes poke through the soft lid making you want to scream or scrub her face with Vim to get rid of the mortal signs, this flaking and sore human redness. Then other times it melts out into soft focus like there is a thin layer of light just under the skin or round the periphery of her face so it glitters; the lips full like plum flesh under pale membrane, little cracks on the skin so you could almost touch them, run a finger over to feel the texture. I have woken next to Rona's face in Salisbury and Leith, watched it mottle with cold walking for miles to save bus fares in Arran, Amsterdam and Gouda, seen it feed itself cheese sandwiches in Munich, Helsinki, Copenhagen, and Kirkwall. It has found me a puppy carved out of yellow stone, roses in the dark, sunflowers and

ah god.

Cramp sears through one buttock and makes me sit upright, out of a slump. I order another two drinks and wonder if this is a good idea. No it isn't. Of course it isn't. But I do it anyway. Tomorrow we will go to the cathedral and find Rona's zodiac carvings, sit with one coffee in the pub and

och wait and see Cassie

wait and see.

Dear god.
Creases round my eyes. No, I wasn't coming out of a darkened
room, it was just the way the cathedral was even at that time
in the morning. Overcast and no candles. I wasn't feeling as
bad as that looks och that's a lie I was so but I was trying to
make it not matter. Anyway we were on the way out, getting
ready to pull the big door open when a noise like a cold air fan
started up, something whirring away right over our heads. A
bird. A trapped bird had settled on the beam above the North
Door and every so often battered itself against the beams,
trying to get out. You could only just see it in the gloom in
there, fluffing up its wings to look braver. I couldn't think
what to do for a moment. Obvious things escape me out of
habit. Then it dawned. Just open the door. I held the big
metal handle and started pulling, letting the light in, white
light from the overcast sky outside. I figured even if it was
blind it would feel the fresh air, it would know which way to
go without hurting itself. And it did. We didn't have time to
even see what colour it was. So that's me, standing at the door
after I opened it, looking up: my back fading into the
darkness and my front bleached out, looking up to see where
the bird had gone. I couldn't of course but that's me doing it
anyway. You can see the sore head just looking at it. Serves me
right.

Rona rearranges flakes of pastry off her front, picks up the coffee cup with the same hand.

ROUEN, she says. It says here Rouen is a beautiful city with exceptional historic monuments discover history the 10th Century Viking Rollo, William the Conqueror, Joan of Arc, Corneille and Flaubert, cathedral, fine Arts Museum, plenty churches, Art School, place they burned Joan of Arc, carparks within easy reach of historic heart of old Rouen. We don't need to see the cathedral if you don't want though.

She shuts the book, pushes the specs up the bridge of her nose and says I'll drive then, will I?

Joke.

Tom with a pair of trousers on his head. Stag night. He seemed to feel the need to send me it along with a wedding photo. She looks perfectly ok, doesn't she? Horribly young. And married to Tom. You never know. She might still be. Anyway. Tom with a pair of trousers on his head. Expressing himself.

> Despite constant heavy traffic and a naturally damp climate, ROUEN is a beautiful city. Much of the old was, infamously, bombed heavily during WW2 and many new shopping and pedestrian malls now occupy old sites. There is still much of history (the 10th Century Viking Rollo, William the Conqueror, Joan of Arc, Corneille and Flaubert are a few of the famous associated with the city's legend) though present glory rests in ROUEN's importance as a thrusting business and industrial centre, a triumph of reconstruction after the dreadful damage sustained throughout the Second

World War. DON'T MISS the Place du Vieux Marché, the centuries old market place where Sainte Joan was burned at the stake in 1431 – avoid paying the inflated café prices if you can!

You missed a lot of this out Rona.

Rona knows.

After four, we reach Rouen.

sixteen

Big orange flowers with grey leaves cover the walls. There are green brocade curtains, a grey carpet with overlapping brown blobs and a chandelier. Cassie dumps the case on the bed and pushes open the toilet door, shouts A BATH RONA A BATH. Spreadeagled at the window, a curtain in each hand like Samson, Rona finds a view. She does not check the bath, I do not check the view. Fine, we say. Fine. We'll take it.

The Musée des Beaux Arts/Museum voor Schone Kunsten/ Museo de Bellas Artes/ Museum der Schönen Künste/Museo de Arte says it has a fine selection of paintings from every European tradition. We see only paintings by the men of that tradition. They've painted lots of women to make up. There is a

Woman (attrib)
Woman at a mirror
Woman at her toilette (pastel)

Woman bathing
Woman drying herself
Woman powdering herself
Woman lifting her chemise
Woman seated in a garden
Woman sewing
Woman in a hat with veil
Woman in a dress
Woman in distress
Woman on her deathbed, eyes red-rimmed and skin going green.

Right, says Rona.
I look at her, she looks at me.
Culture fatigue, she says. I vote we go back to the room and look at each other.

Enough. We've had enough.

The curtain makes a noise like old rolling stock, rusty as hell. Between the fan of her own feet, splayed apart on the end of the spread, Cassie watches Rona pull the second across and put it into neat folds before padding through to the bathroom. Blisters on the ceiling. A spring under a shoulderblade twangs inside the mattress. Cassie kicks off one sandal, the other.

Christ I'm tired.

The toilet flushes. Bathroom. We have a room with bath. I shut my eyes thinking about the bath through where Rona is, imagine it full. Neck-deep. I could run such a bath and soak there, the steam softening my face for an hour, get out, roll myself in thick towelling to dry and slop around in satin, eating delicacies from silver dishes. Opposite, the church, the stained glass and the boules pitch will lengthen and fade while I savour wine and the sky turns a sameness of sea-deep velvet shot with a promise of stars. Elegant. Self-contained. Unlikely.

Ah god.

Come again? Rona in her bra and knickers looks down from the side of the bed. I didn't catch. You said something and I missed it.
Just ah god.
Rona misses it again, opening the case, searching for something clean to put on. I watch her throwing things about under the lid and know what will really happen. Rona will put on a T-shirt and go shopping. Then I'll get up, push the card table to the window, spread the spare sheet for a tablecover and hunt for flowers. There is always a bathroom tumbler and there are always flowers. I've found them straying out from under hedges, in churchyards, edging their way round dustbins in back alleys and growing out of cracks between the paving; in gutters and ditches, fallen from windowboxes and hidden among treeroots. Weeds count. We've lunched over a single dandelion, the odd daisy or stem of cow parsley. I'll find something floral and make the table nice. Then I'll run a bath and lie in it listening for the key turning, the rustle of paper, the wee noises that mean Rona has brought parcels of food. There will be opening and closing of drawers. I will lie in the still bathwater listening, imagining her under the plastic chandelier, raking through batteries and lengths of string, spare travel adaptors, elastoplast and Diocalm for the bottle-opener. I'll be listening for the silence. The silence that always comes before she sees the table and laughs like it's a surprise. On her own in the other room she'll say it out loud: I don't know how you do it Cassie, I really don't, laughing at me/with me/for no reason I'm ever clear about except it doesn't seem to be anything harmful. Whatever the reason is, it's ok. But that is to come. For now there she is at the end of the bed, cased in cerise and white, turning to let her eyes find mine.

241

We need more cash, she says, bouncing the purse in one hand. Then I'll get us some food while I'm out. Want me to run you a bath? Seeing everything I'm thinking. Knowing fine.

The door clicks shut. I get up and go across to the window, watch her cross the road. Lipstick stripes band her chest: I couldn't miss her if I tried. On the road in front, a couple walk hand in hand. Just as I'm about to leave the window, something happens. The couple. He pulls her towards himself so violently, she almost falls. They both stop walking, locked. It takes a moment before I realise what he's doing. It's a kiss. His hat tilts back as his mouth encloses hers, one leg of the navy uniform trousers a brace so she does not fall. Merely a kiss. Rona pulls alongside and past them, hardly altering her stride. Shockproof. She just keeps going.

Eglise de St Ouen. Right outside the window. It would have hung around outside the window whether I bothered with it or not but I thought I'd take it anyway. What I seen on my holidays by Cassie Burns aged 39½. Just a photo.

By late evening the sound of traffic outside makes hairpins, individual crescendoes that rise and fall from a distant wash. A bike with the baffles out, birds arguing, a diesel train. Rona sits up, shadowy against the wallpaper marigolds, reaching for the jar of gherkins. The packet of German biscuits with the Italian name is at her elbow, the other bottle of cider on top of the bedside table. Within easy reach. Rona wears her vest and blue knickers: Cassie, a white-going-grey cardigan over her red satin. A piece of gold brocade trim is peeling from the nearest curtain, the threads that held it loose as laces near the open edge. Cassie pours, drinks, settles back against the pillow wondering if this is what they call a companionable silence. Whatever it is, we share it: Madame Bovary open between two lumps on the bedcover, Rona's brown bag, the car specifications manual. Maps and POTTED FRANCE. We have been this way forever.

This is the life, says Rona.

Nothing else happens for five minutes, then Rona pours us both some more cider. Still holding her glass, she slides down the bedcover into a prone position, the free arm above her head, tumbler resting on her chest. Ah, she says. The life. Another five minutes. Eventually, Cassie says

Rona?
Mmm? She doesn't look over.
Cassie waits till she's ready, sipping. See your grandad's letters?
Mmm?
What d'you make of them?
What d'you mean, what do I make of them? She lies flatter on the spread, rolling her head to ease the muscles in her neck.

I mean what d'you make of them? As in d'you think he was normally like that? I mean normally affectionate?

Rona lies still for a while, flexing her wrists in the air till the bones make a soft cracking noise.

Dunno. He could have been affectionate but I don't know. Why d'you ask?
I was just thinking. I was just thinking about that bit at the end where he said something about being spared to come back and be better for her or something like that.
Hold on. Her hand flaps out. It's here somewhere. Here.
Desiccated paper flutters onto Cassie's chest, a dying moth.

Right here.

Cassie opens it to show willing but the writing is too fine. There's not enough light. She takes another sip of cider, peers some more.

I can't see it right, Rona. You know the bit I mean though. Where he says he was glad he ran away because it was the only way to see her. And something about hoping he'll get back so he can do more for her than he had in the past. You know the bit I mean.
Mhm. She sniffs, puts her hand out, open. Give me a try.
Rona. What makes you think you can read it if I can't. You're the one that wears specs. If I can't read it –
Rona snorts, pushes the open hand out again. Give.

Cassie hands it over, sighs, sips. Rona sits up, squinting hard, humming and muttering.

Right. Royal Warrant 5 days CB only for 1 days absence I something something got round the orderly something giving him 1/- for a drink so that . . . um . . . shows . . . god.

She changes position, lifts the letter so it almost touches her chin.

I was very glad I ran away de da de da for the sake of the bairns is that bairns for the sake of the bairns it is hard times something something here it's Here it is. I will always be thinking of you and the bairns no matter where I go to. Now Maggie I will bid you farewell I hope to be spared to come back & to do more for you than I have in the Past.

She emerges having proved something from behind the paper. Is it that bit? she says. Knowing fine.

Cassie listens to the birds outside. After a while she says Yes slowly. Yes. That's the bit. So what d'you think it means?

What do I think what means?

244

The thing you just read. The wanting to come back and do more for her thing. Is it guilt or what? I mean who d'you think he wrote it for?

Rona's travel alarm ticking.

Ok. What I'm asking is d'you think it's about some kind of guilt he's getting off his chest in which case, it's for himself, or is it affection? I mean is it *really* for her?

Rona cracks a knuckle then lies very still.

Well. Another finger cracks. I suppose it's some kind of affection. But there's something about hoping she doesn't mind him saying it that sounds kind of embarrassed. I don't think it could have been all that natural for him.

Ticking.

Hellish isn't it? Hellish.

What? Rona lies down again, stretches full out beside me. Our toes touch.

Och everything. Having to bribe somebody to let it be ok you ran away to see your wife. The army trying to make sure anything that resembled tenderness had no legitimate place in case it got in the way of getting them to fight. Repression. The idea that was probably the most affectionate he ever managed to spit out, maybe even the most meaningful thing he ever said to her in terms of him letting her know what she meant to him then he never got to come back. Then he never got to act on it. The whole thing is hellish.

Ticking.

Och he maybe never would have acted on it anyway. Rona sits up, pours herself more cider, lies back. Maybe he was only able to find out he thought that because of the situation. He was maybe only able to say it precisely because he thought he wasn't coming back. Extremis. Like drink. You can say anything you like then and get

245

dispensation later. Maybe that's just my experience though. I don't know. I don't know what kind of man he was at all. She never talks about him. Not like that anyway. Not anything revealing.

Hellish.

Hellish.

Agreed, we make gullet noises into the ticking for a while, let it get darker. We both look up, imagining the ceiling.

Rona?
What?
How come you don't bother with men much? I mean you never seem to miss not having one around.

I feel the split second going ear to ear, tightening in my chest before I know it was ok to ask.

Well there was Iain.
I know there was Iain.

Something parks under the window outside. Doors open and close. Rona swallows.

I suppose that was enough. I've just never wanted to repeat it badly enough. Och sure some things would be nice but I think . . . well it's just too big a drain on your time. You know? You only get the one shot at things and men use up too much energy. It's just too easy to miss out on what your own life might be about with one of them about the place. They need a lot of attention, one way and another. I suppose there's other things I'd rather be doing.

Is there nothing you miss though? Really and truly nothing?

Rona swallows again, coughs, moves her feet.

Sex, I suppose.

Cassie looks at Rona, a nose lying next to her sheeny in the thickening dark.

Sex is only sex though. I mean you've got to be able to talk about something afterwards and that starts up a relationship. Dependencies build up, then the power games: the moral blackmail, the intellectual blackmail, the guilt, the guilt – it goes on forever. Trying to make him take on his fair share of the work involved, and I mean the emotional work as well as the cleaning the toilet stuff. I don't want it. Not all that. I can't be bothered. The idea of having a man in my life is attractive all right. If I'm drunk or something. The idea can be fine. But that's all it is. I'd rather keep it that way. The actual thing is another matter entirely.

She pulls herself on to an elbow, looks over.

I always liked the smell of aftershave though. Old Spice. My dad used to wear it. Apart from that, and the possibility of kids, the answer's no. I don't miss anything. Not since I grew up. Nothing at all.

I look at the ceiling changing shape, rods and cones filtering dwindling light. Rona takes another sip of her drink.

The question is, she says and I turn, see a face delicate under wet hair; her eyes heavy, lips full. The question is how come you *do* miss them, Cassie? How come you *do*?

Ticking. A key being tried in a lock somewhere close, tumblers falling into place. My head running movies.

Ticking.

Ticking.

247

I miss

the warm male scent of skin from the shower and him with a towel round his middle.

I miss the look on his face, the shared knowledge of what we are about to do.

I miss the thing a kiss is, opening up for another mouth that way. I miss the silk of his belly, my fingers barely touching its surface, circling my nails over his breasts. I miss easing back, cupping a hand under his balls to feel the living skin there crawl, the slither of secrets inside and I miss I miss the feel of his penis in my mouth, that vulnerability; his intake of breath and the thrust of his hips to meet me, his pubic hair scouring the tip of my nose like a hat veil, like net and I miss folding my lips over the tooth edges, shielding him from sharpness that drew blood from my own tongue, the taste of that blood with his fullness in my mouth. I miss the way he slid down over my stomach, trailing my open thighs with his tongue, the taste of his kisses when he came back; I miss the weight of him, him under me, the slide of the glans against the melted butter I became. And I miss after, the evidence of bone under my cheek, embracing the bowl of his hips, the soft penis, the thick scent of the two of us warm against my face till I reach, close him up in one hand and feel the blood come again, the tip nosing like a plant shoot till my hand opens, an eggshell, and our eyes lock and smile. I miss the smile and what it means. The length of his body in the morning, the bolt of hard softness stretched out next to where I am, brushing against my boundaries. That contact

that other living body turning to cover me

my skin taking over

the feeling of sharing a language for once and

Ticking.

Ticking.

Ticking.

Godknows, Cassie says. I hear her saying it. Godknows.

Rona's breathing is even. She waits silent with me in the meting out of seconds till I hear an admission coming up and out my mouth. A single word.

Sex.

Rona says nothing.

There is definitely a weakness in that area, Rona.

Rona says nothing.

It's not the whole story though. I sometimes like to forget it isn't but it isn't. I think I also have a problem getting over the training, all sorts of addictive shite I learned from fairy tales and bride dolls and out the Jackie and every bloody pop song since the year dot and godknows. I keep thinking Love is possible. That it might vincit omnia. The thing is. The thing is though. Sometimes I think I don't even like them very much. That it's a whole other sex out there and they are Not Us, Rona. They don't have the same priorities, to be able to organise their priorities in a compatible way with ours. There's no getting away from it. They're Not Us by which in gerneral I mean they're selfish bastards. Ok I know I know, you can't say you don't like a whole sex just like that or that they're all the same. You can't. Of course you can't. But I think it sometimes anyway. I think about the emotional dishonesty that passes for normal male behaviour, the laziness and evasion and I get angry. I get mad as hell. Dearchrist Rona fancying men and not liking them very much must be a common enough complaint. The world must be full of us. And the bastard is Rona, the REAL bastarding thing is that most of us think our experience is just our individual bad luck or something. And it fucking isn't. There are millions of us for godsake, feeling the same fallout. Not able to bridge the contradictions, the tearing involved. I know all that. But I can't get the fairy tales out my innards, the child in there pining for happy ever after. It's not even much I want for godsakes. Company. An arm to dunt when I'm watching a good film. Somebody to ask what I've been doing all day at the office, to talk all night to and take pictures of. To teach me to drive. I know. It's daft and politically incorrect enough for a jail sentence and I'm supposed to be a big girl now and not want the impossible any more. But I'd prefer it. I'd trade a lot for tenderness. I really would. So what's wrong with them, Rona? Why won't they eh? Why won't they?

The room tilts, swings back like a hammock.

Christ.

A big mouthful of cider finishes the glass. I pour more.

It is me though.

Sip.

I mean it must be. You manage fine. Maybe I'm just maudlin. Maybe if I work on it. It might yet be possible to come to terms with the awful truth. The knight on a white charger is never going to come, Rona. You know why? Because he's down the pub with the other knights, that's why. Or on the bloody golf course or at the football or constructing Great Art or some such bloody thing that has nothing to do with the forging of sound interpersonal relationships AT ALL. HA! Heterosexuality, Rona. A sick joke right enough.

Ticking.

Cassie breathing between the strokes.

The paint on the ceiling throbs through the gloom. I watch it pulsing, feeling my own heartbeat in my wrists, my mouth opening and closing no reason I am aware of. And I hear my own voice saying

You know what we could do Rona?

We could make a go of it ourselves. Look after each other. A big flat on the Southside maybe: one with corniced ceilings, a tiled close and a drying green. Imagine. Cut costs, save fuel, half the time you spend washing up; enjoy stimulating conversation and witty exchange at any time of the day or night with an in-house companion. What d'you think Rona?

Rona?

The horrible stillness knows I have gone too far. Waiting for answer which does not come.

Rona?

A mild rasping noise, like a drill several streets away. Only it is night and there are no workmen. The mild rasping noise repeating in lungfuls. I look over. Rona leans against the wall, propped upright in the candlelight. Snoring.

The curtain edge is rimmed with pale light. Barely visible on the floor, my clothes. Melted blue bodies abandoned by shapes they no longer remember. The open legs of Rona's shorts make dragon nostrils on the chair.

Rona? I shake her shoulder. Rona, cmon. Bed.

She struggles sideways and under the duvet in one fluid motion. I think about telling her she hasn't brushed her teeth then don't bother. We can both have a night off. I get in too, worm down between unfamiliar sheeting.

After a moment or two, Rona moves.

She rolls from her back on to her side, the other side, the original side again, on her face, back on the original side again again, arms over her head, under her head, feet outside the cover, back inside, then clutches the pillow. She clutches the pillow as though she thinks someone might come and steal it. When she relaxes, the snoring starts. Snores and the twitching of feet. Cassie lies on her back throughout, unflinching.

From another room a rhythmic tapping becomes louder.
The moans and sighs of unmistakable thrust and withdrawal, thrust and withdrawal. These walls are paper fucking thin.

A small voice escapes from under cloth, muffled.

Cassie?
What?
I'm just thinking.
What?
I'm thinking did we leave the travel kettle in Amboise? I can't remember. Did we

The end of the sentence never comes.

The couple in the next room just keep going.

252

seventeen

That's

forget now. Anyway that's Rona outside it, metal roof with
bolts sticking out like Boris Karloff's neck and a vegetable stall
underneath. Carrots and pyres of tomatoes. Further along,
this. Joan of Arc. We must have walked by her the previous
day and I hadn't even noticed. The bloody great cross right on
the spot where the burning happened is totally unmissable but
not her. Less than lifesize, cuddled into the wall of this modern
block with lattice windows, arms folded like wings over a flat
chest and the wee boy haircut. The curly things are
representational flames, not causing undue concern. I know
they were trying for transcendence but even so. You think
someone on fire would tend to notice more. The skin can't
keep its distance from that much reality. Suffering is not made
nobler by being unobtrusive: just less inconvenient. If I'd
made her she'd have looked different. Skin reaming, blistering
hopelessly to repair itself, eyes rolling, you wouldn't have had

to look twice to find her. I'd have had her screaming her fucking head off.

Rona eating pizza. No that isn't a bit of the cathedral. It's C&A. Me behind dark glasses, tired and emotional, outside C&A.

I need to lie down, Rona. I really do need to lie down.

She walks ahead of me, all Calvinist stoicism. As hung over but more stubborn. Rona. I can't bring myself to shout. The bugger knows fine.

The cathedral is dark, rubbed over with industrial soot. Inside too. Rona walks round alone, takes pictures while I sit with my eyes shut, unwilling to focus.

Look at this. It got hit by a bomb and they've been restoring it all that time. Years of work researching the right techniques. All that trouble.

I hear the click of the shutter, Rona taking a picture of an information board for me to read when we get home.

Clever though, she says, sitting. You can't differentiate between the original and restored bits at all. All that effort. I think it's wonderful.

An odd note in the voice makes me open one eye. Behind the polaroids, hers glisten.

I think it's wonderful they don't just leave things falling to bits. They put them back together again.

She stops, eyes filling up. I touch her hand and it threatens to get worse. No good. There are no paper hankies in my pocket, only something hard. I bring it out and look. Yeti's Feet sweeties. I offer them, watch her take one. It turns over in her mouth three or four times before she digs a hankie out of her pocket, spits the thing inside and folds it out of sight. Christ Cassie what do they put in those bloody things? she whispers.

Outside she reads the tin for five minutes then flings it in a rubbish bin. Learning from past mistakes. She saves only one to give me.

Here. Cure your headache.

Walking back to the car, I take her advice. Medicine and punishment. Making me fit for the road.

We move through the Seine Valley. I know it is the Seine Valley because Rona tells me. She says she knows because she read the book, boning up in secret before we left the hotel. I just like to know where I'm going, she says. When the Seine finally appears, there is an enormous boat on it. Gunboat maybe, horrible shade of yellowy grey. To mark the occasion, I finish the last chapters of Madame Bovary and feel awful. Rona tells me it's because reading in a car is bad for your inner ear. That's what causes car sickness, she says and I say it's not that, it's this thing. It's the story.

She killed herself. I just didn't expect it. Not that way anyhow. Arsenic poisoning. It takes ages with him trying to make her vomit and she can't and they bring her wee girl in and it's just terrible. She kills herself as a favour to other people, Rona. It's awful.

I know, she says. I read it at university but never liked it much. Flaubert sets her up. Charles as well. He constructed them to keep their field of possibilities as narrow as possible. All that stuff about women who read certain kinds of novels, literary point-scoring. He

255

never takes her seriously. Reading it in the original it's even more brutal somehow. French is such a bald language.

I look at her, astonished. Rona and her secrets. I don't know the half.

In somewhere we don't bother knowing the name of, Rona changes money and fills up the tank. I stay in the car, tidying. It's a tip in here, Rona, I say as she walks away. A tip. I find a tape under the back seat: Neil Sedaka. I can't work it out. It must be one of Rona's. I slot it into the player, watch the spindles turn. After a cool six-bar piano introduction, Neil starts singing. *Fremd bin ich eingezogen, fremd zieh' ich wieder aus* in a terrible German accent. I take the cassette out, check. Winterreise. Peers and Britten doing Schubert in the wrong case. Mine. Time I got Rona sorted out, never mind anything else. I'm getting a cassette rack for this car.

The hill was going on forever.

Every turn, Cassie sat up, hoping for a fresh view. Every turn, there was more hill. It was daft. Watched kettles never boiled etc. But for three more turns after she said it was the last time, she kept watching anyway. There were only three more bits of hill. The radio wouldn't tune in. After tidying up, there were no cassettes handy: only an orange and a half bottle of mineral water in the passenger door pocket. Cassie opened and shut the glove compartment and sat back upright. Everything was blue. Blue widening out on all sides, stretching to the furthest point of visibility. The sea. Dear god, the sea, shimmering into sight and everywhere the minute her back was turned. Typical. Absolutely bloody typical.

drive along the sea-line, secure. Now they have found it, it won't go away. Cassie looks down as though over a cliff edge while the sound of water rises through shut windows, through the engine revs. Wilder and bluer, filling up the whole world. Her laughing starts Rona too. Rona laughing and accelerating, throwing her head back so her teeth show. She can't know what for but she joins in. Typical.

VEULETTES arrives before it has any right.

We park on the sands and emerge from the plastic interior, creaking. I check both legs are still where they should be, that nothing has fallen off. It's all there, just sore. And that passes. It always does. Breathing deep brings the sour smell of seaweed into my chest. Bits of it stay there even after I exhale. Rona points and bathing huts appear in a line along the sea wall, like Lyme. Lyme with the cob I walked along pretending to be Meryl Streep in The French Lieutenant's Woman, wondering how she kept her balance. Rona's got a picture of me doing it, coiled up in a duffle coat and peering out behind the hood, my nose dripping. We had cream tea in a chip shop and slept in the car in a place I was convinced was deserted countryside. Daylight made it the verge of an airport runway. It's astonishing what gets past you in the dark. Rona looks at me.

LOOK, she shouts. It's exactly like Lyme.
I know, Rona. I know.

Behind the counter of the Hotel Stella Maris, a Viking hands over a key. They invaded here too, Rona says. Looting and pillaging. They got everywhere. The Viking's key works first time. Inside the room, I open the case, locate the single jersey I brought

257

and leave the rest. It'll be in a washing machine tomorrow. Rona's. I don't have one. Anyway, a washing machine. At home. Rona unearths something huge from the brown bag. An aran. I shake my head, smiling, freeing my shoulders up. She pretends not to notice.

In the only shop we buy a dry baguette, crisps and yogurt, leaving enough francs for breakfast tomorrow. Thinking ahead. We carry the picnic up on to the shore cliffs while the wind gathers, not able to hear each other speak for being out of breath and trying to chew. Gusts suck the words away. There is a stone sun-dial at the top of the hill, its arm broken. The sound of the sea is overpowering. Without knowing why, I start to run on the way down, gathering momentum on the narrow path between the windbreaks then wait, chest searing, by the side of the ice-cream van for Rona. My face must be crimson. The two teenage boys on the road couldn't care less. They dive between gaps in the traffic, their fingers interlaced. Two men holding hands. I can't work out whether this is a charming French custom or enviable disregard for societal disapproval. Either way it cheers me up. By the time they're on my side, buying cones, Rona arrives. A blur charging past, shouting COOEE, laughing like a monkey on speed.

We walk along the prom and back to the car. Rona wonders if we should move it.

Salt, she says. It'll rust.

I stand looking at the car not sure about the chemistry of the thing and a man stops beside us: a man in an anorak with the hood up, black skin on the backs of his wrists puckered with goosebumps.

Bonjour he says. Bonjour. All three of us look at the car.

C'est votre voiture?

Oui, says Rona.

Algerian, he says, knowing we're too stupid to be natives. Je ne parle pas Anglais.

We smile a lot. He smiles back. Je suis étudiant. A Paris.

We smile some more. Nous ne sommes pas étudiantes: trop vieilles.

He smiles, looks at his feet in case it wasn't a joke.

Nous sommes voluntary workers, I say. Welfare Rights. Je ne sais pas le mot en Francais. Welfare Rights. I shrug, hopeless. But he doesn't mind. He comes with us.

We walk the length of the beach with the silent Algerian. When we're back where we started, he turns and shrugs.

Eh bien, he says. Eh bien. Et au revoir.

He holds out his hand. Rona shakes it and asks his name.

Aki, he says. His face is luminous with pleasure. Aki.

Rona. Et voilà Cassie.

His fingers are warmer than mine when our hands touch. I check but the goosepimples are still there. He's warmer than me and still frozen. Still holding my hand, he looks to Rona.

C'est votre soeur?

She looks at me. I look at her.

Oui, I say. Ma soeur.

Me and Rona on the beach at Veulettes. A student we met took it. We're huddling in like that because it was so bloody windy, my hair blowing over her face so she could hardly see out. I bought him an ice-cream. Could only have been about nineteen, probably trying to get out of national service. Went off down the beach holding it. Milk running over dark knuckles. A trail of white dots in the sand.

Rona and me. We sit on the shore wall with our backsides numb. Evening has come down, our sandals are full of shale and cold toes. But we keep sitting.

Christ, Rona says. I'm tired.

We sit some more.

Rona?
Mhm?
What are you thinking?

The sea coming in.

Things you don't want to hear.
What though.
Well. A sigh. I'm thinking the answer'll be back about Elna McKay's attendance allowance. They'll have done the assessment. The mobility allowance thing as well. I'm thinking about it waiting on my desk.

The sea.

I'm thinking Morag Conlan will have gone back with her man and that she'll be black and blue the next time we see her. Her eye never healed right from the last time either. I'm thinking –
Ok. Enough.

Enough.

We sit some more.

Right, she says. Might as well get the good of the ozone.

She sniffs hard, drawing in as much of the place as she can manage. Then she jumps down on to the shale, walks to the edge of the water, her shoes crunchy. All the time she keeps her eyes down, searching. I watch her bend and straighten, picking something out from the debris at her feet.

Skiffers, she shouts. I'm looking for skiffers. Want to come?

She holds a flat stone up to what is left of the light, checking to see if it'll do, stows it safe in the jeans. Then moves off to find more. My nose is runny. I sniff too, launch off the low wall and walk, my feet precarious across the pebbles. The hand searching for a hankie doesn't find one. If finds something else instead. Something hard. It's a tiny conch: iron-grey shell dappled with white, pink swirling dark and sheeny inside. Clean as a lover's mouth. I rock it between finger and thumb, a relic from somewhere I don't recall, think about setting it to my ear. A redundant reflex. The real sea is here. Wave after incoming wave, washing louder all the time. Shaking my head to hear less of it doesn't work. It only makes me dizzy. When I open my eyes again I can't see a bloody thing. Just hair: a mesh of auburn-grey where the horizon should be. Suddenly it lifts. A hand that isn't mine is pushing it back, fishing my face free. A hand with four and a half fingers. I hadn't even heard her coming. Rona peers in to where I am, blue irises ringed with pale green. Close and getting closer. Black lashes brush my temple: her fingers rest on the back of my neck.

Wondered where you'd got to, she said. Are you ok?

The warm scent of spit on tissue: Rona dabbing my cheek.

I don't know, she says. I don't. Here. Do it yourself if you like. She hands me the hankie, already a tangle of rags. Pink for a girl. Blow your nose as well while you're at it.

And our eyes lock. Smiling. We embrace.

We embrace.

It takes only moments. Then we get on with practicalities.
Cmon then, Cassie says, pulling away. Be dark if we don't get a move on.
Rona knows. She begins walking back towards the sea, over what is now sand, stones clicking from some place.

Come on yourself. There's serious skiffing to be done.

And she stands at the water's edge.

I look up clear and there she is: Rona, one arm raised against the sky. Choosing her moment. I watch her, concentrating on the task in hand, and know two things. I know we'll manage. Me and Rona. We'll be absolutely fine. And I know I'll ask her again. Sober this time.

Then wait and see.

I'll wait and

Rona cheers, interrupting.

The stone. I hear it, the sound of solid matter ticking over an insupportable surface: faint blips and splashes. That the skin of water should be tough enough is a constant surprise. I turn to watch and can't help it. I cheer too. Another scuds out, headed for where Dunkirk might be, or home. It could be going home. Godknows. I've no sense of direction, me. I haven't a bloody clue. Rona and me. We stand in separate places, looking out over water that is just water. Rona takes fresh aim, laughing. Defying gravity.